ICEHOLE

ICEHOLE

Kiera Dellacroix

A Fortitude Press Novel

Fortitude Press, Inc. is grateful to Mike and Dianna of Raydog for the cover art. Raydog can be contacted at 49 Potter Hill Road, Grafton, MA 01519.

This is a work of fiction. Names, characters, places and incidents either are the product of the author's imagination or are used fictitiously, and any resemblance to actual persons, living or dead, business establishments, products, events, or locales is entirely coincidental.

Published by Fortitude Press, Inc. For further information about this or other titles, please contact Fortitude Press, Inc., P.O. Box 112, New York, NY 10268-0112, or visit our website at www.fortitudepress.com.

ISBN: 0-9741378-0-4

First Edition, June 2003
Printed in the United States of America

Edited by Cindy Cresap
Cover design by Raydog
Interior design by Ryan Daly

In honor of H.P. Lovecraft whose work inspired this tale.

Another small piece of paper was torn off the tablet on her desk, and the scrap found a temporary home in the Commander's mouth. Her first salvo of missiles had missed their target—a dilemma she felt she would soon rectify as she zeroed in on the back of Ensign Taylor's neck.

The brown-nosing little shit was completely unaware of her previous assault, and she scowled as she loaded her weapon. The spitball was chambered into the end of a soda straw with a minimum of fuss, and she took careful aim. Unfortunately, her prior efforts had lacked both altitude and distance, so she took the time to meticulously calculate all the environmental factors. Taylor sat at his desk, roughly twelve feet away, with his back to her. Her projectile would have to possess the power to travel through the door of her office and have enough altitude to carry it on to her intended victim.

Finally confident, she inhaled deeply and leaned back in her chair to discharge her weapon. She watched the moist little wad of paper sting the back of the ensign's neck with a satisfying splat, and she turned rapidly to the computer on her desk, innocently feigning productivity.

Instead of finding the monitor, her eyes landed on the figure of her commanding officer, and she silently cursed the painfully transparent glass walls of her office. Judging from the distinct look of displeasure on his face, he had witnessed the entire incident. Fooling no one but herself, she tried vainly to pretend she didn't see him and industriously began to type nonsense on her keyboard. She noted movement out of the corner of her eye and grimaced in anticipation of the inevitable confrontation.

"Commander," he said from the doorway. "I'm going to go get a cup of coffee and return to my office. I strongly suggest you be there waiting for me by the time I arrive."

"Yes, sir," she said quickly, rising from her seat.

The admiral turned and strode away, deftly navigating a maze of cubicles. She trailed after him, changing course halfway across the room to take the shortcut to his office and arriving quickly at the desk of the attending yeoman.

"Admiral Eaton requested that I wait in his office."

The yeoman smiled knowingly. "Go right in, Commander."

She tried not to sigh as she entered the room and stood at attention in front of his desk, waiting several minutes for the sound of an opening door. Prudently keeping her eyes focused straight ahead, she waited for the man to seat himself behind his desk. A long and increasingly uncomfortable silence ensued as he studied her with a mixture of disappointment and frustration.

"Your resignation is tabled," he said finally. "I'd like you to consider an alternate command for a period of at least one year. If after that time, you still wish to resign, it will be honored."

"I don't understand, sir."

"You're a damn good officer when you're not being a complete jackass. Your operational record is nothing short of outstanding, and I'd be willing to bet your name will be on the promotion list for full commander within the next eighteen months. I'd like you to take this assignment and use the time to reconsider resigning your commission. The Navy would like to keep you."

A moment of silence followed.

"Yes or no?"

"Where?"

"Antarctica," he replied. "A Joint Task Force command."

"Antarctica? Isn't that in violation of—?"

"Yes. It's a classified operation and facility. The construction finished ahead of schedule, and the interim civilian leader down there abruptly decided not to winter over. You weren't on the list of original command candidates, but none of those who were considered are available at such short notice. In desperation, I recommended you for the job. Surprisingly, your nomination was unanimously accepted."

"Why?"

"Because I want to keep you, but I don't want to put up with you any longer."

She grinned. "When?"

"Eighteen hours. All information will be provided in text, due to time constraints. Yes or no?"

Another thoughtful silence. "Yes."

"Good," he said. "Your flight leaves from Andrews at 0600 to Christchurch, New Zealand. From there, you'll hook up with 109th Air Mobility Wing, which will transport you to McMurdo. You can take the rest of the day to get your shit in order."

"Very well."

"Dismissed, Commander."

She sketched a salute. "Take care, sir."

"You too, Commander," he said, allowing himself to smile.

Tired eyes slowly surveyed the people gathered within the mess hall, and Larry Daniels cleared his throat, waiting patiently for everyone to get settled. The news he had to deliver would be met with some hostility, even though they all knew it was inevitable.

His gaze landed briefly on each person. He favored every set of eyes with a small smile and an approving nod.

"What's the scoop, Skipper?" Dr. Rivers asked cheerfully when everyone had quieted down.

He gave the little doctor a grin; the woman was as cute as she could be. If there was anyone he would miss above all the others, it was Corky Rivers. Her popularity among the staff was second to none, and he had developed a fierce paternal affection for her. Lucky if she stood an inch over five feet tall, with shoulder-length black hair that lived in a constant state of disarray, the diminutive figure contained twelve feet of "don't fuck with me" attitude. She was friendly and fiendishly brilliant, but woe to the individual who pissed her off.

"Show some patience, Corky," he chided. "Is everyone here?"

"All the civilians spending the winter are," Corky replied.

He sighed. She was going to take the news hard. "Then we're all here."

"Why is that?" Corky asked.

Bracing himself for the explosion that was only minutes away, he seated himself on top of a folding table in front of the crowd, letting his legs dangle freely.

"Well," he started slowly, "as you know, I was originally assigned to this project to supervise construction. Now that it's complete, and we can concentrate our efforts solely on excavation, the administration of this facility falls into military hands."

He registered a number of resigned sighs, shaking heads and, finally, a pair of brown eyes burning brightly under a mop of unruly black hair. He could tell from Corky's reddening cheeks that an outburst was building. She took a deep breath, and he acted quickly.

"Save it, Corky. Everyone knew this was going to happen, and it's a stipulation we all agreed to before signing on."

Corky subsided, crossing her arms over her chest childishly.

"I tell you this now because I won't be wintering over this year." He held up a hand against the beginning protest. "I'll be leaving tomorrow with the arrival of the new skipper."

"Goddamn it, Larry," Corky said. "All U.S. operations on the continent are under the purview of the NSF."

"That is true," he said. "However, each and every one of you knows the classified nature of this facility and was aware that the military would eventually take control here. There will be a drastic increase in both civilian and military personnel next season, and since I recently decided not to winter over, they're sending the new boss ahead of schedule."

"Who are they sending to replace you, Larry?" Dr. Stokes asked in his gruff voice.

"No doubt some jarhead with a roll of quarters stuck up his ass," Corky mumbled, getting a few hesitant chuckles from her colleagues.

"Actually, you're not getting a jarhead; you're getting a sailor," Larry replied quietly, throwing a disapproving look at Corky.

"Coast Guard?" Clovis asked.

"No, Navy."

"What?" Corky sprang from her seat. "I thought the Navy ceased operations on the continent some time ago. How could they be in charge?"

He sighed. "This entire facility is being funded by the Department of Defense. They can send anyone they want."

"How the hell does a sailor fit in here?" Corky asked.

"You'd be surprised, Dr. Rivers," he said with a hint of warning.

"What's his background?" asked Dr. Lenard, a small and fastidious man who wore a pair of glasses that spent more time being cleaned than they spent on his face. He took them off and began to polish them as he awaited Larry's response.

"He is a she," Larry replied as he pulled the orders from his pocket and consulted them. "One Lieutenant Commander Malory Q. Lovecraft. Assigned to Naval Intelligence since her graduation from Annapolis."

"Is that all the info you have? Why would they assign an intelligence officer?"

"The commander's posting was last minute, so I don't have a lot of info," Larry said. "Although I can tell you that her most recent fitness report described her as unorthodox."

"That's just great," Corky mumbled. "A Section Eight sailor trapped in the dark with us for eight months."

"Dr. Rivers," Larry said sharply, "I suggest that upon her arrival, you treat her with respect if you expect to receive any in return. I wasn't going to mention it, but now I feel I should. Commander Lovecraft is a decorated officer and is held in high regard. She may not find your comments as amusing as you might hope."

An irritable grunt was his only reply.

"Look, people, the fact of the matter is that this facility would not have been a possibility without military intervention. What is of the utmost importance is the excavation, which is why the majority of you are here to begin with. The United States is not the only government with interests here, and you all know that if this complex were discovered, it would be in direct violation of the Antarctic Treaty. I might also remind you that it was the NSF itself that asked the military for their involvement. If we had not done so, we would now be competing over this site with an untold number of foreign governments."

He looked over his audience and was gratified to note that even Corky had quieted. "That this facility remains a secret is due solely to the military's efforts. The NSF does not and did not have the means to construct this site without its being detected by foreign satellite surveillance. At this point in the game, the military is assuming command and is here to administrate, provide continuing security and evaluate the ongoing needs of this operation." He sighed and allowed himself a small smile. "Give the new commander a break, let her do her job and hope that I don't get a bad report from her on any of you when I return in the summer."

His smile grew affectionate as this news was met with a happy response, most notably from the shining brown eyes of the group's medical doctor.

"Now that we have that out of the way, I've arranged for a little party," he said. "Break out the booze, and let's all hope I've provided enough munchies."

His hand came up again to forestall the rising cheers. "But first," he added in a stern voice, "I'll need to see Dr. Rivers in my office, please."

Corky sighed and rose to follow her boss, trying her best to ignore the impressively unmusical chorus of her co-workers.

"Corky's in trouble. Corky's in trouble."

Larry sat down behind his desk to await the arrival of the troublesome doctor. He had finished packing his things shortly before summoning everyone to the mess, and he spared a remorseful glance around the room, the bare walls and shelves a not-so-subtle reminder that come the morrow, this office would no longer be his own. He looked up at the quiet knock and noted the sheepish look being cast in his direction.

"Sit down, Corky," he said, gesturing to a chair in front of his desk and waiting until she seated herself before continuing.

"I know you have a bug up your ass over military involvement here, and for the most part, I've ignored your rather contemptuous attitude toward the servicemen already among us," he stated quietly. "What I don't understand is why."

Corky shifted in her seat uncomfortably, avoiding eye contact.

"In the past, I've let you get away with it, and I probably shouldn't have. The men here have been nothing but polite to you, yet you treat all of them as if they're barely tolerated enemies."

She opened her mouth to speak but was silenced by an upraised hand.

"If you think for one minute the new boss will let you get away with such behavior, you're gravely mistaken. How do you think it will feel to have your security clearance revoked and spend the rest of your tour confined to quarters?"

"She wouldn't dare."

"Don't fool yourself, Corky. The U.S. has a lot at stake here, and there's no reason why someone with your attitude would be tolerated. With that thought in mind, you can rest assured that they wouldn't send an idiot to take charge here. I would assume Commander Lovecraft to be quite formidable."

Corky fidgeted in her chair.

"I'm waiting."

"Waiting for what?"

"Waiting for you to explain just what your problem is so I can help you save your job."

He watched the woman struggle with a myriad of emotions, noting at last the determined and stubborn clenching of her jaw.

"You're not leaving this room until you come clean, Corky."

Her eyes narrowed for battle.

He sighed and reached out to enter the intercom code on the phone in front of him. "This is Daniels," he said, his voice reverberating down the halls outside. "Would PO DeSoto report to my office, please?"

Corky's eyes widened. DeSoto was the communications officer.

"It's rather late in the game to request a doctor, especially one with your skills, but hopefully we can acquire another before winter sets in."

Corky shrank in her seat, assuming a repentant posture and injecting a healthy dose of sugar into her voice. "Larry..."

"Don't give me that. I have two daughters. You're wasting your time playing the sweet-and-contrite card."

Thwarted, Corky scowled. It would be a matter of seconds before DeSoto arrived.

"You're running out of time."

Corky wanted to growl in frustration. *Who knew that Larry could be so ruthless?* His approval had come to mean a lot to her; she both admired and genuinely cared for him and didn't want to disappoint him by revealing anything. Yet she knew staying on her current course wouldn't win her any brownie points, and she would most likely not only disappoint him, but lose her job as well.

"All right, Larry," she said reluctantly a split-second before the doorway darkened.

"You called for me, sir?" DeSoto asked.

"Yes, but I don't think I'll need anything now," Larry said, giving Corky a questioning glare, gratified when she nodded slightly. "I'm sorry to have bothered you."

"No problem, sir."

Larry waited a moment and leaned back in his chair. "Let's hear it."

Corky took a deep breath, hoping she hadn't underestimated him. "Well..."

Mildly interested eyes watched the world speed by from within the confines of the helicopter. The view now was the same as it had been twenty minutes ago, when they had lifted off from McMurdo: an endless landscape of ice, occasionally highlighted with light and shadows from the low sun of polar summer. The sun would soon disappear and leave the continent in darkness for the duration of the winter season. Not that it would matter. She would be spending that time underground—or, more accurately, under the ice.

Malory returned her attention to the papers in her lap, skimming the details of her new command. She would be taking control of a recently completed, impressively vast, self-contained complex that would shelter a winter population of twenty-nine people, the majority either belonging to or employed by the National Science Foundation.

Six years in the making, her new home had been a massive and enormously costly undertaking that had required a considerable amount of stealth.

A signatory to the Antarctic Treaty, the United States was well aware of its violations. Forty-five nations participated in the treaty, twenty-seven of which regularly had representatives on the continent, and all member nations had the right to go where they pleased; access any area; and inspect all stations, installations and equipment. It was also required that notice be given before any military personnel were introduced.

Fortunately, Antarctica was a very remote, notoriously hostile portion of the planet that in the most hospitable season boasted a population of roughly four thousand people who were scattered over an area larger by half than the United States itself. This meant that the rules were seldom enforced, and for the most part, adherence to the treaty was regulated by the honor system. Yet in the interest of caution, all transportation of manpower and material had been carefully timed to prevent detection by foreign satellites, and located along the same flight path, the façade of another outpost had been created more than a hundred miles away from the actual construction site. The powers that be could point to these few uninhabited props in case questions were asked or anyone noticed something they weren't supposed to.

When all the necessary resources were safely entrenched underground and not openly exposed to detection, the bogus outpost disappeared, and construction of the actual complex began in earnest. Now that the station was complete, a skeleton crew would be spending the winter underground, preparing for the arrival of more than a hundred people scheduled to appear with the change of seasons.

Malory shuffled through the papers in her lap until she found the list of military personnel, noting that if she included herself in the total, they numbered thirteen: five from the Coast Guard, six from the Air Force, one from the Army and, of course, one from the Navy. She thought that a little odd, but then again, the whole endeavor struck her as odd, considering that the ultimate goal was to investigate several anomalous sonar readings almost a kilometer below the ice. If all went as planned, excavation would reveal the discovery to human eyes by October. There were pages of text describing why the scientists were in such an uproar over the project, but they might as well have been written in Latin as far as she was concerned. She only skimmed the first few paragraphs before tossing them aside and declaring herself a layman. The scholars were creaming their jeans over the expected find, but she couldn't muster an ounce of excitement, considering relics and fossils to be about as interesting as watching a lump of shit dry in the sun.

She was more concerned about how she was to occupy herself underground for the next eight months. As soon as the pilot dropped Daniels at McMurdo and returned, the entire facility was to be sealed, allowing no one entry or exit until flights resumed in the far-distant summer. She groaned and again turned to watch the scenery fly by in a never-ending white blur.

1220 hours

Corky looked up from her computer with a frown when the flashing red light on the ceiling caught her attention.

So our new monarch arriveth.

Her first thought when she got out of bed that morning had been to avoid the new boss lady for as long as she could. However, memories of the scathing lecture she had received from Larry the night before soon assailed her, and she thought it prudent to at least give her the benefit of the doubt. She smiled a little, remembering that she had indeed underestimated the man and was going to miss him terribly. Not wanting to give Larry any more reason for worry, she grabbed her jacket and started making her way to the entrance, joining several of her colleagues in the halls. They were all headed in the same direction and obviously eager to meet the new cheese.

Malory watched with detachment as the helicopter began to descend between two men who were standing with flares in the middle of apparently nowhere, their figures a stark contrast against a solid white background. She glanced around for any other hint of population or machinery and came up lacking. Upon touchdown, she removed her seat belt and made to open the door but was called up short.

"Commander," Lieutenant Ring said from the pilot's seat, turning to look at her. "You can get out, but don't stray away from the aircraft. It's a long drop."

She stared at him for a moment and nodded slightly in agreement. When her boots hit the snow, one of the signalmen approached her and saluted. He was a young man with blond farm-boy good looks.

"Commander," he said loudly over the dying roar of the helicopter blades. "I'm Staff Sergeant Hanson. Please don't wander. Are you ready to enter the facility?"

"Yes, carry on," she said distractedly, more than a little curious to see how things unfolded.

Hanson looked for a thumbs-up from the pilot and another from his counterpart on the other side of the helicopter before speaking into his headset. "We're secure. Let it drop." Then he added, "Commander, please stand inside the barriers."

She let her gaze drop to her feet and was surprised when the ground began to sink underneath her. The barriers made themselves obvious as she found herself on a platform about the size of a tractor-trailer. Within a few seconds, a wave of warm air washed over her, and she chuckled as the platform lowered them, helicopter and all, into the facility two stories beneath them.

"Cool," she whispered.

Corky looked on with interest as the platform began its descent, her eyes searching for the woman who would no doubt be a thorn in her side for the duration of the rapidly approaching winter. She wasn't alone. It appeared that the entire staff was in attendance.

Her eyes tracked to the woman standing next to the helicopter, whom she assumed was soon to be their fearless leader. As the platform got closer to the ground, she frowned. The woman was wearing a large, flamboyant, battered black Western hat that had the front brim rakishly pinned back to the crown by the little gold insignia of her rank.

"She looks unorthodox from here," Clovis grumbled good-naturedly beside her.

"No kidding," she replied, scrutinizing the woman. Corky couldn't make out her features, due to the sunglasses that covered her eyes and the shadow that her ridiculous hat cast on her face.

When the platform completed its journey, Corky watched grimly as Larry approached the commander and offered her his greetings. She wished she were close enough to hear what was being said.

"Commander Lovecraft," Larry said, offering his hand, "I'm Larry Daniels. It's good to meet you."

"A pleasure," she said with a smile.

"We need to get the platform back up. Hanson and Terrel will get your gear stowed in your quarters," Larry said, gesturing at the assembled personnel. "It seems everyone came out to greet you. Any objection to introductions?"

"Not at all. Lead the way," she said and followed him off the platform to the group of people waiting in the distance.

"Great. Afterward, I'll give you the nickel tour." He looked at her for approval and got both a nod and another smile.

"Here she comes, Rivers," Clovis whispered. "Square those shoulders, and puff out that chest."

She swatted him playfully. "Shut up," she added as she watched the woman stride gracefully in their general direction. They came to a halt in front of Dr. Isaaks, and her eyes widened in appreciation as the sunglasses came off and the hat was swept back to hang from a cord around her neck.

Oh, my gosh. She's stunning.

Corky's eyes took in the wealth of thick, dark red hair that suddenly flowed over the woman's shoulders, the hair framing a face that was classically beautiful and home to a pair of startling pale-blue eyes.

She was jarred from her thoughts as the woman stopped in front of Sergeant Major McNeely, who saluted her crisply. She turned to Clovis and brought a finger to her mouth in a gagging gesture, getting a subdued laugh from her companion.

Malory saw the pantomime out of the corner of her eye and covertly studied the two as she continued making her way through the line of introductions. She caught the undeniably attractive and dark-featured little woman rolling her eyes more than once. About the fourth time the gesture was repeated, she was more than a little irritated.

"This is Clovis Stokes, our senior archaeologist," Larry said as they came abreast of a sandy-haired, monolithic man who was easily six inches taller than her own five-foot-ten-inch height and, from the look of him, almost two hundred pounds heavier.

"A pleasure," she said, her hand disappearing within the enormous grasp of his greeting.

"Nice to meet you, Commander," Clovis replied.

Corky assumed an expression of mortal boredom as they moved to stand in front of her.

"This is—"

"No need for introductions here, Dr. Daniels," Malory interrupted. "I would recognize the janitor anywhere."

It took several long seconds and a few audible snickers from those close enough to have heard the comment for Corky to get past the initial shock of being so blatantly insulted.

Malory beat back a pleased smile as the woman visibly ground her teeth.

"Actually, this is Corky Rivers, our M.D.," Larry said carefully, afraid that his own amusement might show itself.

The commander shrugged indifferently. "My apologies," she said, extending her hand in the brunette's direction and waiting until Corky's grasp was within her own before adding, "It was an honest mistake."

Corky paled in the effort to keep her composure. "Charmed," she managed, quickly withdrawing her hand.

"Of course you are," the commander said as she moved on to the next person in line, purposely dismissing the doctor as insignificant.

What a fucking bitch! Corky fumed silently as the woman moved away.

"And this is..." Larry continued, but Malory's thoughts were miles away. *It looks like the next eight months won't be so boring after all.*

1330 hours

The tour ended with Larry showing her to her quarters, consisting of two rooms, one of which served as her office. She noted that her gear was stacked neatly against a wall, and she took a seat in one of the two chairs positioned in front of the desk, gesturing for Larry to take the other.

"The facility is impressive, to say the least."

"Yes, it is," Larry agreed. "Any last minute questions?"

"A few, if you don't mind," she said. "I understand you're flying out tonight?"

"That's correct. I'm looking forward to spending some time with my family and lounging around in a warmer climate for a few months."

Malory chuckled; she liked the man. "Well, then, I won't keep you any longer than I have to."

"What would you like to know?"

"The military personnel. What are their current duties here?"

"Would you like specifics or just an overview?"

"An overview would be fine. I'm not quite up to speed on all I should be."

He grinned. "Ahh, the joys of a last minute posting?"

"Yeah," she said, giving him a grin of her own.

He leaned back in his chair. "Let's see. From the Air Force, there's Lieutenant Ring, the helicopter pilot. The lieutenant is usually invisible until it's time to fly."

Malory nodded knowingly. "Typical pilot."

"Then there's Technical Sergeant Alvarez, Staff Sergeants Hanson and Terrel, and Airmen Daly and Cohen, all of whom are assigned to flight operations, supply, equipment maintenance and mechanical."

She grunted. "And the Coasties?"

"Senior Chief Reynolds, the station engineer," he replied. "The chief's been here from the beginning and has been invaluable. He knows all there is to know about the facility."

Her eyebrows rose. "He's been present since initial construction began?"

"Yes."

"Long time to be on the ice."

"The chief didn't winter over last year, so he did get a bit of a break. However, his absence was felt, and with the onset of summer, the other engineers were screaming for his return."

"Impressive. And the others?"

"Petty Officers DeSoto and Butler, who maintain computer operations and communications. Petty Officers Percy and Coy are paramedics."

"And Sergeant Major McNeely?"

"Yes, another invaluable man. He oversees day-to-day operations and takes care of all ordnance and demolition. The Army Corps of Engineers sent us the sergeant major, and Excavation, Receiving and all the wonderful corridors you see in the ice are his work."

"So he's been here for some time, then?"

"About as long as the chief."

"Sounds like a good crew. Any problems I should be aware of?"

"Not a one."

"Glad to hear it. Care to give me a civilian breakdown?"

"Sure," he said easily. "At the present time, the NSF employs a kitchen and maintenance staff of six. The remaining ten civilians are members of the NSF and are specialists of different types assigned to study and excavation."

"Specialists?"

"Mostly of the archaeological and geological variety."

"Who are the top dogs?"

"Doctors Stokes and Lenard have seniority. They'll be the most vocal, as everyone else tends to complain to them, and they in turn complain to me—and now to you."

She snickered. "Very well. I'll take the time to meet with everyone over the next few days. Is there anyone I should keep an eye on?"

Larry thought carefully, assessing the woman across from him. There was no mistaking the warning volley she had fired at Corky earlier; indeed, it was the rare person who could flummox the volatile little doctor as easily as she had. In fact, Corky had been suspiciously missing from her post when he had shown the commander the medical facilities.

"Dr. Rivers."

"I kinda figured. What's the story?"

"It's complex."

"I kinda figured that, too. Gimme a summary."

"Let's just say she's had the military run roughshod over her on a few occasions. Some of it's very personal, and she's still bitter."

"Good enough."

"Commander, I would be remiss if I didn't point out that if she were incapable of doing her job, I wouldn't have approved her position here. Despite any personality she might throw at you, underneath it all, she's a very outgoing and friendly person."

"Don't worry, Dr. Daniels. She'll still have a job when you return."

Larry sighed in relief. "I was worried. She knows how to push the envelope."

She laughed. "Sounds like a challenge."

1500 hours

Malory watched with a nagging feeling of foreboding as the men pulled the ski-equipped helicopter off the platform with elbow grease and the assistance of an ATV. It was the last thing to be done before the platform was raised for the winter. She didn't know why, but suddenly, the idea of being trapped underground was unnerving. They had the means to travel in the event of emergency, but that was entirely too dependent on the violent Antarctic winter. They were more than a thousand miles from any established outpost, on an area of the continent that had an average temperature of eighty-seven degrees below zero and that was, more often than not, buffeted by wind speeds ranging from forty to one hundred twenty miles per hour.

She tried to suppress a shudder as she surveyed the cavernous chamber that served as the entrance to Receiving. She estimated the area to be an acre or larger, and the white walls that had been carved from the ice seemed to be a great deal more ominous now than they had when she'd arrived. Irritated with herself for her case of the creeps, she was glad to hear Sergeant Hanson yell out to her.

"Commander, we're ready to seal her up!"

It took her a second to give the order. "Do it."

She watched as Hanson spoke into his headset and gave a thumbs-up in the direction of a long, narrow window that was situated several meters off the ground in one of the far walls. The distance made it impossible to identify the figure behind the glass of Operations, but she assumed it to be Chief Reynolds.

The platform started its ascent, and she abruptly decided that she didn't want to be present when it completed its journey. Her first thought was to return to her quarters and begin the tedious task of unpacking, but she changed course impulsively. She had seen Daniels off earlier, watching with interest as everyone had materialized to bid farewell to the man. Of particular note was the little figure who had rushed forward to embrace him, eventually letting him go and quickly retreating down a hallway, wiping her eyes.

Malory entered Medical unnoticed. Dr. Rivers was speaking to the man she remembered as Petty Officer Percy, and both had their backs to her. Content to remain unobserved, she waited patiently and took in her surroundings, her attention eventually landing on a specimen jar filled with a vile green liquid. Morbidly intrigued, she stepped closer and examined the contents of the container, unable to identify the squishy-looking organic mass floating within. Engrossed in her study, she was startled when her presence was finally noticed.

"Commander!" Percy exclaimed, coming to attention and throwing her a salute.

"Percy," she said. "Lose the salute, or it's gonna be a long winter."

"Yes, ma'am," he said, standing a little easier.

"Lose the 'ma'am,' too," she added, noting that the doctor hadn't bothered to turn around. "'Commander' or 'Lovecraft' will do in a pinch."

"Very well, Commander."

"Pass the word, will ya? I don't wanna have to go through this with everyone."

"Will do," he said. "Is there anything I can help you with?"

"Nope. Was hoping to have a word with Dr. Rivers."

"Oh," he said, standing uncomfortably in place for a moment and then lighting up in sudden understanding. "Oh, of course. Excuse me, Doctor," he added hastily, skipping into a less-than-graceful exit.

Finally alone with the doctor, Malory was a little miffed that the woman still hadn't bothered to acknowledge her. Not wanting to be the first to give in, she hopped up on one of the examination tables, reclining with her hands behind her head and crossing her feet at the ankles.

The silence stretched into minutes, and still the doctor carried on as though no one else were present. Grinning at the woman's back, Malory lifted her eyes to the ceiling and began to count the little holes in the tiles above.

A full twenty minutes passed, the silence finally broken when Clovis burst through the door.

"Hey, Corky. I..." He trailed off when he noticed the lounging commander. "Uhm...excuse me."

Corky finally turned and opened her mouth to speak.

"Quite all right, Dr. Stokes," Malory interjected. "Dr. Rivers informed me that she wanted to see me naked at the earliest opportunity."

"Uh..." Clovis stuttered but quickly thought better of continuing. With a confused look, he simply turned on his heel and left the room.

Malory almost laughed as she watched the doctor struggle with her temper. When Corky finally spoke, her voice came out as a strangled rasp.

"What is it you want?"

"Nothing, really," Malory said, smoothing a pretentious finger over an eyebrow. "Was just looking for a place to rest the feet. My dogs are killin' me," she added with a wiggle of her boots.

Corky's eyes narrowed to slits. "I thought maybe you had come to apologize."

"Apologize?" she said in mock confusion. "Whatever for?"

Hands clenched into fists. "Does being in charge entitle you to be a bitch?"

"Nope," Malory replied easily. "I just get off on it."

"Metaphorically or sexually?"

"Perhaps both."

"So our little conversation excites you in some manner?"

"Too early to tell."

"Odd," Corky said thoughtfully. "Scientifically speaking, I was of the understanding that a frigid bitch like yourself couldn't get wet in the shower."

"Oh, that's more like it," Malory exclaimed, raising herself to a seated position. "Now I'm definitely turned on. Would you like to confirm? In the interest of science, of course."

Corky wrinkled her face in disgust and stormed out of the room.

Mission accomplished, Malory swung her legs around and dropped to the floor. Smiling brightly, she made tracks for her quarters to begin the menial task of unpacking.

The next two weeks passed quickly for Malory as she spent the time familiarizing herself with the staff, summoning a few people each day and getting to know them and their assigned duties. She soon came to the conclusion that she would seldom be needed. The staff members all knew their jobs and were dedicated enough that supervision really wasn't required. That suited her just fine; the less she was needed, the more time she would have for herself, and now was as good a time as any to indulge. She reached for the phone to summon the only person she hadn't spoken to formally.

"I'm telling you, Corky," Clovis said over his coffee cup, "she's not as bad as you make her out to be."

"Yeah, right."

"I spoke to her for almost half an hour. She's kinda nice. Not what I expected at all."

"She's an asshole," Corky proclaimed, getting a laugh from her friend.

"You're just mad because she's got your number."

Corky frowned. "I am not."

"You think she's cute?" he asked mischievously.

The frown deepened. "I think she's an infuriating bitch."

"Okay, okay," he chuckled. "Do you think she's a cute infuriating bitch?"

She regarded him coolly and drew in a sharp breath.

"This is Lovecraft," the intercom sounded. *"Dr. Rivers, would you report to my office, please?"*

"Looks like the commander saved me," Clovis said cheerfully.

"You're not off the hook, Stokes," she grumbled. "I wonder if she'd be pissed if I didn't show up?"

"Probably. She's called everyone in to talk to them. Hell, Corky, everyone likes her but you."

"Hmmm."

Clovis grinned. "Go see what she wants."

"Oh, all right," she sighed. "I hope I don't regret this."

Her thoughts were dark as she reluctantly made her way through the halls. She had gone to great lengths to avoid the maddening woman since their encounter in Medical. The bitch was an enigma to her. She had never met anyone who took such an obvious delight in being irritating. The first words out of her mouth, and almost every word since, had been insulting. What was even more annoying was the fact that the woman had seemingly singled her out of the crowd and targeted her for torment. For the life of her, Corky couldn't figure out why.

As she approached her destination, she took a moment to work up a bored and indifferent expression. With a deep, cleansing breath, she traveled the last few feet and knocked on the doorframe.

"Ahh," Malory said. "Come in, Dr. Rivers. Have a seat."

Corky entered warily and gently placed herself in the same chair in which she had received Larry's final lecture. "You wanted to see me?"

"Yes, I did. I've talked to everyone on the staff but you, and I was hoping we could take this time to get past any differences you and I might have. After all, we'll be working together for quite some time."

Corky eyed the commander suspiciously. "I wasn't aware that I had done anything that might have given you offense."

She chuckled. "It usually takes more than one day for someone to muster the nerve to call me a bitch to my face."

"And I suppose you did nothing to warrant such an action?"

"I, of course, admit nothing," she replied with a disarming smile. "But I called you here with the intention of calming the waters."

"How do you propose to accomplish that?" Corky asked, bewildered that she suddenly found the woman to be rather charming.

"I thought you might start by telling me what your problem is with people in uniform."

Corky tensed.

"I had a chat with Dr. Daniels about you before he departed," Malory continued, studying the woman carefully. "Don't worry; he didn't say anything he shouldn't have."

"Then you won't be offended if I say I don't know you nearly well enough to have that conversation with you?"

"Of course not," Malory said, beaming her best smile. "I wouldn't presume to put you in such an uncomfortable position."

To Corky's dismay, she couldn't help but smile in response to the one being directed at her. "Then I don't understand."

"I have a solution to our problem."

"Oh?"

"I was pretty sure you'd refuse to tell me, so I thought you might tell my XO."

Corky gaped. "Huh?"

"Just try to keep an open mind, okay?"

"I don't get it."

"Just try," she asked again, begging her with her eyes.

"Okay," Corky relented. "I'll try."

"Great!" she exclaimed, suddenly bending over and digging in a desk drawer.

Corky watched in confusion, half of her wanting to know what the woman was up to and the other half almost positive that she was being set up for something. Her lips tightened when a small tape recorder was placed on the desk in front of her. However, the stinging comment poised on the tip of her tongue died quickly, and she was struck dumb as another item was placed on the desk. Her eyes almost refused to register the sight before her. Within arm's reach sat a Chatty Cathy doll with a bad red dye job, clothed in a childish copy of a naval uniform, complete with a miniature version of the commander's asinine hat.

"Now, I know what you're probably thinking," Malory said. "But I've used this approach successfully many times in the past. I'll just hit Record and go find something to do for about an hour. Little Lovecraft is a good listener. Feel free to tell her anything you want."

Corky could only stare, all traces of color gone from her face.

Trying to remain passively disinterested until she was out of the room, Malory turned the recorder on and made a hasty exit.

It took several minutes for a nonviolent thought to enter Corky's mind. *The bitch suckered me right in! And to think for a second there, I thought she was charming. Why me? What the fuck is her malfunction?*

She was suddenly aware that her hands hurt, and she dropped her gaze from the doll to find her knuckles white from the death grip she had on the arms of her chair. Her fingers uncurled themselves gingerly, and she grimaced slightly as circulation returned. When she had regained some feeling, her eyes again traveled back to the idiotic doll, taking note of the little cord dangling from her neck.

Do I dare?

She hesitated, but in the end, she couldn't help herself. Knowing that she was going to regret it, she reached out and pulled the string.

Malory watched from her hiding place as the doctor stormed out of her office and stomped off down the hallway. She made herself wait until the woman disappeared before she ran back to her office, chuckling when she found Little Lovecraft in the garbage can and both lying across the room. As she had hoped, Corky had forgotten about the recorder. She picked it up to rewind it and plopped down in her chair to listen.

"Roses are red. Violets are blue. Don't you just hate it when I fuck with you," came the childishly sung tease.

"Fuckin' bitch," Corky hissed.

"I know you are, but what am I?"

The final taunt was followed immediately by the sound of Little Lovecraft landing violently in the trash can and then a thud and crash as both were obviously kicked across the room.

Malory fell back into her chair with a howl of laughter.

The next few weeks passed slowly, and life for the commander had become exceedingly dull. She was rarely sought out for anything other than the most trivial of matters. Worse, Dr. Rivers had managed to avoid any contact with her, going so far as to leave the mess every time she entered, whether she was finished with her meal or not, and taking the precaution of slipping on a pair of earmuffs so she couldn't listen to her the one time she had approached her in Medical. Among other things, Malory decided, the woman was a poor sport.

She was in the midst of another losing hand of computer solitaire when Petty Officer DeSoto appeared in the doorway.

"Commander," he said in greeting.

"What's up?"

"External communications are down. I'd like permission to go outside and clear the dome."

Malory perked up. "Alone?"

"No, I was gonna take Butler with me."

"Cut him loose. I'll go," she said, happy to have a project.

"Very well, Commander," he said warily. "It's quite a hike, and the weather is pretty ugly."

"Looking forward to it," she said, hopping out of her chair. "Give me a few minutes, please."

"I'll be in Receiving when you're ready."

"Meet you there."

Ten minutes later, she arrived at the platform, feeling burdened under the weight of all her arctic clothing. She was excited to see what the outside looked like in the winter.

"Ready, Commander?" DeSoto asked.

"Yep. Lead the way."

"I kinda thought we'd drive, Commander."

"Excuse me?"

"The silo is about a mile away," he explained.

"I thought you said it was a hike."

"It will be going up."

She chuckled. "Okay. Give me the scoop."

He pointed to a distant door in the ice. "We take a snowmobile down that corridor to the silo. Once we're there, we climb to the surface, where the dome is situated."

"Ahh. So who's driving?"

"You're the commander."

"That I am. Show me to my chariot," she ordered the dark-featured young man.

Several minutes later, his arms were clinging desperately around her waist as they rocketed down the narrow passageway at a blistering pace. He conjured up images of what he would look like if they crashed, and he pictured his body a mass of compound fractures lying at the end of a long bloodstain that stood out sharply in the snow. He was immeasurably relieved when they made it to the end of the corridor still intact.

Malory leaped off the snowmobile and turned on her flashlight so she could investigate her surroundings. A few yards away was a ladder that disappeared into a circular hole in the ice.

"How far up?" she asked.

"About a quarter of a mile. Don't let any exposed skin touch the metal of the ladder."

"So it would be a bad idea to lick one of the rungs?"

He chuckled. "Only if you want to have your tongue amputated."

"Think I'll pass," she said with a grin. "Want me to carry any of the gear?"

"I got it."

"You're the boss. Lead the way."

A few minutes into the climb, she was beginning to think that she would have been better off bored in her office. It was frightfully cold, and her hands were starting to hurt, the chill of the metal ladder effortlessly penetrating the insulation of her gloves. The atmosphere of the tunnel was claustrophobic, and it was creepy in the dark.

When they finally reached the top, she decided that DeSoto had been correct; it was indeed quite a hike. They emerged into a small—but, fortunately, much warmer—room filled with a variety of cabling and electronic equipment. She noticed that space heaters were installed in the walls, and she turned to DeSoto.

"These heaters run on a timer?"

"Yes," he replied, shedding his backpack. "They run just enough to keep the equipment from freezing over."

"All of this powered from our own generators?"

"Yes."

"Why so far away from the main compound?"

"Because we needed an outside landscape that could camouflage our equipment. The area above the compound is flat ice. It's hard to hide the dome."

She looked to the ceiling. "Are you telling me we're standing under a glass roof?"

"A special kind of glass, yes. You wouldn't be able see this place from the outside unless you stepped on it."

"Wow. You guys really went all-out here. Communications go down regularly?"

"Yeah. In the winter months, the dome has to be cleared two or three times a week."

"That often?"

"We get a break with the change of season."

"I see. So what is it we need to do?"

"Unfortunately, we have to go outside and shovel the snow off the dome."

"That sounds like fun," she said dryly. She was still cold. "How much snow?"

He shrugged. "Depends. It's not really snow. We don't get a lot of that here.

Winds from the coast blow ice into the interior, so the landscape is always changing. Maybe four feet; might be a little less."

"Great," she said, now certain that she should have stayed in her office.

"Well, we get Mexican tonight for dinner," he offered. "Dr. Rivers makes a mean plate."

"Excuse me? Dr. Rivers is making dinner?"

"Usually once a week, a couple of people give Mr. Jones and the kitchen staff a night off. Dr. Rivers always does Mexican."

"Really?"

"Yep."

"Hmmm. Then let's get after it."

She tried to hide her frown when he handed her a shovel.

1800 hours

Malory trudged back to her quarters and flopped face-down onto her cot in all of her clothes, immediately covering herself with blankets. She had never been so cold in her life. It had taken most of the day to clear the snow from the dome, due largely to the fact that they had to work in shifts. They were unable to endure the weather for more than ten minutes at a time. It had been pitch-black outside, and the wind could only be described as evil. She knew for a fact that she wouldn't be volunteering for another project, no matter how bored she might become.

She peeked out from under the covers to glance at the clock, a little grin twitching at the corners of her mouth. "Almost dinnertime."

Corky stood behind the counter, jovially filling the passing trays with food. This was one of her favorite activities; she loved to cook and enjoyed the friendly banter of her colleagues. Being the chef also provided the benefit of indulging her ego, and she gleefully soaked up the compliments she received for her culinary efforts.

In fact, now that Larry was gone, she had grudgingly decided that things weren't as bad as she had predicted. It had taken a lot of effort, but she was finally able to admit, despite her personal feelings for the insufferable commander, that everyone seemed to genuinely like the woman. She didn't intrude, was easygoing and pretty much let everyone do their own thing.

Her own feelings, however, contrasted starkly with public opinion. She hated— more accurately, *loathed* —the bitch to the point of being unable to devise a death for the redheaded slag that would be suitably tortuous. Even more maddening was the fact that she couldn't figure out why the commander would go to such great lengths to torment her. She would probably like the woman her co-workers described, but she had yet to see that person, and it didn't make her feel special to be singled out for such abuse. The whole thing both pissed her off and perplexed her.

"Uh-oh, Corky," Clovis said, coming up from behind to deliver another platter of food from the kitchen. "Word of your table has reached the ears of the commander."

"What?"

"Here she comes," Clovis said with a nod.

Corky looked over to see that the commander had entered the mess hall, and she tensed. *Trapped!* She couldn't very well storm out while serving the food she had prepared for everyone. She scowled as it occurred to her that the bitch probably knew this and was using it to her advantage.

She tracked the woman covertly as she made her way toward the counter, scoffing internally at the way she was dressed. *What a slob.* Her boots were untied, the laces dragging behind her on the floor. Her blue fatigue pants were half-tucked into one boot, as if she were too lazy to bother. And she wore a gray Annapolis sweatshirt that was covered liberally with white paint stains. Even her hair gave the impression of slothfulness. It was tied up but falling out all over the place, and it secretly chapped Corky's ass that the woman was pretty enough to get away with looking so slovenly. It bothered her even more that her appearance probably did nothing but endear her to the male population. *God, I hate her!*

She hastily summoned her most impassive expression as the commander grabbed a tray and sauntered forward.

"Good evening, Doctors," Malory said cheerfully. "Be generous with the grub; I worked up an appetite today."

Corky snatched Malory's tray silently and handed it to Clovis to fill.

"I heard you went outside with DeSoto today," Clovis said. "How was it?"

"Cold," she replied with a shiver.

"I'll bet." He chuckled, handing her a tray filled to the brim.

Malory's gaze fell to the food in front of her, quite aware of the brown eyes watching her intently. "What's this?"

"An assortment of Mexican dishes," Corky said stiffly before Clovis could answer.

Malory studied the tray suspiciously. "It looks like Pancho Villa puked in my plate."

Corky's irritation rose sharply at the sound of Clovis's quickly stifled chuckle. She simmered silently as she watched the commander poke the food experimentally with a fork, her face twisted in disgust. Finally, she raised a portion to her mouth, grimacing painfully.

"Oh, my God. It tastes like barbecued shit!" she exclaimed with a gag, letting the food slowly dribble out of her mouth to land with a moist splat back in her plate. "Jesus, I wouldn't allow a pig to swill in this," she added in revulsion, backing away from the counter with a shudder.

Clovis watched the entire spectacle, his jaw clenched tightly to keep from laughing. He had seen Corky start to pale and had noticed her mouth drop open slightly in horror as the commander let the food fall from her mouth. He turned wary eyes on her as Lovecraft left the room and noted that the little doctor looked mad enough to chew through enriched uranium.

"That miserable cunt," she finally rasped, reaching out to grab the tray of food the commander had left behind and then storming after her.

It was his first thought to stop her before she did anything foolish, but Clovis suspected that the commander knew what she was doing. Instead, with Corky safely out of the room, he finally let out the laughter that had been strangling him.

Corky stomped through the halls, her anger growing with every step. As she rounded the last corner, she caught sight of her target heading for her quarters, and fury threatened to burst from every pore. *The bitch was skipping! Fuckin' skipping! I want her dead. I want her family dead. I want her house burned to the ground.*

Malory entered her office and kicked off her boots, a huge smile plastered on her face. Suddenly sensing a presence behind her, she turned to find Dr. Rivers standing in the doorway.

"You forgot your goddamn dinner," Corky growled, launching the commander's dinner tray into the room with deadly accuracy.

Malory didn't have time to do anything but bring her hands up to protect her face as the tray hit her elbows and coated her from the neck down in Mexican cuisine. She peeked out from behind her hands to see the doctor breathing so heavily in the doorway that she was practically snarling. She couldn't help it; she laughed. She laughed so hard that she doubled over.

The commander's amusement was simply too much for Corky to handle, and she rushed into the room, raising a hand with every intention of wiping the dumbfuck smile off the woman's face. By the time she was in range, anger transformed the intended slap into a from-behind-the-back haymaker that she let fly with as much strength as she could muster. She was stunned when the blow was stopped by a powerful grip around her wrist. Startled, she looked up to find pale-blue eyes appraising her, and abruptly, two crimson eyebrows waggled at her suggestively.

"Gimme some sugar, baby," Malory rumbled, darting forward to place a kiss on the flummoxed doctor's lips.

With a gasp, Corky backed up a step and tore her wrist from the woman's grip. "You horrid bitch."

This time, Corky was so fast with her slap that it darted past the commander's defenses. She let her teeth show in satisfaction as the woman tried to shake off the blow.

"Wow," Malory said after a stunned second. "I kinda liked that. If I kiss you again, will you slap the other cheek?"

Corky gaped at her. "You're fucked in the head."

Malory shrugged. "Are you afraid of me?"

"No!"

"You're shakin' like a dog shittin' peach pits."

"Maybe I'm just pissed off."

"Wanna take a shower with me?"

"I've gotta get out of here," Corky exclaimed, spinning and running from the room.

Malory watched her go with a smile, bringing a hand up to rub her stinging cheek. "Gotcha."

Dr. Watkins leaned on his shovel at the bottom of Excavation and surveyed his surroundings. A day of labor had not agreed with him, and the hole in the ice certainly didn't have a smooth, circular bottom. At any given time, half of it was chopped into levels of different depths. The thought of making yet another trip across the man-made arctic Stairmaster was enough to leave him feeling exhausted.

He squinted in response to the ungodly glare coming from the portable lights and released a deep breath that, in the frozen air, was as visible as cigar smoke.

"I already miss the summer crew."

"You just don't like to work," Dr. Isaaks replied.

"True," Watkins admitted with a shrug. "How did we get stuck with shit duty, anyway?"

"We drew straws, remember?"

"Oh, yeah."

"A little exercise will do you good."

"Right," he grumbled. "You know what I want to know?"

"Pray tell."

"Why isn't the military down here, armed with shovels and picks?"

"Excuse me?"

"I mean, isn't learning how to dig a latrine the first thing they teach you in Basic Training?" he asked, smiling at his own wit. "I'd think they'd take to this kind of work like a fish to water."

Isaaks shook his head sadly. "One of these days, the wrong person is going to overhear one of your comments and not appreciate it."

He clutched his chest in mock horror. "God forbid."

The other man chuckled. "If it weren't too painful to watch, I think I'd enjoy being present when you're confronted with the inevitable rude awakening."

"Yeah, yeah."

A shout from Clovis caught their attention, and they looked in his direction to see him wave a hand in front of his neck and point a finger skyward.

"Looks like we're calling it a day," Isaaks said.

"Thank God."

Isaaks stretched to work out the kinks in his back. "Looks like our friends agree with you," he said, gesturing toward his retreating colleagues. "They're already on their way back up."

Watkins dropped his shovel and started after them. "Let's go."

"Uhm...care to give me a hand with the gear?"

Watkins came to a halt and sighed; he was going to have to make another trip after all. He changed direction and gave Isaaks a dispassionate glare as the man rolled his eyes and began the journey across the floor of the excavation.

They were halfway to their destination when the ground seemed to move beneath Watkins's feet, and he froze in his tracks. Not sure he hadn't imagined it, he took several cautious steps forward and froze again as he experienced another, much more distinct tremor. His eyes landed on Dr. Isaaks, but the man was still moving forward and apparently hadn't noticed anything amiss.

He spun on his heel and, without uttering a word of warning to his companion, burst into a headlong sprint for safety.

Corky had spent the past few weeks in constant fear of another confrontation with the commander. She had been left suspicious and confused after every encounter in which she was met with a polite nod or greeting. The woman baffled her to no end. Apparently successful in her mission to incite a riot between them, the commander was now very cordial, no longer going out of her way to illicit any emotion or response from her, granting her both distance and respect. Corky wasn't sure that the bitch didn't have a doppelgänger. Yet she would die before letting her guard down again, often considering the notion that the woman had some sort of grand scheme to drive her insane slowly.

In another galling development, Lovecraft was becoming ever more popular with the staff. She often spent time in the mess hall laughing lewdly with the men, obviously sharing coarse jokes and tomfoolery. It left Corky feeling somewhat ostracized, considering that they were the only two females in the compound. To add insult to injury, her best friend, Clovis, was unable to hide the fact that he adored the fucking woman. It made her want to vomit every time she saw him make goo-goo eyes at the bitch.

Corky slammed her coffee mug on her desk, thinking—not for the first time—that she should call the commander on the carpet and force her to admit the details of her insidious plan. She was so lost in her thoughts, she almost screamed in surprise when the station alarm went off.

"Dr. Rivers, POs Percy and Coy, and all military personnel report to Excavation immediately!" McNeely barked over the PA system. *"Move it, people!"*

"Oh, boy."

Minutes later, she was sprinting down the corridor, pausing as she passed through a heavy fire door to wiggle into a safety harness and strap spikes to her boots. The metal tiles of the hall abruptly gave way to ice only a few feet past the door, and she clamped onto the guide rope that led down the tunnel to the excavation site.

The corridor made for slow going. It was completely carved from the ice and led down at a severe angle for almost a quarter of a mile. One slip, and it would be a long slide on her ass to the bottom before she was called up short by the safety rope. She moved along as quickly and as cautiously as she could, becoming aware of others making their way down the tunnel behind her.

Almost ten minutes later, she reached the end and emerged into the circular chamber of the main dig site. The room was a little over one hundred yards in circumference, and a shelf about fifteen yards wide made up the perimeter of a gigantic hole in the ice that spiraled downward for another quarter of a mile. A rather narrow pathway cut from the ice wound down the interior to the floor of the pit.

She was soon assaulted by an unimaginably foul odor, so strong that it made her eyes water. "Where's the fire?" she yelled to get everyone's attention, relieved when Clovis emerged from the crowd.

"Stand by, Doctor," Hanson said as he rushed by.

"What's going on, Clovis?" she asked.

"We hit a pocket in the ice," he explained. "The bottom fell out."

"Oh, God. Anyone down there?"

"Isaaks. He was the only one in a bad spot when it happened. He's trapped. We couldn't reach him."

"Is he okay?"

"Seems okay, but if he slips, he won't make it," Clovis said grimly. "The pocket looks to be about forty or fifty yards deep."

Corky broke away from her friend and pushed through the spectators to see for herself. She looked over the side to see that the cave-in had taken a good portion of the walkway with it, making it impossible to get to the bottom—where, unfortunately, Dr. Isaaks clung desperately to the ice, precariously close to the edge of a nasty drop.

"I'm going over. Start feeding me slack," the commander's voice barked over the radio in Chief Reynolds's hands. *"Get everybody on the ropes. He's gonna be heavy from this distance."*

"We're on it," Reynolds replied. "Slack to come slowly," he added and turned to start issuing orders to the men working on a complicated series of ropes.

Corky gasped when she realized what was happening and turned to take a closer look over the edge, following the path of the ropes to the figure in a black hat dangling from the end. Anxiously, she watched the commander drive an anchor into the wall and level a rifle across the void directly at Dr. Isaaks. Instead of a bullet, the rifle fired a bolt and cable that shot across the distance between them, burying itself in the ice about three feet from the man's head and creating a horizontal bridge between them.

Corky chewed on her lip nervously as Malory spent several minutes working on her end of the cable before she let go of the wall and started pulling herself across. It was slow going; it took nearly a quarter of an hour for her to get to the other side and get Dr. Isaaks into a harness.

"I'm not convinced the bolts will hold both of us at the same time, I'm sending Isaaks across first," Malory's voice came over the radio. *"He fell several meters and took a beating. Be gentle with him."*

"Will do," Reynolds replied.

Malory dug some footholds into the wall so she could remove her weight from the line and attached Isaaks's harness to the cable.

"You ready, Dr. Isaaks?" she asked.

He looked at her with wide eyes.

She chuckled. "Don't sweat it. The harness will hold your weight; all you have to do is pull yourself across. When you get to the other side, clamp onto the ropes the guys have dropped for you, and they'll pull you up."

He tried a grin. "Easy as that, huh?"

"Yep. If I can do it, you can do it."

He nodded, took a deep breath and gingerly left the relative safety of his perch to dangle in the air by the seat of his pants. An anxious moment later, he was situated and threw an uncertain glance over his shoulder at Malory.

"I think my arm is broken."

She nodded. "No hurry, Doctor. Do the best you can."

Isaaks's progress was slow but ultimately successful and above, Chief Reynolds turned to the men on the ropes. "Pull him up, but go easy. He's injured."

Corky looked over the edge, trying to assess the man's injuries from a distance; then she turned to get Percy's attention. "Did we bring a stretcher?"

"Yes, ma'am," he replied, and she nodded in approval.

"I'm headed across," Malory said over the radio.

"Understood," Reynolds replied and turned to address the laboring men. "Watch the commander's ropes. She's moving."

By the time Isaaks was pulled over the edge, Malory was three-quarters of the way across the cable. Percy and Coy rushed forward to assist the man, and Corky's eyes returned to the laboring commander, watching in horror as the bolt on the far side broke free from the ice. "She's falling!"

"Brace!" Reynolds bellowed.

Corky covered her mouth with a hand as the commander tried to get her feet in front of her to soften the impact. She was only partially successful and was slammed against the wall with stunning force, the men on the ropes grunting with the effort of her falling weight.

"Get her up here now!" Reynolds ordered, dropping his radio onto the ice and running over to grab a spot on the rope.

Every available man rushed over to lend his strength to the effort, and Corky nervously watched the commander for any signs of life, surprised by the relief she felt when Malory lifted an arm and spoke into the radio.

"I'm okay. Go easy."

Reynolds clapped Clovis on the shoulder and rose to retrieve his radio. "Good to hear."

"Dr. Rivers," Percy said, "Isaaks has a broken arm. Other than that, just a few scrapes and bruises."

"Get him to Medical. I'll be along shortly."

"Right away."

Corky loitered for a few minutes, feeling it her duty to hang back and see whether the commander needed any attention. At least, that was what she kept telling herself. Then the men rushed forward to help the commander over the edge, and she stood shakily, leveling a grin at everyone present.

"Fuckin' A, that hurt," she exclaimed boisterously, receiving a round of relieved laughs and chuckles.

"Chief Reynolds!" she barked after the laughter had subsided.

"Commander," he said, coming to attention.

Malory studied him carefully, again struck by the chief's uncanny resemblance to a younger Sean Connery. "Tomorrow, you'll explain to me why the people working down here didn't have radios, forcing someone to run all the way to the compound to raise the alarm."

"Yes, Commander."

"Well done, Chief." She looked around. "All of you, very well done. Is Dr. Isaaks okay?"

"A broken arm. He'll be fine," Corky said. "I'd like you to report to Medical at your earliest convenience."

"All right," she agreed, and Corky turned to begin the climb back to the compound.

"I want to speak to everyone tomorrow at 0800 in the mess hall," Malory said. "Excavation is put on hold until I make some decisions, and this area is off-limits until that time."

A few faces appeared to protest, but she cut it off quickly. "No exceptions," she warned. "Sergeant Major, a word, please."

Nearly an hour later, Malory walked into Medical, feeling bone-tired. Dr. Rivers was still working on her patient, so she slumped into a chair by the door and waited. Behind the divider, she could hear Corky talking to the injured man in low tones, and her eyelids started to grow heavy. She thought about going back to her quarters, but her shoulder was screaming at her to stay put. Reluctantly, she acquiesced to the demands of her body and leaned her head against the wall, closing her eyes.

When Corky emerged, she was surprised to find the commander asleep with her idiotic hat in her lap. After much consideration, she decided to let her be and quietly summoned Coy to help Dr. Isaaks back to his quarters.

It was the arrival of the young petty officer that woke Malory, and she suffered a few seconds of disorientation, regaining her bearings as Dr. Isaaks was being ushered past. He stopped in front of her and held out a hand. She stood to take it.

"Thank you, Commander," he said. "That was a brave thing you did."

"You're very welcome."

"Commander, would you join me back here, please?" Corky asked.

"I'll let you get to it," Isaaks said. "Thanks again."

"Any time," she said, waiting for Coy to lead him from the room before turning to face the doctor.

Corky stared at her for a long moment. "Are you injured?"

"Yes."

Corky chewed on her lip. "Have a seat," she said, gesturing to the exam table behind her.

"Would you summon Dr. Stokes first?" she asked. "I was going to do it, but I fell asleep."

"I think if you're hurt, we've put it off long enough."

"Please."

Another long stare, this one of a curious nature. "All right," she said, moving over to the phone to summon Clovis.

They waited in uncomfortable silence, both fidgeting uneasily until the man stuck his head in.

"What's up, Corky?" he asked, his eyes lighting up when he noticed the commander. The reaction didn't go unnoticed by the doctor, and she felt a twinge of jealousy.

"Actually, I wanted to speak with you," Malory said. "At the meeting tomorrow, I want you to explain to me, as if you were talking to a child, exactly what it is you expect to find under the ice."

He looked confused. "You weren't briefed?"

"I'm not one for deciphering scientific texts, Dr. Stokes," she said. "That's why I want you to explain it to me tomorrow in Fisher-Price terms."

A scathingly insulting comment was perched on Corky's tongue, but with an effort, she swallowed it. She could see how tired the woman was, and it occurred to her that she was vastly overmatched in the bitch department if hostilities were to flame anew.

"Okay," Clovis said.

"Thank you. That's all, Dr. Stokes."

He knew a dismissal when he heard one. "Good night, ladies," he said with a departing smile.

Corky waited until the door closed behind him to speak. "You ready now?"

"Yeah," Malory mumbled, walking over to the table to take a seat.

Corky moved to follow her but was called up short.

"Lock the door, please."

"Why?"

"Just do it, please."

Corky pursed her lips thoughtfully and did as she was asked. "All right. What's the story?"

"My left shoulder."

"Let's lose the jacket and shirt so we can have a look."

"You'll have to help me," Malory admitted. "I can't raise my arm more than a few inches."

"Jesus. Why didn't you tell me something earlier?"

"Because I was needed, and there was another in worse shape."

Corky shook her head and gently helped her out of her parka. "I'll have to cut off the sweatshirt if you think it would be too hard to lift over your head."

"Cut it off."

Soon, the sweatshirt was reduced to a rag, and Corky examined her quickly, noting the faint outline of surgical scars along her collarbone and shoulder. "What happened here?"

"Old injury."

"I see. You have a hell of a bruise. I'd like to X-ray."

"Okay."

Twenty minutes later, Malory was lying down on the examination table, staring up at nothing and waiting for Corky to deliver the bad news. She could hear her grunting over the X-rays and had come back to the table once to poke and prod her with what Malory suspected was a little more force than absolutely necessary.

"Well, Commander," she said, walking back to the table and hovering above her. "It would seem to me—"

"You can call me Malory."

Corky blinked. "Excuse me?"

"You can call me Malory."

"Why would I want to do that?"

"Because it's my name?"

Corky looked at her thoughtfully. "I think I'll stick with 'Commander.'"

Malory sighed. "Sorry to hear that."

"Uh-huh," Corky said. "You ready to hear your diagnosis?"

"Shoot."

Corky straightened into her most professional stance and spoke solemnly. "It seems you're suffering from...an owie."

Malory rolled her eyes. "Can I get a second opinion?"

Corky chuckled. "In a few months, sure."

"And what treatment would you suggest for this heinous injury?"

"Amputation, of course."

"Why am I not surprised?"

Corky smiled. "Nothing's broken, but you have a sprain. You've had a lot of prior work done in there. Must have been pretty bad."

"Yeah."

"Hmmm. I'll give you some meds for the pain, but it'll get better quicker than you think. Just don't overuse it or abuse it."

Malory nodded.

"Can I ask you a question?"

"Okay."

"What does the 'Q' stand for?"

"What?"

"As in 'Malory Q. Lovecraft.'"

"Oh. It stands for 'Quinn.'"

"Quinn?"

Malory smiled slyly. "Yeah. I was named after a song. Wanna hear it?"

"I'll pass," Corky said quickly. "But are you up for another question?"

"I guess."

"You sure about that? If you answer honestly, there'll be another question. Maybe a few."

"Go ahead. I'm lying here in my bra; you have me at your mercy."

"Why did you single me out for abuse?"

"Because I figured the sooner I got past your attitude and forced a confrontation, the sooner we could be friends."

Corky had been wary of the answer and was actually surprised by the quick and seemingly honest response. "I see."

Malory turned eyes in Corky's direction. "Is there another question?"

"Why did you kiss me?"

"Because I'm attracted to you."

"What made you think I would want to be kissed by another woman?"

"Nothing. I just wanted to do it."

"So you didn't know I was gay?"

"Had no idea."

"That took guts."

"Perhaps."

"Why did you have me lock the door?"

"Because I'm the commander," she said. "Now, as much as I enjoy the interrogation, I'd really like to go to sleep. Could you help me get my parka on so I can return to my quarters, please?"

Corky stared at her for a long moment, finally nodding her consent and helping her with her jacket.

Chief Reynolds reached out and gave the door a short rap before stepping inside.

"Howdy, boys," he said in greeting, fanning a hand in front of him to clear a path though the cigar smoke that assaulted him. "Christ, how do you guys breathe in this shit?"

McNeely chuckled and pushed a bottle of Jack Daniels across the card table. "Have a few belts, and you won't notice, Chief."

He grinned. "Don't mind if I do. Make a hole, gentlemen."

Sergeants Alvarez and Terrel made room, and the chief took a seat between them. "What's the game?"

"Seven-card stud, Chicago low," Alvarez replied, giving the cards another quick shuffle. "Ante up."

Reynolds poured himself a drink and waited for Sergeant Hanson to stack the allotted amount of poker chips in front of him before tossing one into the middle of the table.

"What's your read on the new boss, Chief?" Hanson asked.

"Still a bit early. Can't really say."

"First impression?"

"Well, I think I'd like to get a look up her dress before I answer that."

"What?" Hanson asked around a chuckle. "Why?"

"Because I suspect she's hiding a pair of brass balls under there."

"No shit," Alvarez piped up. "She went over the edge to get Isaaks today in a heartbeat. Didn't even think twice about it."

"My point exactly," Reynolds agreed.

"That's true enough," Terrel said. "But I gotta wonder what she did wrong to end up down here."

"You're way off base there, my friend," McNeely said.

"How so?"

"Look around," he replied. "This is a state-of-the-art, multibillion-dollar facility. Granted, there are only twenty-nine people wandering around down here at the moment, but bear in mind that in a few months, there'll be close to one hundred and fifty. So the better question is, why did they entrust the administration of this station to a lieutenant commander?"

"Good question," Reynolds said. "What's the answer?"

He shrugged. "Our CO is a decorated Naval Academy graduate and an officer who, with this command, is operating at least two levels above her current rank. She's on the fast track."

The men silently pondered McNeely's reply as a new hand was dealt around the table.

"You know what I'd like to know?" Terrel asked after a moment.

"What would that be?"

"How do ya hide a woody from a CO that's built like a brick shithouse?" he asked, receiving a round of chuckles.

"Wear a jockstrap," Alvarez suggested. "It'll keep you...uhm...confined."

Terrel grinned. "Not exactly standard issue. Where would I find one of those around here?"

"Ask the kitchen staff."

"The kitchen staff? What, is a jock required apparel for kitchen service?"

"No, but they're the people to talk to if you need a custom-fit peanut shell."

The barrage of resulting laughter resulted in a slow fade of the smile Terrel had been wearing.

"Damn, boy," Reynolds said, clapping the young man on the back. "You should've seen that comin' a mile away."

Malory shuffled out of her quarters the next morning and made her way down the hall, entering the mess and going immediately for the coffee, refusing to acknowledge anyone until she satisfied her craving.

Once the coffee had provided her the required early-morning energy, she turned to face the crowd and seated herself at the front of the room. "Chief Reynolds, you have an explanation for me?"

Dr. Lenard spoke up in a rush. "Commander, it seems that several of us are to blame for the lack of radios. We...uhm...often forget to take them."

"I see," she said. "Sergeant Major, your opinion, please?"

"It'll take a week or more to re-create a safe working environment. I'll need some help."

"Very well. Use whoever you need. I want to see a duty list by the end of the day."

"Done," he answered with a nod.

She considered for a moment. "When the sergeant major informs me he is satisfied with the conditions in excavation, we can resume our dig. No one is to be found in that area without his permission until that time."

She looked around for objections and was pleased when she saw none.

"Also, in the future, anyone caught working down there without a radio or a safety rope will be relieved and confined to quarters for a time to be determined by me. Any questions?"

No questions were forthcoming, so she turned to Clovis. "Dr. Stokes, you have a lesson plan prepared for me?"

"You bet."

She stood and gestured for him to take the floor, taking his chair when he got up and shooting a wink at Corky, who had been seated next to him. To her dismay, the doctor pretended not to notice.

"Okay," he said gruffly, clearing his throat. "What we expect to find, what we *hope* to find, is a spacecraft—or, more accurately, pieces of a spacecraft that we assume crashed into the ice at some point in the very distant past."

Malory was dumbfounded. "What?" she blurted in surprise.

Clovis blinked at her.

"I'm sorry. Please continue," she said, embarrassed, choosing to ignore the few quiet snickers.

"From sonar readings and estimated projection, it seems the craft crashed into the ice with enough force to break apart at impact."

"How long ago was this?"

"Impossible to tell," Clovis replied. "It would depend on a lot of variables. We suspect that the ship crashed with enough force to bury itself. We believe the force of its collision with the Earth resulted in a sizable crater, flash-boiling the ice it landed in. Subsequently, the water from the melted ice soon refroze over the wreckage and removed the impact crater from the landscape, essentially disguising its age under the natural formation of the ice pack."

"I don't understand."

"Okay," he said. "Imagine that five thousand years ago, someone dug a hole in the ice and threw their wristwatch inside. Instead of covering the watch with ice, they just filled the hole with water. What would happen?"

"It would freeze, right?"

"Exactly."

"But can't you tell how old the ice is?"

"We can estimate, yes. But it's not an exact science, especially considering what we theorize of the circumstances surrounding the crash. You see, there are a multitude of factors that—"

"Make a guess, Dr. Stokes."

"Uh…well…the ice we're currently digging in is thousands of years old, and we're several months away from reaching what we consider to be a significant portion of the spacecraft."

She leaned against the back of her chair thoughtfully. "All right, why do you assume it to be a spacecraft?"

"Because we've already uncovered several small fragments of material that apparently broke off the main craft. It's of a composition we can't identify. The atomic structure is extraterrestrial."

"And the main craft? Is it still intact?"

"We believe there are three large sections still relatively intact," Clovis said. "It is from those pieces that we hope to gain the most knowledge."

She grunted. "So how did we find this thing?"

"Mostly luck. A routine expedition took some core samples that had traces of an unidentifiable material. Further study, ground-penetrating radar, advanced sonar, deep core drilling and a detailed exploration of the area eventually led us to where we are today."

Malory gave this a moment of thought. "Okay. Off the subject, why did it smell so bad in there yesterday?"

"I would assume stale air."

"You don't sound convinced."

"We haven't had the chance to investigate."

She rose to her feet. "Thanks for the education, Dr. Stokes," she said, giving him a nod. "It looks like we have some work to do. So let's get after it."

May 1 - 1730 hours

Four days later, Corky decided to bite the bullet. She wasn't sure whether it was the right decision, but she felt that she owed it to herself to try. The commander clearly had a multifaceted personality, and there was no denying that she found the woman intriguing, no matter how hard she tried to convince herself otherwise. She suspected that under all the bravado the woman displayed, there lurked a person she would like to know. The only question remaining was whether she could stand to be in her company long enough to find out.

With this mission in mind, she waited until the end of the work day and marched determinedly to the commander's quarters. She found a closed door and took a minute to cement the binds on her temper before knocking. When she received no response, she knocked again and poked her head in to find an empty office. She walked a few paces into the room and was surprised to hear singing, or what passed for it, coming from the woman's quarters. Corky winced; it was painfully apparent that vocal talent wasn't on the commander's list of abilities. She went to rap on the door but paused when she caught sight of Little Lovecraft sitting in the chair behind the commander's desk. Her eyes narrowed, and she had to take a moment to forcibly remind herself why she was doing this.

She turned and pounded on the door a little more loudly than she had intended. She quickly grew annoyed when her knock wasn't answered and she was assaulted by another verse being sung in the other room.

"Hush, my darling, don't cry, my darling, the lion sleeps tonight!"

"Jesus, it sounds like she's boiling a fuckin' cat," Corky whispered in disgust and knocked on the door again.

"A-wimoweh, a-wimoweh, a-wimoweh..."

"God help us all," she exclaimed, coming to the abrupt decision to just open the door. "Commander?"

Corky had to clamp a hand over her mouth to keep from laughing. The woman had headphones on and was singing into her toothbrush as she stood in front of her little sink and mirror. Dressed in her fatigue pants and bra, she swayed her ass back and forth in time with the music.

Finally, she turned to see that she had unexpected company, and Corky couldn't contain her laughter when Malory yelped and jumped in surprise, almost falling down. When Malory got over her shock, she ripped the Walkman off angrily, her eyes flashing indignantly.

"Don't you know how to knock?" she asked and was none too pleased when the doctor indulged in a fresh gale of laughter. "What's so damn funny?"

Corky could barely summon the breath needed to answer. "Your face."

"What about my face?"

Corky raised a finger and pointed at the mirror.

Malory frowned and turned to take in her reflection, immediately flushing with a new wave of crimson. "Goddamn it," she hissed, reaching for a towel to wipe away the toothpaste that covered her chin and was running down her neck.

"Do you..." Corky struggled. "Do you often foam at the mouth?"

Malory stomped her foot, ignoring the comment and afraid that the doctor's laughter might be contagious. "You might as well come in," she said sarcastically, picking up a T-shirt from the floor to put on.

Corky took a deep breath and wiped her eyes before walking into the room. She looked around for a place to sit, but there wasn't a square inch of space that wasn't covered with something.

Malory saw the dilemma and walked over to throw the clothes covering the room's single chair onto the floor. "Have a seat."

Corky admired the disheveled room with amusement. "How do you walk around in here?"

"When it gets tired of me stepping on it, it just gets out of the way. Was there something you wanted to see me about?"

Corky smiled. The commander was doing an admirable job of ignoring the blush that still clung to her face. It made her task a little easier. "I was wondering if you wanted to go to dinner and maybe watch a movie."

Malory gaped. "I'm sorry, what?"

"Please don't make me ask again. It was hard enough just to decide to."

It took a moment for Malory to wipe the befuddled look from her face. "Sure. I'd like that."

1800 hours

Corky picked a spot in the mess that was somewhat secluded and sat down across from the commander, who had been uncharacteristically quiet. Whether she was still embarrassed about being caught goofing around or merely perplexed by the developing situation was yet to be determined. She watched the woman play with the food on her plate, and it suddenly occurred to her that the enigmatic commander was probably used to being in charge and wasn't sure how to act. Corky decided to press the perceived advantage.

"So where you from?"

"Uh...Boston."

"Interesting. You don't have an accent."

"No, I moved around too much to develop one."

"How old are you?"

"Thirty."

"What's your favorite food?"

"Pussy."

Corky's cheeks ballooned in an effort to stifle a bray of involuntary laughter. She covered her mouth with her hand and looked away in sudden embarrassment. When she had composed herself, she turned an accusatory glare in the commander's direction.

"Have you no shame?"

"Why did you ask me out?"

Corky shook her head sadly. "Because despite the fact that you can be an atrocious bitch, I sense a likable person underneath."

Malory raised an eyebrow. "Does this mean you think I'm a hottie?"

Corky sighed. This was going to be more difficult than she expected. "Can you at least *try* not to be an ass?"

"I'll do my best."

"Your best can be very good when you put your mind to it."

"What in the world does that mean?"

"It means I've watched you," Corky said. "You're intelligent, capable, undemanding and brave. I watched you risk your life to save Dr. Isaaks, and unfortunately, I watched you be the most unendurable person I've ever met. Why can't you be the person that everybody likes and admires to me?"

"Maybe it's a case of teasing the girl you like."

Corky chuckled. "We're not in grade school here. Your idea of teasing and mine are quite different. I've never hit anyone in anger until I met you."

"I had it coming."

Corky stared at her. "You enjoyed it, and you enjoyed pissing me off, didn't you?"

"I can't say that I enjoyed being struck. But yeah, it was a hoot watching you get madder than a one-legged cat trying to bury shit on a frozen pond."

Corky tightened the grip she had on her fork. "Do you ever think before you speak, or are you this tactless and tasteless with everybody?"

Chastised, Malory reviewed her part of the conversation. "I guess I could've phrased that differently," she admitted, shoving a heaping forkful of food into her mouth.

"Are you a virgin?"

"What?" she exclaimed around her food.

"You heard me."

Malory hurriedly swallowed. "Why would you ask that?"

"Because you come on stronger than cheap aftershave but don't have the faintest idea how to be flattering," she explained, watching the woman wolf down another huge portion of food. "Plus you have despicable table manners, a crass vocabulary, and you're a slob. I would imagine those qualities don't appeal to many women."

Malory took the diatribe in stride. "You're the one who asked me to dinner, so I must appeal to you in some way."

Corky considered her response and decided to use the commander's tactics against her. "Sure. You've got an awesome set of tits."

"I knew you thought so," she replied triumphantly.

Foiled, Corky frowned. "So you didn't answer my question."

"What question was that?"

"Are you a virgin?"

"Would it make you happy if I said yes?"

"I don't know. It might answer some questions I have about you."

"Are you?"

"Am I what? A virgin?"

"Yeah."

"No, I'm not."

"Are you a slut, then?"

Corky took a deep breath. "No. Are you?"

"No, but I'm willing to learn."

The smile came without permission. "You kill me."

"Thanks...uhm...I guess."

"So tell me about yourself."

"What do you want to know?"

"Anything you want to tell me."

Malory propped her chin on her hand thoughtfully for a moment. "I like needlessly violent movies, and I vote Republican."

Corky laughed at her brevity. "Is that all you want to share?"

"I guess," she replied. "I'm not very good at this. If you want to know something, it would be easier if you asked me."

Corky shook her head. "You vote Republican?"

"Of course."

"Why would a gay officer in the military vote Republican?"

"Who said I was gay?"

Corky gaped. "Aren't you?"

"Well, duh."

An exasperated sigh. "You're being an ass again."

"Thanks for pointing that out," she said dryly. "I vote Republican because I believe in the bigger picture."

"Care to explain?"

"I won't endorse a party out of selfishness. I try to balance between what's good for me and what's good for the country as a whole."

"For instance?"

"Take gun control, for example. It's the very height of stupidity to believe that taking that right away from me will take guns away from criminals. The men and women who have fought and died for our country's ideals did not give their lives so I could be shot down defenseless in my home because some political hack convinced a majority of Congress that I should no longer have the right to bear arms."

"And this serves the bigger picture how?"

"How do I vote for a party that claims to want equal rights for homosexuals, but at the same time wants to take rights away from the nation as a whole? That's the very definition of selfishness. I get something for me at everyone else's expense. That doesn't serve the bigger picture."

"Nice speech."

Malory shrugged. "I can ride a soapbox when I have to. Your turn."

"My turn for what?"

"Tell me about you."

Corky smiled engagingly. "What would you like to know?"

Malory leaned forward excitedly. "Where are you from? Where did you go to school? Do you have a family? Will you kiss me good night? Do you have a pet? How old are you? Do you have a home somewhere? Where do you want to go when you leave here? What kinda music do you like? What's your favorite—?"

"Wait!" Corky exclaimed. "Lemme catch up."

"Okay."

"Let's see," she said. "I'm from Corpus Christi, I went to Texas A&M, my parents live in Arizona now, no siblings, maybe, no pets, twenty-nine, I sublet my apartment, I haven't thought about it and classical."

Malory filtered through the responses carefully and smiled slyly. "You will."

"I will what?"

"So what do we have in the way of movies to watch?"

When they entered the small lounge, it was empty with the exception of Lieutenant Ring, who was sitting up asleep on the couch, his mouth hanging open. Malory walked over and nudged him from behind.

"Looks like your show is over," she said, gesturing to the blue-screened television when he groggily turned eyes in her direction.

"Uh...yeah," he mumbled, lumbering to his feet and sleepwalking out of the room without another word.

Malory watched him go with an amused smile and turned to her companion. "So what's playing?"

Corky opened a large cabinet containing a huge assortment of DVDs. "You choose," she offered diplomatically.

Malory's eyes widened when she saw the collection. "Oh, cool."

"You don't seem to know a lot about this place, for being the one in charge," Corky observed.

"I'm pacing myself," she replied, extending a case. "Let's watch this."

Corky looked at the cover and sighed. "Can we pick something else?"

"What's wrong with *Reservoir Dogs*?"

Corky rolled her eyes.

"Fine. You choose," Malory said, walking around and flopping down on the sofa.

"Okay," Corky said cheerfully, spending a few minutes going over her possible choices. "How about *Hope Floats*?"

"What's it about?"

For an answer, Corky walked over and handed her the case to read, waiting for acceptance.

"I think I'd rather set myself on fire," Malory proclaimed, tossing the case on the coffee table as though it offended her.

Ten minutes later, after a series of offers and rejections, they finally agreed on *Kingpin*, a movie that Malory enjoyed immensely and that Corky endured with sighs, eye rolls and occasional chuckles.

As soon as it ended, Malory spun around in her seat unexpectedly, ending up on her back, her legs dangling over the end of the sofa and her head in Corky's lap. She stared up at her surprised companion hopefully. "You wanna make out now?"

"You're unbelievable," Corky said, amused.

"So is that a yes?"

"I think I'll pass."

"Come on. You know you want to."

Corky brought a hand up to smooth an errant lock of hair from Malory's face. Surprised at herself, she tore her hand away and displaced the woman from her lap roughly as she stood and took several steps away from the sofa.

Almost thrown to the floor, Malory resituated herself and turned an annoyed look on her companion. "Well, gee. A simple 'No' would've sufficed."

Corky threw her a regretful look. "I'm sorry. Maybe we'd better call it a night."

Malory frowned but nodded her acceptance reluctantly. "Come on," she said, standing up and gesturing to the door. "I'll walk you to your quarters."

Corky nodded and preceded her into the hall, glancing over her shoulder occasionally at the obviously moping woman. Coming to a decision, she turned when they reached Medical and held out a hand, which Malory took with a quizzical expression.

Corky pulled her forward and stood on her tiptoes, planting a gentle kiss on her cheek. "Good night, Malory," she said and quickly disengaged to retreat into her quarters.

The commander watched the door close and broke into a goofy smile, bouncing off down the hall.

"A-wimoweh, a-wimoweh, a-wimoweh."

The next morning, Malory entered the mess and was disappointed to find the doctor not in attendance. She poured herself a cup of coffee and took a seat with the educated types, hobnobbing with them for nearly an hour. When they eventually broke up to go make themselves busy, she rapidly found herself bored. Torn between returning to her office to do nothing and paying the doctor a visit, she chose the latter.

She burst into Medical with a happy smile, only to have it slowly change into a frown; the place was deserted. Disenchanted, she was turning to leave when she spotted an abandoned stethoscope on a countertop. Excited by the discovery, she wasted no time experimenting with it, immediately putting it on and listening to her heartbeat. When that activity became dull, she began placing it on every object she could find, hoping it would make a noise. She was in the process of clicking Corky's desk lamp on and off in the hope that the light bulb would make a cool sound when a throat being cleared signaled that she had been caught playing.

She turned to find the doctor staring at her from the doorway, her face a mixture of curiosity, peevishness and amusement.

"Uhm...I was just...uh..." She struggled, noting Corky's raised eyebrow, and finally opted for the truth. "Okay, I was fuckin' around."

"No kidding?"

Malory shrugged.

The doctor set her coffee down and walked over to grab the end of the stethoscope dangling on Malory's chest.

"This is not a toy," Corky said sternly and, for good measure, flicked the sensor sharply before pulling the scope from the commander's ears.

"Oww!"

"What are you doing in here, anyway?" Corky asked, trying not to be amused by the chastised look she was receiving.

"I guess I wanted to see you."

Corky looked at her for a long moment, unsure what to say in response. "I—"

"Commander?" the radio on Malory's waist squawked.

Irritated at the interruption, she snatched it from her belt. "What?"

"Uhm...Commander, are you alone?" McNeely asked.

"No. Should I be?"

"I think that would be best, Commander."

"Very well," she said. "Five minutes."

"Understood."

Malory's brow wrinkled as she put the radio back on her belt.

"What was that about?"

"No idea. Uhm...I have to go," she said, making tracks for the door.

"Malory?" Corky said before she could leave.

"Yeah?"

"Drop by my quarters tonight, if you want," Corky said shyly.

"Should I wear something sexy?"

"Do you own anything sexy?"

"Just my birthday suit."

"Come fully dressed."

Malory walked the last few paces to the bottom of Excavation, breathing heavily. The conversation with McNeely had been cryptic, saying only that they had found something and that her presence was required. She took the last step and let out a relieved breath. The going down was tiring and painfully slow. The men were standing about fifty yards away.

"Sergeant Major!" she yelled. McNeely broke from the crowd, starting an easy jog over to meet her, and she observed him as he approached. Easily a decade and change older than she was, the man moved with an easy grace that spoke of a lifetime of physical conditioning. Other than the dark brown hair above his ears that had started to gray, one would suspect the man to be at least ten years younger than he actually was. His green eyes sparkled with intelligence and hinted at barely suppressed sly humor.

"What's the big deal?" she asked when he arrived.

"Just come take a look."

She started forward, McNeely falling into pace beside her. "What's with the cloak-and-dagger shit, Sergeant Major? What the hell did you find, and why does it smell like a whorehouse at low tide down here?"

McNeely shook his head. "You'll need something to cover your nose; the smell is worse over by the guys."

Malory watched as he lifted a rag to cover his mouth and nose. Thinking it best to follow the man's advice, she dug in her pockets for a handkerchief and followed suit.

"I want some answers, Sergeant Major."

"I wish I could give them to you."

She was about to call the man up short but paused as they came in range of the rest of the men. She suddenly felt uneasy as she took in the expressions on their faces. The crowd parted for her, and she walked through them to see what they were all so bothered about, coming to an abrupt halt and tightening the grip on her handkerchief.

Her mind almost refused to process the sight in front of her, and she felt her knees go weak. When she finally found her voice, it came out sounding as alien as the appendage protruding through the ice.

"What in the *blue* fuck is that?"

No one answered her, and eventually, she recovered enough poise to study what the ice had revealed. About six feet away was what she assumed to be part of an arm, the skin greenish-black in appearance. At the end of the limb was what she guessed was the creature's hand, although it had only two fingers and a lethal-looking claw that served as a thumb. The fingers themselves were arachnid in structure, multijointed and curled around the sides of the wrist like a ram's horns. The smell was overpoweringly foul.

Finally, she turned away from the scene and surveyed the faces surrounding her. "Anyone not here that knows about this?"

"No, Commander," McNeely said. "I wouldn't let anyone leave."

"Good call," she said. "Cover that thing and mark it. Then all of you join me by the ramp."

She marched off, her mind already putting up walls to distort what she had seen.

When she reached the ramp, she plopped down on the ice and took off her hat. The portable lights were hot and so bright that she wished she had brought her sunglasses. Some of the men had walked back with her, and they followed her example as they waited for the ones who had stayed behind to arrive.

Eventually, McNeely and Alvarez walked up, and she stood to address them. "Okay, I guess we all knew they were digging up a spacecraft. We shouldn't be so surprised to find one of the passengers. Personally, I never stopped to think about how alien an alien might be."

"No shit there," Alvarez commented, getting a few reluctant chuckles.

"Sergeant Major, how satisfied are you with the safety of present working conditions down here?"

"Went faster than I thought it would, Skipper. I was gonna give the green light by the end of the day."

"Very well," she said. "Let's keep this under wraps until tomorrow, and I'll address everyone in the morning. I'm sure more than one of the geeks will get a hard-on over this. However, I feel the need to take some precautions—"

"I concur with that, Commander," Reynolds interrupted, looking at her questioningly, and she nodded for him to continue. "We have no idea what we're dealing with here, no telling what that thing is gonna look like or be capable of when they dig it out."

"Are you suggesting that it might still be alive?"

"What I'm saying is we don't know a damn thing about it. It looked pretty preserved to me. Who knows what its constitution might be if it thawed out? I would suggest an armed detail to oversee the excavation from this point on and to stand guard over anything biological they might pull out of here."

"I agree with Chief Reynolds, Commander," McNeely said.

Malory played with the brim of her hat for a moment. "Okay. Starting tomorrow, I want all military personnel issued side arms, to be carried until they are deemed unnecessary. Also, I want the men providing security over the dig to be issued rifles. You'll see to this, Sergeant Major, and I'll want a full accounting on a daily basis."

"Yes, ma'am."

"Additionally, I want to make damn sure that everyone has radios with them at all times. Let's also see to it that we have constant communication with McMurdo, even if this means going outside daily to clear the dome for the communication dishes. And start keeping a closer eye on the weather. Chief, this is your responsibility."

"Yes, Commander."

"Lieutenant Ring isn't down here, but I also want the helicopter in a constant state of readiness in the event of an emergency. I'll inform him when we get topside. Is there anything else that needs to be brought to my attention at this time?"

She looked around expectantly.

"All right, then, if an issue comes up, take me aside before I address everyone in the morning. Any questions?"

There were none.

She put on her hat. "Let's get the hell out of here."

Malory scrubbed herself thoroughly in the shower, attempting to wash away the uneasiness that still lingered. When she was finished, all thoughts of space monsters were pushed aside in anticipation of an evening spent with the doctor, and she hurriedly made herself presentable. Unable to contain her enthusiasm, she arrived at Corky's quarters only fifteen minutes after the duty shift.

When the door opened, Malory beamed what she hoped was her most attractive smile. "Hi there!"

Corky tried not to laugh. "A little early, aren't you?"

"Am I?" Malory asked in mock surprise. "Can I come in?"

Corky considered. "Okay."

Malory immediately brushed past the little doctor and flopped down on the cot. "You would think that with all the money they poured into this place, they could provide more than a cot for everyone to sleep on," she said, casting a come-hither look in Corky's direction.

"Make yourself at home."

"I will, thank you."

Corky shook her head. "You know, I haven't even had time to take a shower."

"I don't mind waiting. Go ahead," Malory said slyly. "I like to watch."

Corky didn't know whether to be upset or amused. "I don't think so."

"Why not? I'd let you watch me."

She chuckled. "Why don't I meet you in the mess in about half an hour?"

Malory frowned in disappointment. "I thought you asked me to come to your quarters."

"I did, but I'm not taking a shower with you in the room."

"Would it make you feel better if I joined you?"

Corky laughed. "No."

"Why are you playing so hard to get? I know you're warm for my form."

Corky's mouth dropped open. "God."

Malory grinned shamelessly.

"I can't believe you. Do you honestly expect to win me over so easily with your ham-fisted charm?"

"Well..." Malory considered, raising a finger to her lips thoughtfully. "Yeah," she said, as though it were obvious.

Corky's eyes flashed. "Not too long ago, I would've pissed all over myself in joy if you were to have suddenly died, and now you expect me to just jump in bed with you?"

"What better way to bury the hatchet?" Malory asked, spreading her arms invitingly. "Come get some."

She drew a sharp breath. "Get out."

"Huh?"

Corky pointed to the door. "Get out."

"But—"

"Get out, Commander."

"But—"

"Now."

Malory rose from the cot slowly, belatedly realizing that she had painted herself into a corner. Plans to rectify the situation raced through her mind, but one look at the doctor's red face told her anything that she might say or do at this point would not be welcomed. She shuffled past the fuming doctor and stepped into the hall, the door slamming shut behind her.

Shit.

Still sulking from the night before, Malory emerged from her quarters and sat down in her chair, displacing Little Lovecraft and setting her on the desk in front of her.

"Well, my friend, looks like I screwed the pooch. Any advice?"

She stared at the doll as if she expected it to answer. "Any comments, then?" she asked and reached out to pull the string.

"Like I give a shit," Little Lovecraft said sarcastically, and she chuckled.

"Thanks," she said with a smile. "You always cheer me up."

The sound of approaching footsteps prompted her to stuff her companion into a desk drawer. McNeely paused at the doorframe to knock but stopped when he saw her at her desk. She gestured him in, and he placed a holstered .45 and two magazines on the desk.

She stood to attach the weapon to her belt. "Everybody equipped?"

"Yes, Commander. You were the last."

"Anything I need to know this morning?"

"Not that I'm aware of."

"I want everybody to take turns watching over Excavation."

"I'll prepare a duty list. I have Sergeant Alvarez and Airman Cohen slated for the job if the geeks go down today."

"I'm sure they will," she said knowingly. "I guess we're ready. Let me call in the troops, and I'll meet you in the mess shortly."

"Very well."

Clovis burst into Medical excitedly. "Corky!"

She looked up from her desk, smiling at the boisterous greeting. "What's up, Clovis?"

He walked over and whispered conspiratorially. "Something's goin' on. Lieutenant Ring and Chief Reynolds were in the mess this morning."

"So? They not allowed to eat?"

He gave her a condescending look. "They were armed."

"What?"

"They were wearing guns, Corky."

"What for? Did someone attack us in the middle of the night?"

He laughed but stopped suddenly, shooting her a knowing grin and eyeing her carefully. "I kinda doubt that. But since you and the Macho Nacho are so chummy, I thought I'd get you to ask her what's going on."

"Chummy? How would you know?"

"Gimme a break, Corky. Gossip flies around in here at the speed of light."

"Gossip?" She chuckled. "And I thought women were bad."

He shrugged. "So will you ask her?"

"Why would she tell me?"

"God, Corky. You graduated from medical school. You can't be this dense," he said, shaking his head. "The woman's gorgeous. Every guy in the place is at half-mast when she walks by, but the only person she notices is you."

"Isn't that special," she said sarcastically, still miffed at the arrogant woman.

"Would all personnel assemble in the mess by 0800, please," the commander's voice blared over the intercom. *"Attendance is mandatory."*

"Hmmm. Looks like I won't need you to take advantage of the commander's affections."

"Clovis..." she started in annoyance.

Malory strode into the mess five minutes later and purposely avoided glancing anywhere in the direction of the doctor. She took a seat at the front of the room.

"There's been a development," she stated. "Yesterday, the crew working in Excavation uncovered part of what we guess is a corpse."

A few seconds of silence were followed by a burst of energized whispers.

"Why weren't we informed immediately, Commander?" Clovis asked in annoyance, his colleagues nodding their approval of the question.

"A couple of reasons. First, the sergeant major had yet to inform me that he was satisfied with the conditions down there, and second, the corpse isn't human."

"What do you mean, not human?" Clovis asked, barely containing his excitement.

"In my opinion, not of this Earth."

"When can we view the specimen, Commander?" Dr. Lenard asked.

"I'm prepared to allow personnel to return to Excavation today. However, there will be stipulations."

"Such as?" Clovis asked.

"There will be two armed men overseeing the dig at all times," Malory said. "This is just a precaution until we're certain there's no threat. This is nonnegotiable."

"What are we in danger of, Commander?" Dr. Ballenger asked.

"The...life-form...was remarkably preserved. And it was brought to my attention that we know nothing of its capabilities. Until I'm convinced that it, or anything else biological we find down there, is not a threat, it's always better to have and not need than to need and not have."

"What are the other stipulations?" Clovis asked.

"As I said before, if anyone is found not in possession of a radio, they will be confined to quarters with nothing but a radio to keep them company. This is for everyone's safety and is also nonnegotiable. In addition, those same consequences will be imposed on anyone working in Excavation without a safety rope. This goes double for Dr. Isaaks," she added with a smile in the man's direction. "Any other questions?"

She looked around, but no one seemed inclined to speak up. Everyone but the soldiers wore eager expressions. "Okay, I'll let you get to it," she said finally, and her audience practically leaped from their seats.

"Some last minute advice," she said loudly over the rising clamor. "It smells like angry diarrhea down there, so take precautions, and don't give me a reason to get pissed off at anyone."

They fidgeted anxiously, and she waved them away. "Dismissed," she said, unable to keep from grinning at their enthusiasm.

She stayed in her seat, using the moment to compose scenarios she could employ to approach Corky that didn't give the impression of desperation. When the last body filtered by, she saw the doctor had also remained seated, and she felt a spark of hope. Perhaps she wouldn't have to grovel after all.

The minutes passed, and finally, Corky got up to go refill her coffee mug. Malory watched nervously as she refreshed her beverage and walked over to stand a few paces away, staring at her with the same neutral look on her face.

The commander couldn't take the silence. It was only a matter of seconds until she broke and begged for forgiveness. She cut it off at the pass.

"What? Do I have a booger?" she asked, bringing a hand up to rub her nose.

Corky fought it, but the smile came anyway. "I don't know why I bother."

"It's the magic that is me."

She sighed.

"Because I want you just as much as you want me. But I'm honest enough not to beat around the bush about it."

"That's probably true."

"So why fight it?"

She took a deep breath. "If you think you can behave like something other than a randy adolescent, we can talk about it tonight."

"Really?"

"Really. Show up at least an hour after duty shift."

"Okay," Malory said happily. "There's no one here but us. Can I talk you out of anything other than a 'Good night, Malory' cheek peck?"

Corky looked around the room guardedly and closed the distance between them, leaning over the commander seductively, bringing her mouth to within an inch of Malory's.

"No."

"That wasn't fair," Malory whined as the doctor turned and strode from the room with a cavalier wave.

1545 hours

Near the end of the day, Malory was sitting in her office playing Tomb Raider when the radio squawked.

"Commander?" Alvarez asked.

"Go ahead."

"They uncovered the...uh...alien. They want to transport it to the lab."

"I see," she said slowly. "What's it look like?"

"You don't want to know."

She shuddered. "I'll take your word on that. What would it take to get it up here?"

"A lot of time. It's in some sort of fucked-up chair. Stokes wants to send someone back for a stretcher."

"Tell them to leave it in the ice until tomorrow. My order."

"Will do," Alvarez said. *"Do you want me to report to you when I get topside?"*

"No, thank you. I think I can make it through the night without a description. I'll see it soon enough."

"Understand that. Out."

She returned the radio to her belt and checked the time on the computer, a smile in the works. She hopped from her seat to go get ready.

By the time she knocked on the door to Corky's quarters, she had devised a new plan, the meat and potatoes of which consisted of her thinking very carefully before she opened her mouth. It wouldn't be easy, but she was determined.

She waited what she deemed was a polite amount of time and knocked on the door again, the thought that the doctor might still be in the shower entering her mind. Debating carefully, she decided to knock one more time before she poked her head in, well aware that a Peeping Tom incident would not be looked upon kindly.

"Dr. Rivers?" she called out hesitantly.

Receiving no reply, she entered to find an empty room. Scowling slightly, she exited and walked one door over to Medical, only to find it deserted as well. The scowl deepened as she wandered from room to room, finally ending up in the mess, still with no sign of the elusive doctor. Puzzled and disappointed, she returned to her office, where a clue flew in and hit her in the head. She reached for her radio.

"Sergeant Alvarez," she called.

"Go ahead."

"What's your status?"

"Still in Excavation, Commander."

"Why?"

"They're still fawning over the damn thing."

She could almost see the compact Hispanic man rolling his eyes. "Is Dr. Rivers down there?"

"Yeah, she's here."

Malory sighed. "Very well. Give them a little longer and then tell them to wrap it up."

"Will do," he said, obviously happy to get the order.

"Lovecraft out."

She leaned back in her chair and sighed again, deciding that she would pass the time with a movie.

It was after midnight when Corky got out of the shower. The smell in Excavation had been hideous, and being in such close proximity to the creature had made her clothes stink as well. Earlier, Clovis had called her down to take a look at it, and she found herself unable to resist. Caught up in her own curiosity and everyone's excitement, she had let the time get away from her—that is, until Alvarez had informed them in no uncertain terms that it was bedtime and that they could play with their new toy tomorrow. It was then that she realized how late it was and that she had unwittingly stood up the commander.

Hoping that Malory would still be awake so she could at least apologize, she got dressed and slipped out the door. When she entered the commander's office, it was dark, and no light was coming from under the door to her quarters. With a sigh, she turned to leave and took a few steps into the hall before turning impulsively, walking back into the office and quietly entering Malory's quarters, closing the door behind her. She stood silently, letting her eyes adapt to the dark and then using the light from the clock to guide her to the commander's cot. Praying that she was making the right decision, she stripped to her panties and T-shirt before climbing in next to the sleeping woman. She had to nudge her a few times to make room for herself and ignored the sleepy grumbles of protest as she slipped under the blankets.

So far, so good. She snuggled up next to a delightfully naked back, putting a tentative arm around Malory's waist and cautiously burying her face in clean-smelling hair. She caught her breath in surprise when Malory suddenly grabbed her arm, but smiled as her hand was cuddled between a pair of breasts. It took a few minutes for her to realize that the commander was still asleep, but when she did, Corky quickly fell asleep beside her.

Clovis wandered into the mess and found the majority of his colleagues loitering around the coffeepots.

"Couldn't sleep?" Dr. Lenard asked.

"Still a little worked up," he replied, looking over the crowd with a knowing eye. "And it looks like I'm not the only one."

Several of the men chuckled.

"So what's the order of business this evening? Discussion or bitch session?"

"A little of both," Grey said. "Is Corky coming?"

"Said she was going to bed."

"Damn," Watkins said. "How are we going to conduct a proper bitch session without our ringleader?"

"We'll manage, I'm sure," Clovis said. "I guess Isaaks hit the sack too?"

"Yeah. He's still a little sore from the tumble he took the other day," Gallagher said.

"He'd be biased anyway," Watkins said.

"Why's that?" Clovis asked.

"Lovecraft saved his bacon."

"Ah. So the topic tonight is the commander?"

"Yeah. We're not happy with some of the new restrictions, and I for one don't like being supervised by armed guards or told when to stop doing my job."

"Me either," Grey agreed with a nod.

Clovis hummed for a moment and helped himself to a cup of coffee. "I can't say I entirely disagree with you, but I think you may be making a mountain out of a molehill."

"How's that?" Watkins asked.

"Lovecraft has been down here...what? Almost three months?"

"Yeah."

"Have you ever seen her in the lab?"

"Uh...no," he mumbled. "What has that got to do with anything?"

"Not counting the incident with Isaaks the other day, how many times have you seen her in Excavation?"

Watkins's brow wrinkled. "None that I can remember. What are you getting at?"

"I'm saying that we're not nearly as supervised as you think we are."

"Come on, Clovis," Grey said. "Armed guards? Lovecraft may not be looking over our shoulder, but her men are."

"That's only in Excavation and the only thing I personally have a problem with, but only because I don't understand the need. However, the radios and safety ropes are precautions we should've been adhering to all along."

"I'm with Clovis on that, gentlemen," Lenard said. "We could've saved a lot of time getting help down there when we needed it, and if Dr. Isaaks had been wearing a rope, he might not have taken such a bad fall."

"All right," Watkins said. "I'll concede to the ropes and radios, but Alvarez talking to us like children and telling us play time is over gets under my skin."

Clovis chuckled. "Okay, he could've been a little more diplomatic, but look at it from his perspective. The man just spent twelve hours watching us carry on over a creature he probably doesn't care to know the slightest thing about."

"Lovecraft was pulling his strings," Grey said.

"Probably," Clovis said, throwing in a shrug. "So?"

"So," Grey replied, "I'm concerned that as scientists on this project, we're going to end up being nothing but tools for the military."

"It's a two-way street, fellas. We wouldn't have this opportunity without the military. Besides," Clovis rumbled, gesturing with his fingers to Grey and Watkins, "a few weeks ago, you guys thought Lovecraft was great."

"Gee, Stokes," Watkins cooed. "That crush of yours is showing."

He reddened, attempting to ignore the comment and resulting chuckles. "What do the lab boys think? Where are Doctors Tanaka, Dobson and Ballenger this evening?"

"I'm sure they went right to bed to dream about vivisecting the alien," Gallagher quipped. "You know how it is with those in pure research; they rarely take notice of anything outside the scope of their current study."

"True enough," Clovis said with a grin. "Why don't we lose the complaints and talk about our alien?"

"Hear, hear," Lenard agreed. "Can you believe...?"

Malory immediately noticed several things upon waking. First was the floor, which she was staring at because half of her body was hanging over the side of the cot. In addition, there was a warm weight resting on her back, and most surprisingly, there was a possessive grip on her left breast.

Her eyes traveled down her chest to examine the hand that the grip belonged to, and an eyebrow went up in satisfaction. It was a small, obviously feminine hand, and because it wasn't her own, the odds were favorable that it belonged to none other than Corky Rivers.

She craned her head around to look at the clock; it was set to go off in less than a minute. Smiling, she plastered on her most smug expression and waited to see how the doctor would react to rising in such a compromising situation.

The alarm went off with an irritating electronic wail. Corky's eyes grudgingly opened and then almost instantly widened as she found her cheek resting on a naked back with a pleasant softness that could be only one thing filling her hand. She froze in horror, immediately wishing that she had thought her impulsive decision from the night before all the way through. She hadn't given a moment's thought to how awkward it would be to wake up uninvited in someone else's bed, let alone to be caught fondling the body that the bed belonged to.

The alarm continued to blare, and Malory could feel the tension running through the body resting on top of her. She decided to make the most of it.

She cleared her throat loudly. "Uhm...if it isn't too much of a bother, could you let go of my boob long enough to turn off the alarm?"

Corky flushed with embarrassment, silently removing her hand and turning to slap the alarm behind her, instantly wishing she hadn't, as she found the resulting silence even more uncomfortable.

Malory was anything but uncomfortable, enjoying the situation immensely. "There's some Kleenex on the nightstand. Would you mind wiping the drool off my back?" she asked, almost laughing when she heard the horrified gasp her request produced.

Corky's eyes dropped to Malory's back in mortification, but after a quick examination, they turned to the ceiling in annoyance. "Funny," she said finally, bracing herself against the inevitable laughter.

She was surprised when it didn't come, and Malory turned around, wrapping her arms around her and pulling her close. "I haven't woken up so happy in years."

It was the last thing Corky had expected, and she buried her face into the crook of the commander's neck with a relieved sigh.

Malory ran her hands inquisitively through Corky's hair, enjoying how soft it felt as she waited for the doctor to emerge from her refuge. Eventually, she stirred and lifted shy brown eyes up to meet hers. "I knew you could be sweet if you wanted to."

Malory smiled. "I'm not the ogre you make me out to be."

"I never called you an ogre."

Malory shrugged indifferently. "So can I have that kiss now?"

Corky chewed on her lip thoughtfully.

"Oh, come on! It's the least you can do after feeling me up."

"I was asleep," Corky said, looking away in embarrassment.

"If you kiss me, I'll let you feel me up any time you want."

Corky chuckled. "Okay," she relented, bashfully moving forward.

Her mouth had almost completed its journey when a hand blocked the way, obscuring the lips below hers.

"Wait!" Malory said, her voice muffled by her hand, and Corky backed away uncertainly, looking at her in puzzlement.

"Could you brush your teeth first? Your breath would make a dung beetle barf."

Corky went limp in exasperation, her face falling into the blankets as the commander's chuckles washed over her.

"You just can't make it easy, can you?"

"Nope."

"Corky, where you at?" Clovis's voice blared from the radio on the floor.

"Oh, shit." Corky sprang upright in alarm.

"Corky, you there?" Clovis asked. *"You better have your radio with you, or the boss is gonna be pissed."*

Malory chuckled and reached down to retrieve the radio from the floor. "You better answer him, or I might have to discipline you."

Corky snatched it from her hand. "Go ahead, Clovis."

"Where the hell are you?"

She bit her lip. "Where are you?"

"I'm in Medical."

Malory snickered and received a slap on the arm. "I'm in the mess," she offered, crossing her fingers.

"I just left there. I must have missed you. No biggie. On my way back now."

"Shit," Corky said, jumping over the commander and gathering her pants from the floor in a panic.

Malory reclined on the cot, watching the show with interest as Corky frantically wiggled into her fatigues.

"Goddamn it," she exclaimed, tossing dirty clothes aside. "Where's my other boot? How do you find anything in this shithole?"

"You'll never get there before he does."

"Shut up," Corky said. Then she squealed as she found her other boot and dropped to the floor to pull it on.

"What the hell, Corky?" Clovis said. *"Where'd you go?"*

"Told you."

Corky froze, totally at a loss.

"Tell him you're in my office, and you'll get back to him shortly," Malory offered.

She slumped over in relief. "Sorry, Clovis. The commander wanted to see me. I'll call you back in a minute."

"All right, got lots to do today. See ya in a few."

She fell onto her back, lying in a pile of discarded laundry. "Jesus."

"I'm glad you came by last night," Malory said.

"I am too."

"Will I see you again tonight?"

"Only if you clean this place up or come to my quarters."

"I'll come to your quarters."

Corky chuckled and rose to finish lacing her boot, glancing up to meet blue eyes watching her intently from a few feet away. "What are you staring at?"

"You. You're a beautiful woman," she replied, smiling at the resulting blush.

"So are you," Corky said, trying to ignore the heat on her face. "Most of the time. When your mouth doesn't get in the way."

Malory chuckled.

"I'd better go," Corky said, rising to her feet.

"Okay."

The doctor debated for an instant and then hastily stepped forward and leaned in to place a peck on the commander's mouth, withdrawing swiftly and rushing through the door without looking back.

1655 hours

The commander had been checking the time regularly for the past hour, unable to concentrate on anything but the approaching end of the current duty shift. She was down to counting the last few minutes when McNeely's voice from the radio demanded her attention.

"Commander?"

She sighed, knowing she would probably have to put her plans on hold. "Go ahead."

"They were going to page you, but I thought I'd give you a heads-up. They want you in the lab."

"And the heads-up would be?"

"Hope you haven't eaten recently," he said.

She winced, knowing that if the man thought to say something, the alien would be a dreadful sight. "On my way. Lovecraft out."

She arrived at the lab a few minutes later and found the sergeant major waiting for her right inside the door. The laboratory was actually the largest room, or series of rooms, in the entire complex. The main door opened into a glass-enclosed lobby of sorts, where visitors had to pass through a vacuum-sealed door to gain access to the facilities inside.

Staff Sergeant Terrel and Airman Daly stood behind McNeely, hands tight on their rifles. Their attention was fixed on the activity inside. Malory avoided looking for as long as she could, glad that several of the scientists were hovering around the creature, partially obstructing her view.

"Commander, you'll want to put this on," McNeely said, offering her a clip for her nose. She looked at the man, noting that he was already wearing one.

"Thank you," she said. "Let's get this over with."

McNeely pushed through the door, and she followed him inside. Dr. Lenard turned at the sound of their entrance and beckoned her over with a wave. The crowd parted to give her a full view of the exam table, revealing the creature in its entirety.

The thing appeared to be equal parts insect, humanoid and technology. Its skin, where visible, was the same greenish-black that she remembered. It seemed to be sitting backward in a chair—not all that surprising, considering that its trunk resembled the hindquarters of a cat, only attached in reverse and covered sparsely with thick, coarse hair or antennae. Its arms projected outward as thought it were trying to protect itself from something. The torso was covered in a carapace, like that of a huge cockroach, and seemingly fused to the strange-looking chair. Tentacles protruded from an orifice in the neck and wrapped themselves around the shoulders and groin. The actual head of the alien was the most disturbing feature to behold, resembling a snail's shell with no other visible features except a frighteningly wide mouth consisting of three rows of triangular teeth, which looked razor-sharp and protruded in all directions.

"God," she said. "Look at the choppers on that thing."

"No kidding," McNeely said from behind her. "I wouldn't want it goin' down on me."

Malory chuckled and looked up at the sound of a familiar laugh, somewhat surprised to find Corky on the far side of the examining table. She shot her a small smile and wondered why she hadn't noticed her when she had first entered.

"Okay, why am I here?"

Dr. Lenard spoke up. "A couple of reasons, Commander. First, you should be aware that it's impossible for this creature to reanimate suddenly. It's very dead."

"And you're convinced of this why?"

He gestured for the others to help him turn the alien on its side. "You'll notice that the back of the head and a good portion of the rear torso seem to be missing," he said, pointing to several gaping holes and missing chunks in the body.

Malory grimaced and leaned closer to observe. "Okay. And?"

"In our estimation," Corky said, "the damage to the creature's body was inflicted by one of its own kind."

"Pardon me?"

"We took a cast of the creature's mouth," Corky explained, producing a hideous plaster representation of the alien's teeth. "As you can see," she said, holding the cast up to the wounds on the creature's back, "these injuries were made by an entity with the same dental framework."

Malory watched the plaster teeth line up almost exactly with the ragged wounds in the creature's body. "So they're cannibals. Or one of them was really pissed off at the other."

"Cannibals would be our guess as well," Dr. Lenard said, removing his glasses and buffing them on his shirt. "A good portion of this alien's internal body mass is missing."

She tried not to visualize. "So there's no chance of this thing getting up and walking around?"

"None," Dr. Lenard said.

"And you're one hundred percent certain of this?"

"Our analysis *is* preliminary," he said cautiously. "The injuries to this creature would've been fatal even if it hadn't been buried in the ice for the past few thousand years. I think we can all agree that it's quite dead."

Heads bobbed in confirmation, and Malory pursed her lips thoughtfully, rocking back and forth on her heels for a moment. "Your opinion, Sergeant Major?"

"I'd prefer to remain cautious," McNeely said. "A lot of unknowns here. The craft might have had more than one life-form aboard."

She nodded in agreement. "Okay, everyone remains armed for the time being, but let's cut the guard in Excavation down to one."

"Very well, Commander," McNeely said.

She looked at the gathered scientists. "Is there anything else?"

Dr. Lenard glanced at his colleagues questioningly. "I don't believe so, Commander."

"Very well, then. Please keep me informed," she said and turned to exit the room, McNeely on her heels.

As soon as they were outside, she reached to pull the clip off her nose, turning to the sergeant major with a sour look. "Is that you or me that smells so bad?"

"Unfortunately, it's both of us."

"Jesus, that's rank."

He nodded. "Some of them weren't pleased by maintaining a guard in Excavation."

"No, they weren't," she said. "But this whole space-monster thing freaks me out. Plus if someone wasn't down there to tell them to call it a day, they'd be at it all night."

"True enough."

She gestured at Sergeant Terrel and Airman Daly. "Stow their rifles, and give them the night off. Apparently, that thing isn't gonna get up and table-dance."

He chuckled.

"Also, we need to get a message off to McMurdo to let them know what we found here."

"External communications are down. According to the chief, a severe weather system has moved in above us."

She chewed on her lip for a moment. "Let's get a status report out at the earliest opportunity."

"Will do."

"Is there anything else?"

"Not at the moment."

"Then I'm headed for a shower. Good night, Sergeant Major."

"Good night, Commander."

"Goddamn it," Grey mumbled the second the door closed behind McNeely.

Corky gave him a confused look. "What's with you?"

He gestured in the direction of the recently departed. "The queen and her henchman."

She stiffened. "What?"

"We told her that our expired extraterrestrial was twice as dead as Julius Caesar, and still, she keeps an armed crony watching over us."

"So? She's simply being cautious."

"We're not children who need supervision, Doctor."

"I don't think anybody implied that."

"Oh," Grey said. "Then why the armed babysitter?"

"What does it hurt?" Corky said, beginning to frown. "The way I understood it was that a guard wouldn't be there to watch over you, but to watch over whatever you guys might find."

"That's an excuse. She doesn't trust us."

"The way you're acting at the moment, I wouldn't either. I hope you're not speaking for everybody," she said, letting her eyes travel around the room.

"No, he doesn't," Lenard said. "I think a guard is unnecessary, but I don't believe the presence of one is as nefarious as Dr. Grey apparently does."

Several heads bobbed in agreement.

"Wait and see," Grey said with a shrug. "This isn't the last restriction she'll place on us. She already has her thugs tell us when to quit for the day, and we risk being sent to our rooms without dinner if we're caught without a radio. And she kicked us out of Excavation the day Isaaks got hurt, and what was the result? A soldier discovered the alien, not one of us. This is only the beginning."

"You're forgetting that she risked her life to save Dr. Isaaks, who is *not* one of her soldiers," Corky said. "You're also forgetting that she kicked you guys out of Excavation for your own safety and sent the soldiers down there to clean up the mess. And if you'd care to notice, the guards outside are gone. She dismissed them right after you assured her that the creature didn't present a danger. I think you're blowing things way out of proportion."

"I agree," Clovis said. "I'd also be willing to bet that the guys who found the alien would have preferred not to. To them, it's a monster, and as long at it stays dead, I'd imagine the majority of them don't really want to know anything about it."

"Can we cut this short?" Dr. Tanaka asked impatiently, not bothering to look up from his microscope. "I'd like to be able to concentrate on these tissue samples."

Several heads turned in the man's direction, but he was already engrossed in his research and blissfully unaware of the attention.

1900 hours

Malory lay on the cot in her quarters, feeling sorry for herself. It had been more than two hours since she had left the lab, and she suspected that she wouldn't hear from the doctor any time soon. It wasn't easy playing second fiddle to some hideous, foul-smelling monster that also happened to be dead. She was trying not to let it bruise her ego.

She looked around the room and scowled. She had even cleaned her quarters for the woman. With a sigh, she rolled over to turn off the light, stopping when a knock came at the door.

"Yes?" she said, a hopeful lilt in her voice.

"Can I come in?" Corky asked.

"Of course."

Corky entered the room, closing the door behind her and projecting a sheepish look. "Sorry," she said. "Hey, you cleaned up in here."

"Are you impressed?" Malory asked, pleased that her efforts had been noticed.

"Yes, actually," Corky said but then smiled knowingly. "You ran out of clean clothes, didn't you?"

"Nope. I did all of this for you."

"Really?"

"Okay, I ran out of clothes, too."

Corky chuckled. "Uh-huh."

"Are you gonna stand by the door all night or come over here?"

Corky swayed indecisively. "Are you naked under there?" she asked, pointing at the blankets.

"Would it make a difference?" Malory asked, smiling seductively.

"Yeah. I was hoping we could talk."

"Wouldn't you rather just sit on my face?"

Corky's jaw dropped. "Jesus, could you *be* less romantic?"

Malory choked back the intended retort. "Sorry," she forced, resituating herself cross-legged on the end of the cot and gesturing to the available space. "Make yourself comfortable, and tell me what you want to talk about."

The doctor sighed and sat down, pulling off her boots. "Larry said you were decorated. Will you tell me about it?"

"What else did Larry say?"

"Only that you were considered unorthodox."

"He shared more than he should have."

Corky turned to face her, pulling the opposite end of the blankets up over her legs. "Will you tell me?"

"Why?"

"Because I want to know more about you. And I know that women in the military aren't typically exposed to situations that result in combat decorations. I also know that a young female officer wouldn't be the choice of many to oversee an installation of this importance."

"I'll tell you if you tell me why you have a problem with the military in general."

"Okay. You go first."

"What exactly do you want to know?"

"How did you get your decorations?"

"I was in a helicopter over Bosnia that came under fire, and I took a hit in my thigh. The aircraft itself took several and was crippled. We were forced off course and crashed into the Adriatic."

"Is that how you hurt your shoulder?"

"Yeah. Dislocated, compound fracture of the clavicle, torn rotator cuff, blah, blah, blah."

Corky winced sympathetically. "And?"

"And what?"

"What's the rest?"

"There were five people on board. Only two survived and made it to the surface. One was a Marine colonel who had broken his back when we crashed. I pulled him from the wreckage and kept him afloat until we were rescued a little over a day later."

"How did you do that with a useless arm and a wounded leg?"

"I did it because I had to."

"I can't imagine how horrible that must have been."

"It isn't something I look back on fondly."

"What were you decorated with?"

"The DSM and a Purple Heart."

"What's a DSM?"

"The Distinguished Service Medal. Now tell me your story."

"It's pretty simple, really," Corky said. "Former lover of three years also happened to be in the Army. I never really fit in with her crowd and always felt looked down upon because I was a civilian. I moved across the country twice when she was transferred just to be with her, even though she was distant and treated me as if I wasn't good enough for her. The third time she was transferred, she told me not to bother to come with her and informed me that she had been seeing someone else for the last two years—not surprisingly, another officer."

"Is that how you ended up here?"

"Pretty much. Larry was a professor I had in college. When I completed my residency, he approached me with the job."

"I'm sorry about your girlfriend."

"I'm not. She was a horrible girlfriend and an even worse officer," she said and looked away, suddenly shy. "She couldn't hold a candle to you. I judged everyone in uniform by what I saw in her and the people she associated with. I look at you and see everything she could never be. Everyone may not always agree with you, but they respect you, and not because you're the boss, but because you're a leader."

Malory smiled. "Can we make out now?"

Corky laughed. "No. Tell me how you got here."

The commander sighed heavily and shrugged. "I'm a promotable officer and was going to resign my commission. They threw me a bone."

"You were going to resign? Why?" Corky asked in surprise.

"Because my whole life has been nothing but the Navy. I was of a mind to see what life was like without it."

"You changed your mind?"

"They made me an offer. Take the position here, and use the time to reconsider. Since I didn't have any idea what I wanted to do once I resigned, I agreed."

"Do you have a girl in every port?"

"Nope."

"Have a girl anywhere?"

"Nope."

"Are you a virgin?"

"I lost my cherry but still have the box it came in."

Corky chuckled. "Where did you get your vocabulary?"

"It was on sale at Sears. Can I see you naked?"

"Maybe. Have you had a lot of lovers?"

"Numerically, you'd be the second, but as far as I'm concerned, the first and only."

"Really?"

"Really on both counts."

"I'm having a hard time resisting you."

"Why would you want to?"

"Do you have any idea what a hateful bitch you were to me?"

"It was the quickest way to solve the problem."

"That's it? No apology?"

"Did you know the minute I saw you I got wet?"

"Could've fooled me."

"Get over it."

"It's not that easy."

"Yes, it is. Just kiss me."

"You think it's that simple?"

"Yes."

"It isn't for me."

Malory threw up her hands in exasperation and abruptly leaned forward, resting on her hands and knees, her face suddenly an inch away from Corky's. "Then I'll kiss you," she whispered, and gently covered the doctor's lips with her own. She prodded lovingly with delicate caresses until she felt Corky respond. Then she greedily accepted what was offered, catching a hesitant tongue and sucking it tenderly into her mouth. She moaned softly at the bodily sensation it induced.

She sighed in a frustration she felt all the way to her toes when Corky began to disengage gently. Struggling with her composure, she didn't fight it and backed off respectfully, waiting with a barely restrained desire to observe Corky's reaction.

Corky leaned back against the wall and caught her breath. The energy radiating off the commander was so extreme, every nerve ending in her body was standing at attention. It was an intensity unlike anything she had ever experienced, both seductively powerful and emotionally frightening.

"I want you," Malory rumbled.

Corky looked up into a blue gaze almost dilated black with longing and knew she wasn't prepared for the passion lurking behind those eyes.

"I want you," Malory repeated. "Let me show you how much."

Corky tentatively reached out to cup her cheek, almost groaning when it was leaned into wantonly. "I want you, too," she whispered. "But I've never felt so...pleasantly scared."

Malory bit her lower lip almost painfully. "Then lie with me and let me hold you."

Corky practically gaped at the sudden transformation; the sexual aura that had been almost tangible receded at the gentle request. The commander resituated herself on the cot and lifted the blankets in front of her invitingly. Silently, Corky stood on weak knees, stepped out of her fatigues and climbed into the offered embrace. The blankets settled around her, and Malory turned to click off the lamp, returning to pull the doctor tightly against her body.

"Thank you," Corky said softly in the dark.

"You're welcome," Malory whispered, her breath tickling Corky's ear. "However, if you wake up in a puddle, it's not because I have a bladder problem."

"God," Corky giggled. "You're so vulgar."

For an answer, Malory placed a gentle kiss on the back of her neck and smiled at the shiver it produced. "Good night, Doctor."

Corky rose without the aid of the alarm and frowned, realizing how late it was. Belatedly, she noticed that the body she held in her arms was about five feet smaller, one hundred pounds lighter and nowhere near as warm as the one she went to bed with. Her eyes narrowed in the dark, and she fumbled around for the lamp. Illumination confirmed her suspicions, and she flung Little Lovecraft across the room in disgust.

Not amused at waking up with the doll instead of the commander, she got up to put her boots and pants on. She was about to enter Malory's office when she heard McNeely's voice on the other side of the door. Trapped for the time being, she sat back down on the cot with a huff. The time passed slowly, and eventually, her eyelids began to grow heavy.

When Malory finally entered, she snickered at finding Little Lovecraft on the floor and picked her up to seat her on the chair. She threw a glance at the cot and smiled at the doctor sleeping in her clothes. Deciding to leave her be, she silently cursed the efficient McNeely and started to undress.

Corky woke at the sound of running water and froze when she realized that Malory was in the shower. Torn between wanting to make a hasty exit and being present when the commander emerged, she fidgeted and cleared her throat.

"Good morning," she ventured.

"Good morning. Decide to get up?"

"Yeah. Why did you turn off the alarm?"

"McNeely showed up first thing. If he heard the alarm being shut off, he would've known someone was in my quarters."

"Oh."

"Your buddy Clovis and crew were up before dawn and down in Excavation. Petty Officer Butler went down with them. He wasn't pleased at being rousted for guard duty so early," Malory said in amusement. "Neither was the sergeant major."

"They're just excited," Corky said. "It's an important find."

"Whatever. Since you're up, wanna join me?"

Facing another dilemma, the doctor considered her options. Part of her wanted to spring from the cot and strip, and another part wanted to run from the room. "I think I'll pass."

"You sure? I know you're dyin' to see if my carpet matches my drapes. I'll let you peek."

Her brow wrinkled in confusion for a few seconds, and then her eyes rolled. "I'm sure," she said, shaking her head and glad Malory couldn't see her grin.

"Okay. Your loss."

"You're such a pompous ass," she said with a chuckle. "I can't believe how full of yourself you are."

"I'd like to be filled by you."

To her dismay, Corky started to blush. "I'm going to go."

"Okay," Malory said nonchalantly. "See ya later."

Corky spent a moment staring at the shower curtain suspiciously. Wary of a trap, she rose and made for the exit. "See ya."

"Heh," Malory cackled when she heard the door close.

Corky spent the entire day in a turmoil of emotions, performing her duties in absentminded automation, her thoughts rarely straying far from the confounding commander. Malory possessed a multitude of repulsive qualities, and Corky was perplexed that she now found them charming when recently, they would have and did offend her. There was also the lingering confusion left over from the night before. The damn woman exuded a hidden sexual energy that could singe the hair off her toes.

Like it or not, she had fallen hard, and her only options were to move forward or to retreat. Retreating became more unappealing with every minute she spent in the commander's company, and moving forward meant forging ahead with a confusing lover that she might never completely understand. It was a frightening prospect with no guaranteed conclusion.

At the end of her shift, she headed for dinner, still halfheartedly debating alternatives, hoping she could share a meal and have a normal conversation with the woman. She figured the odds of an ordinary dialogue were about 50-50, suspecting that Malory herself didn't know what foot to lead with and generally improvised her way through life.

She was disenchanted to find the mess relatively empty, with no sign of the commander or even Clovis to exchange pleasantries with. In fact, the only people present were Airmen Daly and Cohen, so she got a tray and sat by herself, her thoughts instantly returning to and dwelling on her romantic dilemma.

An uncertain amount of time later, Clovis dropped into the chair across from her. "What's with the long face?"

She blinked and glanced at her watch, surprised to see how much time had gotten away from her. "Huh?"

"You're sitting there looking like your dog just died. What's on your mind?"

"Oh, just thinking," she said, trying to sound cavalier. "How did things go down there today?" she added, hoping to distract him.

"The cave-in sped up our progress considerably. We're a couple of weeks away from the first section. We can't wait."

She smiled. "I'll bet," she said, throwing another glance at her watch. "You're up here kinda early."

"We started early, because we suspect our commander has given the order to have our armed escort tell us when to pack it up for the day."

Corky giggled. "I'm sure she did. Have you seen her today?"

"Saw her laughing with the sergeant major outside his quarters when I was coming to dinner."

"Hmmm. Well, I guess I'm gonna go find something to do."

"Okay, Corky," he said, becoming engrossed in the food in front of him. "See ya later."

"Bye, Clovis," she said with a chuckle.

She made her way to Malory's office, and finding both it and her quarters empty, she began a casual stroll around the compound with the hope of running into the woman. Her efforts proved fruitless, as the commander was nowhere to be found. Confused, she returned to her own quarters and flopped into her chair with a frown. *Where could she be?* She thought about using the radio but couldn't come up with a good story to offer in case Malory wasn't alone.

Two hours of brooding later, she returned to Malory's quarters and again found them empty. Her face wrinkled in confusion. She retraced her steps from earlier, and after searching everywhere, she still saw no sign of the commander.

Jesus, it's almost eleven. Where the hell is she? An idea suddenly formed, and she returned to the lounge, finding Lieutenant Ring reclining in his usual spot on the sofa.

"Lieutenant? Do you know where the commander is?"

He turned around sleepily. "Uhm...she's with the sergeant major in his quarters."

"Thank you," she said, exiting the room before a frown of gigantic proportions could take control.

She had stomped halfway back to her quarters when it struck her that she was jealous, and she paused to consider the notion. Tempted at first to dismiss it as overreaction, she returned to her room. Was she jealous, and if so, why? Did she miss something? Malory had said she'd had only one lover, but weren't they talking about women?

The idea of Malory's being with McNeely brought her blood to a boil, and once the thought entered her mind, she couldn't think of anything else. She tried to tell herself that she was blowing everything out of proportion and was probably wrong, but her imagination had taken hold and wouldn't let go.

She glanced angrily at the clock. It was half past midnight. Fed up and teetering on the irrational, she stormed into the hall and returned to Malory's quarters. When she confirmed them to be abandoned, she marched off with a new destination in mind.

Quieting her approach as she arrived and tiptoeing the last few feet, she lurked outside the sergeant major's door, listening closely for any noise that might emanate from within.

Mumbled voices and then the sound of the commander's laughter brought her temper to a boil, and she turned to stomp down the hallway, coming to an abrupt halt when she heard a door open. She shot a furious glance over her shoulder and was surprised to see Malory emerge, followed by Chief Reynolds and Sergeants Alvarez, Hanson and Terrel, all of them chuckling companionably.

Her jealousy instantly vaporized in favor of a very distinct feeling of embarrassment. She tried to slink away unnoticed and winced when she was called up short.

"Dr. Rivers?" Malory called out.

"Yes?" she asked, turning a hopefully innocent gaze in her direction.

"What are you doing here?" Malory asked, as the men filtered by with polite nods.

Corky thought frantically. "I couldn't sleep, so I was taking a walk."

Malory snickered. "Uh-huh. What's up? You looked angry."

Corky sighed. "I was looking for you. What were you doing in there all night?"

"Playing poker. What did you think we were doing?"

"I don't know."

"How did you know where I was?" Malory asked, a knowing look on her face.

Corky shuffled her feet. "I asked Lieutenant Ring," she said, feeling somewhat exposed. "Can we just go to my quarters?"

"Sure," Malory said, gesturing for the doctor to precede her down the hall.

Corky trudged toward her room, feeling monumentally stupid. Worse, she didn't have to turn around to see the smile on Malory's face; she could feel it. When they entered her quarters, the commander respectfully chose the chair and seated herself primly, turning an expectant look on her companion.

Corky sighed and took a seat on the cot, leaning against the wall. "Why didn't you tell me you were going to play cards tonight?"

"I didn't get the chance," Malory said with a shrug. "McNeely asked me this morning, and before I could say anything, you lit out of my quarters like your ass was on fire."

"Oh."

"If you had told me you wanted to get together, I would have turned him down," Malory offered. "You looked mad enough to blow an ovary. So tell me—what's the matter?"

"Nothing."

"Gimme a break," Malory scoffed. "You can tell me anything."

Corky started to play with the hem of her sweatshirt. "It was stupid."

"What was stupid?"

"I thought you and McNeely were...uhm...you know."

Malory grinned. "You were jealous?"

Corky nodded reluctantly.

"My, how territorial."

Eyes flashed. "You don't have to be so smug."

For an answer, Malory leaned down and unlaced her boots, pulling them off and placing them under the chair along with her socks. Then she stood to remove her sweatshirt.

Corky watched nervously. "What do you think you're doing?" she asked, watching the sweatshirt fall to the ground and hands drop to start unbuttoning her fatigues.

"Bustin' a move," Malory said, stepping out of her pants and standing immodestly before the doctor in her underwear.

Corky couldn't find her voice as her body began reacting strongly to the almost-nude commander, who dropped to her knees in front of her and began to untie her boots. She watched helplessly as the boots were removed gently and her hands were grasped, pulling her forward. Powerless, she let Malory lift her arms above her head to remove her shirt and bra. A whimper preceded the removal of her pants, and soon, she found herself naked and waiting to be claimed by the woman kneeling in front of her.

"You're very beautiful," Malory said, grabbing the doctor gently around the hips and pulling her forward.

Corky opened her mouth to reply but was silenced by lips that descended upon her own and hands that wound themselves in her hair. The intensity of Malory's attentions was not to be denied, and she surrendered willingly, pulling her closer and urging her for more.

Malory relished every sensation, delighting in the taste of the doctor's mouth, exploring every crevice with her tongue, taking a sensual pleasure in the texture of her teeth, the roof of her mouth, the softness of her lips and the warmth of her breath as it mingled with her own. Her hands dropped to the small of her back and pulled her gently forward until her thighs rested on the edge of the cot, dropping her attention to the pulse point on her neck and, eventually, to her rapidly rising and falling chest.

Corky fell back against the wall to allow Malory free rein over her body, consumed by the urgent need the commander conveyed and her own soaring libido. She wrapped her hands tightly in Malory's hair when she felt a breast being teased and pulled her close when she was drawn into her mouth. Her body tingled as her nipples hardened painfully and teeth chewed on them lovingly. She gasped loudly in anticipation as Malory began a trail down her chest, her mouth and tongue showing an interest in every detail they encountered, and when a chin urged her legs apart, she complied without hesitation. Malory's arms dropped to assist, and her legs were thrown over the commander's shoulders with abandon, the air surprisingly cold against the suddenly exposed wetness of her thighs. She exhaled powerfully the instant she was tasted, ecstasy making her shiver when Malory emitted a satisfied groan of her own, as if she'd finally been given something long denied.

One of Corky's hands sought out the edge of the cot to brace against the inevitable, while the other tightened its grip in Malory's hair in an unspoken order to remain where she was. The sensation of Malory's attentions was beyond all of her previous experience, and she could feel the commander's pleasure in the act through the ravenous exuberance of the mouth feeding upon her. Malory's moans were almost as loud as her own, and when a hand left her thigh and the commander set her knees farther apart on the floor, she felt the approaching edge. Malory's excitement was so obvious that it was like receiving a shot of adrenaline, knowing she couldn't restrain from petting herself.

When Corky came, it was with a power that left her helpless, and it was prolonged significantly as Malory's arm tightened around her waist, refusing to let go. Her whole body jumped spastically with every caress, and she found herself screaming with the pleasure of it, pulling the hair in her hand possessively to force closer contact. Corky exalted in the vibrations traveling the length of her sex from Malory's muffled cries, her lover entangled within the tremors of her own release and grinding into her. Corky rode the wave until she was unable to endure any longer and finally dropped a hand between her legs to intervene, going limp in exhaustion, her body shining with perspiration.

As she caught her breath, she was pleasantly aware of Malory still diligently trying to get past the blockade of her hand, tenderly sucking on her fingers and occasionally probing for an opening between them. Corky released the grip still knotted in Malory's hair, surprised at how severe her hold had been and wincing sympathetically when the commander whimpered softly at the reprieve.

"Malory," she said, her voice hoarse.

"Hmmm?"

"Did I hurt you?" she asked, petting her head.

"It was a nice hurt," Malory said as she chewed softly on the end of a denying finger.

"I'm sorry."

"Don't be."

"Come lie with me," she said, about to start the process of resituating herself, but paused when she met Malory's eyes.

"I love you, Corky."

Corky's breath froze within her chest, and she was surprised to feel moisture rise in her eyes.

Malory rose and removed her bra, tossing it across the room as though it irritated her, and she stretched like a cat in front of the doctor's desirous eyes. Her outstretched arms returned to cup her breasts and stroke them lightly before sliding a hand into her underwear to touch herself. She sighed lightly at the contact and brought back moist fingers that she sampled with her mouth.

Corky observed her behavior in unconcealed fascination, arousal again stirring within her as Malory suckled her fingers inquisitively, seemingly unaware of being watched so closely. Apparently satisfied, the commander lowered herself onto the cot and wrapped gentle arms around her contentedly.

"Why did you do that?" Corky asked, unable to curb her curiosity.

"I wanted to see what we would taste like together."

"And?"

"Superb."

Corky sighed, bringing a hand up to wipe her eyes and burying her face in the commander's chest, nipping at her breasts playfully. "That was...uhm...that..."

"Fuckin' amazing?" Malory offered.

"I won't argue with you there," she admitted, abruptly going stiff in alarm at a loud, persistent knock on the door. "Oh, God," she whispered, jumping out of Malory's embrace and anxiously looking around for her clothes.

"Hide," she hissed at the commander, who appeared to be amused.

"I'll do no such thing," Malory whispered.

Corky pulled her sweatshirt on over her head and shot the commander a threatening look. "Oh, yes, you will."

"Nope," Malory said, stretching out along the length of the cot.

Corky shot her a venomous glare as she buttoned her pants. "At least go stand over there where you can't be seen," she said, pointing to a spot.

Malory sighed. "Fine," she said, rising and walking over to stand with her arms crossed over her chest.

Corky took a deep breath and ran her hands through her hair to straighten it before she opened the door to find an empty hallway. Puzzled, she poked her head out and looked in both directions. Spotting no signs of life, she stepped back in to close the door and then froze.

"Oh, my God," she said in horror.

At the words, Malory gave up her hiding place and approached the doctor from behind. "What's the big deal?"

Corky could only bring a hand up to her mouth in mortification, and Malory gently nudged her out of the way to see what had caught the doctor's attention. Stifling a laugh, she bent over to pick up the pack of cigarettes, lighter and ashtray that someone had thoughtfully provided.

Leaving the doctor standing, she closed the door and reclaimed her seat on the cot. "I haven't had a smoke in over ten years."

"My God, someone heard us," Corky finally rasped in dismay.

Malory smiled in amusement. "That's not quite right, Dr. Rivers," she said, popping a cigarette in her mouth and lighting it. "I was occupied."

She gasped.

"Yep," Malory said knowingly. "Someone heard *you*. Actually, I'd be surprised if everyone didn't. There's probably not a limp dick in the compound."

"Jesus," Corky choked. "I can't imagine anything more embarrassing."

"Come to bed. I'll kiss it and make it better."

"How do I show my face tomorrow, or the day after?"

"Come to bed," Malory repeated, snuffing out her cigarette and holding out a hand.

Corky rushed over to bury her face between Malory's breasts. "God, what am I gonna do?"

Malory stroked her hair. "Tell you what," she said with a grin. "First thing tomorrow, I'll make an announcement ordering everyone not to make fun of you for twiddling your diddle."

A quickly stifled snicker was followed by an annoyed swat. "That's not funny," she mumbled. "How would you feel if the situation was reversed?"

"I'm the boss. No one would dare say anything to me. They'd just laugh behind my back."

"You're not helping."

Malory kissed the top of her head and reached down to pull the blankets over them both. "Go to sleep. It won't be so bad in the morning."

A pathetic sigh was the only reply, and she reached out to turn off the light.

Malory rose with a luxurious stretch and gently disengaged herself from the soundly sleeping doctor so she could answer the call of nature. She poked around the room when she was finished, interested in everything that had to do with the little woman. She noted the photographs of her parents and smiled at a family of teddy bears that resided upon one of her shelves.

The shrill blast of the alarm clock startled her, and she leaped across the room to shut it off, chuckling at the small arm that was irritably slapping at it from underneath the blankets. She immediately dove under the covers and playfully snuggled up to the waking woman.

"You gonna get up?" she whispered into her ear, leaving a kiss behind.

"No," came the pathetic croak.

"Why not?"

"Were you wearing your gun last night? I need it."

"Why?" Malory asked with a chuckle.

"Because I have to kill myself."

Malory laughed. "Gee, it's not the end of the world. So what if everybody thinks you were in here thumpin' the man in the little canoe? It's not that big a deal."

Corky turned in Malory's embrace to regard her seriously. "Why do you say that?"

"Well, shucks, Doctor. You're a young, healthy and, as far as everyone knows, single woman. What's there to be embarrassed about?"

"I was screaming like I was being burned at the stake," Corky said dryly. "If I had overheard that, I'd wonder what in the name of God that woman had been doing to herself."

Malory snickered.

"It's not funny."

"Geez, you're a doctor. You of all people should know that masturbation is normal, and everybody does it."

"Do you?"

"Hell, no! What do you think I am, some sort of sick freak?"

Corky snorted in annoyance and pulled the covers over her head to hide, ignoring her laughing companion.

"Oh, come on," Malory chortled. "If anyone says anything, you can just tell them you weren't alone."

"What if they ask who?" Corky inquired from under her blankets.

"Say it's none of their business. They'll spend days mumbling among themselves, trying to figure out who the lucky person was."

"What if someone asks you?"

"Asks me what? If I was the one banging the doc?"

"Yeah."

"Corky, no one here would dare ask me to my face about my sex life."

She sighed. "I wish I were the commander."

"No, you don't. The pay sucks."

"Really? I assumed you were pretty well off in that department."

"I do okay. I mean, I make enough to keep me in tampons and 'roid cream."

"You are so disgusting."

"But you love me."

"Did you mean what you said last night?"

"What did I say last night?"

"You know."

"Yes, I do know, and yes, I do. Now, are you gonna come out of there? I'm horny."

"No way!" Corky exclaimed, pulling the covers around her tightly. "Everyone would think I was a pervert."

"I could gag you."

"Shut up!"

Malory sighed. "I should probably go anyway. McNeely will be looking for me any minute."

Corky poked her head out from under the blankets. "Will I see you tonight?"

"I'd like to see you."

Corky smiled and Malory leaned in for a kiss. "Last night was unbelievable. Thank you."

She chuckled. "I should be the one thanking you."

"You will later," Malory said with a goofy grin and rose to start dressing herself.

Corky grinned and then cast worried eyes to the ceiling, trying not to imagine the horrors that were waiting to assail her when she emerged from her quarters.

Malory leaned over again to place a kiss on her cheek. "Ya gonna be okay?"

"I suppose I'll live."

Malory chuckled. "If anyone says anything inappropriate, you come tell me."

"Thank you, but I'm a big girl."

"You sure are," Malory said. "I'll see you later," she added and turned to exit the room.

Corky waited for the door to close and pulled the blankets back up over her head.

1100 hours

Corky had snuck into Medical, forgoing her morning coffee for fear of entering the mess and encountering anyone. As a result, she had spent a cranky morning looking up sharply whenever she heard footsteps in the hall and sighing in relief every time they passed. When she wasn't eyeballing the door and praying no one would enter, she spent the majority of her time either contemplating the consequences of her inevitable humiliation or reveling in the memory of the previous evening with Malory.

She was reminiscing about the latter when the sound of gunshots brought her out of her chair in surprise and alarm. Seconds later, the station alarm went off, and she ran into the corridor, almost being trampled by Reynolds and DeSoto as they raced by, the chief yelling into his radio.

"Say again?"

"They need a stretcher and..." The commander's voice faded as the chief got farther away.

Corky waited in agitation, not knowing what was going on and somewhat surprised that nothing had been said over the intercom. At least she knew that Malory was okay and was relieved to have heard her voice over the chief's radio. She looked up at the approaching lieutenant.

"Dr. Rivers, you'll need to prepare Medical to receive wounded," Ring said.

"ETA?"

He reached for the radio on his belt. "ETA on that, Sergeant?"

"Thirty to forty minutes. Out," Alvarez replied.

"From Excavation, I presume?"

"Yes, Doctor."

"Thank you, Lieutenant," she said and turned to reenter Medical.

The time passed slowly, and she fidgeted with worry, hoping that her friends were okay and wondering why a weapon was fired. Thirty-five minutes later, Percy's voice came over the radio.

"ETA five minutes, Dr. Rivers. Ballenger incoming with suspected hip fracture, possible internal injuries. Currently stable and conscious."

"Understood," she replied. "Anyone else?"

"Nothing priority. Out."

She took a deep breath to prepare for their arrival.

It was a little over two hours later when she emerged from the operating room to find her domain filled to capacity with people waiting anxiously for news of their colleague. Percy followed her, and she caught his arm, standing on her tiptoes to whisper in his ear.

"Excellent work today."

He smiled at the compliment and made his way through the crowd toward the exit.

"Well?" Clovis asked the question everyone wanted the answer to.

"He's okay," Corky said, loudly enough for everyone to hear. "But he's on his back for the duration and will be on the first flight out."

The news was met by communal relief and then disappointment.

"How bad—"

"Move aside," Malory interrupted from the doorway, waiting for everyone to get out of the way so she could enter the room. She strode through the parting bodies and leveled a look at Clovis.

"Dr. Stokes, report to my office, and wait there until I arrive," she ordered, her voice cold. "Now!" she barked when he didn't rush from the room immediately, startling him and sending him packing.

"Airman Daly, report to the hall *outside* my office and stand at attention," she added, her voice harsh, and the young man practically ran from the room. "The rest of you, return to your duties immediately."

She waited for the room to empty before she turned to Corky.

"How is he?" she asked, her voice noticeably gentler.

"Fractured pelvis. Some internal bleeding. Could've been far worse if it had taken much longer to get him here. He'll be fine, but he'll need to go out with the first flight."

"I see."

Corky had a hundred questions to ask but settled for the most important. "Are you okay?"

Malory smiled with an effort. "I'm fine."

"You sure?"

"Yeah," she said with a nod. "I'll see you later. I have things I need to do."

"Okay," Corky said reluctantly, watching Malory hesitate, as though she wanted to say something else, and then turn to walk from the room.

Daly stood in the hall anxiously. The commander had passed fifteen minutes earlier to enter her office, not sparing him a glance and slamming the door shut with enough force to make him cringe.

His only hope was that the tirade she was currently directing at Dr. Stokes would tire her out before it was time to deal with him. Her voice occasionally thundered from inside the room, and earlier, he had heard something smash against the wall with enough power to shatter.

"Sergeant Major, report to my office, please," her voice suddenly blared over the intercom.

He stood ramrod-straight, afraid to let the sergeant major see him at anything less than rigid attention. Shortly, McNeely arrived and paused in front of him to clap him on the shoulder.

"Stand easy, Daly. You might be out here a while," he said, rapping on the commander's door and stepping inside.

Daly sighed, slumping against the wall until the door opened almost half an hour later and Dr. Stokes stepped out, looking as though he'd been spit out of a combine. Daly grimaced internally and braced himself; it didn't look good.

"Airman Daly!" the commander barked. "Your turn. Get in here."

He stepped into her office and stood at attention, noting the shards of a broken coffee cup in the corner. "Commander," he said respectfully, not meeting her eyes as she sat glowering at him from behind her desk.

"Rest easy, Airman," she said in a friendly tone. "Take a seat," she added, gesturing to the chair next to the silent sergeant major.

He did exactly as he was told.

"I'm glad I spoke to Dr. Stokes first, or I would've had a lot of egg on my face," she said mildly. "Since it was my original intention to have your ass removed for discharging your weapon for no apparent reason. However, I've been informed that you probably saved Dr. Ballenger's life. Tell me, were you aware that Stokes allowed Ballenger to unclasp his safety rope?"

"No, Commander."

"That's what I hoped you'd say," she said, rising from her chair. "On your feet, Airman."

She cleared her throat. "In recognition of your quick thinking and action in the performance of your duties, I feel obligated to inform you that a letter of commendation will be added to your file. Do you have any objections?"

"No, ma'…I mean no, Commander," he corrected hastily.

"Good. Now go grab something to eat," she said with a grin. "Dismissed. Please shut the door on the way out."

He saluted crisply, immeasurably relieved and terribly proud of himself.

Corky stripped out of her scrubs and summoned Coy to watch over her patient for the night so she could make a beeline to the mess to collect the gossip. As soon as she entered, she was beckoned over by Dr. Lenard and company, so she collected a tray and hurried over to take a seat.

"So what's the story?" she asked.

"We hit another pocket in Excavation," Watkins said. "Not as bad as the first, but Ballenger was right on top of it without a safety rope."

"I guess that's why the commander was so pissed."

"Yeah. She confined Clovis to quarters."

"Why Clovis?"

"He gave Dr. Ballenger permission to disconnect his rope. It was giving him problems," Lenard explained.

"So what happened?"

"The pocket was situated right above the section we were working to uncover. He fell about twenty feet and landed on an exposed section of the spacecraft. We got down to him as soon as we could, but there was a large sheet of ice pinning him down. We couldn't lift it, so Daly used his rifle to break it in half, and we were able to get him out of there," Lenard reported. "So how is Dr. Ballenger?"

Corky went through the medical laundry list. "We'll have to watch him for the next few days, but I'm confident he'll fully recover."

"Damn," Lenard said. "It'll kill him not be involved in this."

"At least he has his life," Corky pointed out.

"Very true."

"So you found a big piece of the flying saucer?" Corky asked.

"Yeah," Watkins said. "No telling when we'll be allowed back down there, though."

"How come?"

"Lovecraft pitched a fit when she found out Dr. Ballenger disconnected his rope."

"A fit?"

"Oh, yeah. Threw her hat on the ground and kicked it. Then told us all we'd be lucky if she allowed us to return, and if we couldn't follow simple instructions for our own safety, perhaps the NSF could send another team that could."

"Ouch," Corky said. "So how long is Clovis incarcerated for?"

"He didn't say, but he looked like he'd been read the riot act, and I'm sure he's feeling bad about Dr. Ballenger," Lenard said. "He told him to take off the rope only long enough to fix it. It was just freak chance that what happened did when it did."

"Speaking of freaky things," Watkins said slyly, "did you hear that screaming last night?"

Corky immediately tensed and reddened guiltily, flushing darker as the men began to chuckle.

"My goodness, Doctor," Lenard said with a teasing smile. "You shouldn't save it up like that. It's unhealthy."

"Yes," Watkins added. "For all of our sakes, please pace yourself in the future. I was jolted out of a dead slumber, thinking I should run for my life."

Corky crossed her arms over her chest as the men laughed over their jokes, her face solid scarlet. "Are you guys finished?"

"Oh, come on, Corky," Watkins chuckled. "You should take our advice. Dobson here does it twice a day. Isn't that right?"

"Certainly," Dobson admitted. "Keeps me on an even keel, and I don't impose on my colleagues by carrying on loud enough to wake the dead."

Corky was assaulted by another round of laughter, but she set her jaw and held her ground, clamping down on the impulse to flee. "I shall take your suggestions under advisement. Obviously, I'm not as skilled at it as the rest of you."

Her comment delighted the men, and they quickly bubbled over. Grudgingly, she found their antics to be infectious and began to laugh a little herself.

1930 hours

Malory remained at her desk until well after suppertime, attempting to fight off the straggling remains of anger. Since she'd taken command, two people had been injured, and she was feeling responsible. She was so firmly entrenched in her funk, it took her a moment to realize that Corky was waiting hesitantly in the doorway.

"Hiya," she said softly.

"Hi."

"Can I come in?"

"Of course," Malory said with a frown. "You can come see me whenever you want."

Corky entered and shut the door behind her. "You didn't come to dinner."

"I wasn't hungry."

"Someone looks like they're sulking," Corky teased, getting a small smile for her efforts.

"Maybe."

Corky walked around and scooted Malory's chair back so she could plop down on the desk in front of her. "I visited Clovis in his jail cell. He said you were so mad at him earlier, he was afraid you were gonna order him shot."

"I considered it."

Corky chuckled and hooked her feet through the arms of the commander's chair, slowly pulling her forward. "Expecting any company?"

"Nope."

"How fortunate," Corky said, leaning forward to kiss her.

"Well, Doctor," Malory said when she withdrew. "Whatever brought that on?"

"I wanted to."

An evil smile.

Corky's brow wrinkled. "Why are you grinning like that?"

"Because you're mine now."

"Is that so?"

"Uh-huh. You're powerless to resist me."

"Does this mean you're mine, too?"

"I've always been yours. It just took me a while to find you."

Corky absorbed the words thoughtfully. "That was a sweet thing to say."

"It's true. I've waited my whole life for you."

Corky didn't know what to say in the face of such freely offered devotion. It touched her to the point of being unable to form words.

Malory read the emotions on her face. "I know."

"Y…you know what?"

"You love me, too. You just can't bring yourself to admit it," Malory said smugly. "But you'll come around."

Corky smiled. "I want you to come around."

"What?"

In reply, the doctor pulled her feet from Malory's chair and leaned forward to turn the commander's chair around, wrapping her arms around her from behind and placing a kiss on her neck.

Malory leaned into the contact. "Now I see what you meant."

"So if you're mine, can I do anything I want with you?" Corky murmured in her ear.

"Anything."

"I'd like to see if I could get you to be as loud as I was last night," Corky whispered, chewing on her neck playfully.

"I dunno about that. I'm pretty incredible."

Corky chuckled, dropping her hands to softly knead the commander's breasts, pleased when Malory arched her back and purred at the contact. "I won't deny that you're very skilled."

"Gimme a break," Malory scoffed. "I was so good, I almost screamed out my own name."

Corky laughed, momentarily pausing in the application of her attentions. "You kill me," she chuckled, leaning over to unclasp Malory's belt, letting the gun and radio fall to the floor and moving on to the buttons of her fatigues.

Malory's eyes dropped to the fingers at her waist, watching as they lightly completed their task and a gentle hand snuck in under the elastic of her panties. She hooked her knees over the arms of her chair in anticipation, shivering with the sensation of the long-awaited contact and slowly exhaling a soft, contented moan.

"You're very wet," Corky whispered into her ear, withdrawing her hand to verify.

Malory watched the hand emerge, feeling the doctor's interested gaze over her shoulder as she examined her glistening fingers.

"Very wet," Corky confirmed, flushing powerfully in arousal when her hand was seized and Malory erotically sucked on her fingers, her knees wobbling by the time she was finished.

"God, Malory."

"Touch me again."

"Tell me, why doesn't the commander rate a larger bed?"

In no mood to have a conversation, Malory blew out a frustrated breath.

"I mean, it's so hard to fit two on a cot comfortably," Corky said seductively, brushing her hands over Malory's breasts, smiling at the responsive whimper.

"Don't tease. Please touch me again."

"I know a way we can both fit on a cot," Corky whispered, playing with nipples so hard that they stood out proudly through the fabric of Malory's shirt.

"I'll do anything you want, Corky," Malory said submissively, biting her lip at the stir created by the doctor's caresses.

"Would you like to be on the top or bottom?" Corky asked, pinching the nipples between her fingers painfully and gleefully soaking up the stifled chirp of pleasure.

"What?" Malory rasped.

"I want to be on the bottom. Wanna know why?"

"Tell me," she squeaked.

"Because I want all of you."

Malory flew to her feet and shoved the chair out of the way, engulfing Corky within her arms and capturing the doctor's mouth with her own.

Corky wrapped her legs tightly around Malory's waist as she was lifted bodily off the desk, returning the kiss with equal fervor while the commander bounced them off the furniture and walls haphazardly in her haste to enter her quarters.

The first thing Corky noticed upon rising was Malory's ass, which didn't surprise her, since her cheek was resting on it. They were spread out on the floor, their bodies forming a large T in a mass of scattered blankets and an overturned cot. Her gaze traveled down the length of a shapely pair of legs to note that one foot was still wearing a sock. She smiled at the sight and rolled onto her back for a long, satisfying stretch.

Her companion was apparently still dead to the world, as her soft snoring indicated, and Corky rolled back over to place a kiss on her new pillow, happily reliving the memories of the previous evening. Her new lover was relentless in her need to please and be pleased, wonderfully uninhibited, frighteningly passionate, surprisingly submissive and energetically attentive. Abruptly, her thoughts turned dark, and the sated smile she had been wearing slowly transformed into a scowl. Had Malory shared herself with her previous lover in the way she had last night? The idea raised her hackles in jealousy, and she rolled over to glare at the sleeping mop of red hair, deciding to ask her about it when she woke.

Malory's easy confession of love was another thing that bothered her. She seemed so convinced and cavalier about it that Corky felt guilty about not being able to say it back. The commander began to stir, so she put the thought away for later consideration and turned her attention to her waking companion.

"Malory."

"Hmmm?"

"You gonna get up?"

"No."

Corky chuckled and craned her head around to bite her pillow.

"Hey!" Malory yelped.

"You didn't like?"

"It just tickled," Malory rumbled.

"Can I ask you a question?"

"Sure."

"How long were you with your lover?"

"Which one?"

Corky's brows knitted angrily. "What do you mean which one?"

Malory chuckled. "You're so easy."

She rolled her eyes. "I guess I set myself up for that," she said with a sigh. "Are you gonna answer my question?"

"I dunno," Malory said. "I wouldn't consider a few hours of teenage fumbling in the backseat of a car very long."

"Is that it?"

"Yeah, until I was with you."

"But...never mind."

"But what?"

"You seem so experienced."

"I finally found the person I was meant to be with. I love her, and I love being with her. I waited a long time to experience that."

"Malory," Corky cooed.

"Don't get all choked up on me, or I'll have to fart to lighten the mood."

An involuntary snort of laughter. "How romantic."

"Ya think?" Malory said brightly, lifting a hand off the floor and waving it in Corky's face. "Here, pull my finger."

Corky slapped the hand away with a snicker. "Don't be so gross."

Malory dropped the hand back to the floor and shrugged.

Corky raised herself to a seated position and pulled the covers off the commander playfully. She frowned in disappointment when Malory didn't react in the slightest, and she smacked her human pillow, which only resulted in an arousing rise of her hips.

"Oh," Malory purred. "Do that again."

Corky giggled. "Stop. Won't someone be looking for you this morning?"

"Nope. McNeely has a crew in Excavation today with a few of your nerdy friends."

"What are they doing?"

"Drilling and taking sonar readings to assure me that we'll not encounter any more pockets and clearing away the cave-in from yesterday," she explained. "I'll be glad to see the summer."

"Why? You're not going anywhere, are you?"

"No, but they'll be sending a lot more people and installing a long-overdue elevator in that stupid pit."

"It's not stupid," Corky defended. "Think about the advances we could make in technology from a find like this. What we could learn."

"Did it ever occur to you that maybe we weren't meant to find this thing?"

"No. Why would you think that?"

"I find it odd that back in the day when the highest form of life on this planet was probably a lonely protein, those aliens chose the most remote and uninhabitable region on the globe to crash into. What if they did so intentionally? What if they were carrying something that they didn't want found?"

Corky hummed for a long moment. "I never considered that, but I should point out that there are several planets in our system they could have chosen that offered them a better chance of never being discovered. I mean, Earth is the only planet in the system that supports life."

"What kind of life are you talking about? I mean, for all we know, these things might have considered a planet like Jupiter to be paradise. And what if they didn't have the time to make a better choice and took the closest and best option?"

"Is that what you think?"

"I don't know what to think, but I will say I could've lived my whole life without seeing that damn creature you guys pulled out of the ice. It gives me the creeps."

Corky giggled. "You mean our fearless leader is actually a big 'fraidy cat?"

"Maybe."

"How funny," Corky teased. "Wait till the guys hear."

Malory chuckled.

"Speaking of the guys, how long do you plan on imprisoning Clovis? He feels bad enough about it as it is, and he only told Dr. Ballenger to take the rope off long enough to fix it."

"He should have clasped Ballenger to his own harness or instructed Daly to anchor another rope."

"Malory," Corky said, "Clovis isn't a soldier. He did what he thought was best, thinking it would only take a minute to correct the problem. It was a freak accident; the odds of something happening when it did were astronomical. You were awfully hard on him, and he was already coming down hard on himself."

"Did he ask you to plead his case?"

"No. He's a good man, Malory."

"McNeely pretty much told me the same thing," she said around a sigh. "Okay, I'll speak to your pal Clovis later today."

Corky smiled in satisfaction and let her eyes roam appreciatively over the form stretched out in front of her. "You know, if I had known how good you looked without your clothes and that dumb hat you wear, I might have warmed up to you sooner."

"Please. You were hot for me from the start."

"I wanted to kill you."

"Fuckin' kill me," Malory agreed. "In that order."

She laughed. "God, you're vain."

"Nope, I just know the score."

"Uh-huh. And how would you know I had anything else on my mind except your painful death?"

"Because every time you looked at me, angry or not, you had this little twinkle in your eye like someone was ticklin' your cooter with a feather."

"I did not," she said with a mixture of indignity and amusement.

Malory rolled over and cocked an elbow to support her head. "Oh, yes, you did. Now get out from under those blankets and let me look at you."

"No."

She rose to her hands and knees and advanced seductively, watching in amusement as Corky hastily scooted away, only to be trapped against the overturned cot. She lifted the edge of the covers and crawled underneath them, tickling the quaking doctor as she slid up her body, her head emerging from underneath the blankets between Corky's breasts, where she began a trail with her tongue that ended with a kiss.

"I love you."

Any reply on Corky's part was forgotten as the words were followed by a hand that touched her intimately. "Uhm—" she started but was silenced by another kiss.

"Tell me later. I'll be back in a little while," Malory whispered as she disappeared back under the blankets.

1200 hours

Malory almost skipped into the mess to grab lunch. She had seen Corky off about an hour before and was already missing her. The doctor had left her quarters reluctantly to go check in on her patient, and she herself had dropped in on Clovis to let the man off the hook.

She had just sat down with her long-overdue cup of coffee and was eyeballing her burger and fries when her radio squawked for attention.

"*Commander?*"

"This better be good."

"*The interior of the section unearthed yesterday is accessible, Commander,*" McNeely reported. "*They're requesting more personnel to investigate.*"

Malory chewed on her lip. "And your feelings on the subject?"

"*From what we gather, it's about as safe down here as we can make it. Seems to be pretty solid.*"

"Let 'em have at it."

"*Understood. Out.*"

She tossed her radio on the table and dove into her meal with abandon.

An hour later, Malory strode into the lounge and shook her head when she spotted Lieutenant Ring reclining in front of the television. Even though the man was second in rank only to her, she envied him. His one and only job was to be a pilot, leaving him pretty much without a place in the chain of command. He had no responsibilities other than flying the helicopter, and because air travel during the Antarctic winter was a suicidal proposition, he had a lot of time on his hands.

"Lieutenant," she said, "wanna arm-wrestle for control of the television?"

He craned his neck around and gave her a smile. "If I won, would I still retain control of the TV?"

"Nope. Rank hath its privileges."

He chuckled and picked himself up off the couch. "Then I concede to your superior arm-wrestling skills."

"Ahh, a wise officer. You'll have a long and prosperous career."

"Indeed," he agreed and handed her the remote as he passed. "Your command console, Skipper."

"Why, thank you."

She waited for him to leave and ambled over to peruse the available selections, spending a moment in consideration before deciding on an oldie but goodie. She popped it into the machine and made herself comfortable on the couch, managing to stay awake long enough to get through the opening titles.

Voices slowly pulled her from her slumber, and she was dimly aware of being coated with sweat, a nagging fear surrounding her like a malignant mist. She struggled for consciousness, feeling it was just within her grasp as noises were already penetrating the fog; a man and woman were talking only a few feet away.

"But you need no doors to find God. If you believe—" the woman said.

"Believe?! If you believe, you are gullible. Can you look around this world and believe in the goodness of a god who rules it? Famine, pestilence, war, disease and death! They rule this world."

"There are also love and life and hope."

"Very little hope, I assure you. No. If a god of love and life ever did exist, he is long since dead. Someone...something rules in his place."

"Commander Lovecraft," McNeely said urgently.

Malory awoke with a start, springing from the couch in a near panic, gasping for air and tingling from the gooseflesh that covered every inch of her body.

"Commander," McNeely said, worry evident in his voice.

She shook her head violently to clear the cobwebs, unnerved by a clinging sense of dread. She had been dreaming—about what, she couldn't remember. Neither did she especially want to. Her hands were trembling, and she realized that she was scared shitless. She scanned the room frantically, searching for the specter that she felt sure was stalking her.

"Commander, if you don't respond in the next fifteen seconds, I'm tripping the general alarm."

The words had a calming effect on her frayed nerves, and her eyes focused on the television. *That fucking eerie Vincent Price!* Reality slowly began taking hold, and she shook her head again.

"Last chance, Commander."

She reached for her radio. "Go ahead."

"Are you okay? I've been calling you for the last ten minutes."

"I...I'm sorry, Sergeant Major. I must have fallen asleep."

"You need some time?"

"No, I'm fine, thank you," she said. "What's up?"

"They've found something down here they want to bring up."

A feeling of foreboding washed over her, making her shudder. She glanced again at the television and grabbed the remote, powering it off irritably.

"Commander?"

"What is it?"

"I have no clue, but it's fuckin' with my backbone."

She closed her eyes. "Gimme the scoop."

"It appears to be a container of some sort. Reminds me of that little puzzle box from the Hellraiser *movies, but about the size of a washing machine. Know what I'm talking about?"*

"Yeah. Do we know what's in it?"

"It's a transparent box, holding some sort of large crystal suspended in the

middle. Appears to be harmless, but I gotta point out we found an identical container right next to it that is apparently empty."

"Do you believe it presents a danger?"

"I would lean toward no, but this whole thing bugs me a little."

"Very well, let 'em bring it up. But I want it stored securely in the lab, and summon me when they get it stowed. I wanna give it a look."

"Understood."

"Lovecraft out."

The radio took its place on her belt, and she sat down hard on the sofa, running her hands through sweat-dampened hair. She couldn't remember experiencing such intense fear at any other time in her life, and it was still wreaking havoc on her composure. She tried to rationalize it as the effect of having fallen asleep during a creepy movie, but a sinister sense of premonition insisted that it was something else entirely. With a shaky, calming breath, she rose slowly and began the journey to the sanctuary of her office, wanting to be in comfortable surroundings while she waited to see what the hole in the ice had revealed.

1405 hours

The call came sooner than she expected, and Malory found herself in the lab, staring intently at a container that defied the laws of physics. McNeely had sized the object accurately, for it was indeed about the size of a washing machine, yet a perfect cube and almost completely transparent. A material both Gothic and technological in appearance lined the edges of the container to present a visible outline, but it was the item that resided inside that had Malory's total attention.

Floating magically in the center of the box was a long, narrow octahedron that resembled a flawlessly cut gem. It glowed a distinctive Caribbean blue, the intensity probably enough to illuminate the room if someone turned off the overhead lights. Closer inspection revealed the suspended crystal to be a second container that held a substance of its own. A substance within the crystal that flawed its outer perfection with a multitude of grooves that resembled brain matter.

"I was informed that there was an identical container to this one that was damaged," she said to the audience in attendance. "What exactly was broken? The thing floating inside or the cube itself?"

"The outside," Dr. Lenard replied. "Though it wasn't exactly broken. It was just missing the top panel."

"Is it glass?"

"No. Some sort of transparent epoxy, from what we can gather at this time."

"Is the crystal inside holding some sort of material? It appears that way to me."

"That is our impression as well."

"Could it be an explosive of some sort?"

"Unknown, but doubtful."

"Can any of you tell me anything for certain?"

"The technological is not really our area of expertise, Commander," Lenard said dryly. "The majority of people here at the moment are archaeologists and geologists. Excavation was not expected to uncover anything like this until the end of the winter. The team assigned to research and technological development won't be arriving until summer."

"Did we at least think to bring the empty container up as well? I want to look at it."

"They're working on it as we speak, Commander," McNeely said.

She nodded approvingly. "Understandably, no one can tell me anything concrete, so I'd like to hear guesses. Do we think it's a power source of some kind? It appears to me that the box holds the crystal in a sort of stasis. Anyone concur?"

"We tend to believe it's not a power source, Commander," said Lenard, who was obviously the spokesman for the group. "We believe the spacecraft was of a Y construction, and we speculate that the center and most-forward section was responsible for propulsion. In our estimation, any power source would most likely be found in that area. We assume this container to be nothing more than cargo."

"That would be the section as of yet uncovered and buried deepest within the ice, correct?"

"Yes."

"Why do we assume that the forward section would be responsible for propulsion?"

"It's all theory at this time, of course," Lenard said. "But the deepest section is buried a considerable distance from the others, suggesting an impact with an irresistible force behind it. The craft had to be traveling at an unimaginable speed to bury itself so deeply."

"Forgive me for being a layman, gentlemen. But if it was traveling at a speed anywhere near what you suggest, how did it survive so intact? I would think it would pretty much disintegrate on impact."

"The material that the craft is constructed from is impossibly resilient. We've been unable to damage or alter it with any of the means we currently have at our disposal."

"All right. What do you make of this thing, and do you believe it to be dangerous?"

"We're still very much differing in opinions at this time," Lenard said. "But we tend to think that the cube is a kind of automobile airbag for the crystal inside."

"So you think the interior of the cube provides a protective cushion for the cargo?"

"Exactly, Commander," Lenard agreed. "How, we don't know or can even guess at this time."

"Very well," Malory said. "If the crystal inside this thing was important enough to our alien buddies that they felt the need to pack it in a safety box while gallivanting around in an almost-invincible starship, we *will* follow their example. You have until noon tomorrow to provide me with additional information. At that time, if opinion hasn't altered radically, and if you can't come up with anything to convince me otherwise, the container will be isolated and secured from further study until it can be examined or transported to the appropriate authorities for investigation."

"But, Commander—" Lenard started.

Malory held up a hand. "You just stated that you're not the people qualified to investigate a discovery of this nature. Honestly, I have a hard time picturing anyone who *is*, but I'll not have a potentially dangerous artifact being subjected to casual experimentation. You have until noon tomorrow to study it. Then it will be shelved until the right people either take it away or offer me irrefutable proof that it doesn't present a danger."

She paused and waited for her words to sink in. "Sergeant Major, you *will* assign a guard to watch over the find until it is safely secured."

"Aye, Skipper."

"There will be no attempts to breach the interior of this box. The guard will have instructions to intervene immediately if my orders are disobeyed in the slightest. Have I made myself clear?"

She met every pair of eyes in the room to convey her resolve. When she was satisfied, she turned to McNeely. "Join me outside, Sergeant Major."

1800 hours

Corky entered the mess that evening and smiled reflexively when she spotted Malory, a grin that evaporated as she noted that the commander was conferring quietly with her noncommissioned officers and Lieutenant Ring.

Slightly disappointed that she couldn't join her, she got her meal and chose a seat next to Clovis, who was so deeply involved in a discussion with his gathered colleagues that he didn't notice her.

Feeling somewhat left out, she went about eating her dinner and let the surrounding whispers fly over her unheard, as she was quickly immersed in her own thoughts. In fact, she had spent the better part of the day engrossed in the contemplation of her relationship with the infamous Malory Lovecraft. Where once, the mere mention of the woman's name was a death-by-torture offense, it was currently cause for internal celebration. Now that she had fully indulged her attraction to the commander, she couldn't deny the emotions the woman instilled in her. She still wasn't ready to admit the depth of her feelings openly, but internally, she could no longer deny the power of her sentiments.

"Hey, Corky," Clovis said.

"Hmmm?" she asked distractedly, emerging from her thoughts.

Clovis chuckled knowingly. "Are you feeling okay, Doctor? You haven't been yourself lately."

Quiet chuckles rumbled from a few of the men, and she began to color in anticipation of another round of teasing. Fortunately, Clovis took pity on her before it got started.

"Give her a break, fellas. It's been an eventful winter."

She smiled gratefully at her friend, her blush painfully obvious.

"I was just telling my colleagues here," Clovis said, gesturing to the surrounding men, "that as much as we regret the commander's decision, it would be extremely foolish not to honor it."

"What decision was that?"

"To isolate our discovery from study until the arrival of the R&D team."

"What discovery?"

"Where have you been today? It's all anyone has been talking about."

"In Medical, of course."

"I'm surprised you don't know. We were able to enter the section of spacecraft uncovered by the cave-in the other day. We found a container with some sort of crystal floating inside."

"Really? What is it?"

"We don't know. We hadn't had it in the lab for half an hour when Lovecraft informed us that we only have until lunch tomorrow to study it before it goes into storage."

"Why did she do that?"

"Because we don't know what it is or what it's capable of, and admittedly, there's no one present really qualified to make a determination on its safety."

"That seems practical. What's the problem?"

"A few among us feel that we're here for investigation and study, and to deny us that defeats the purpose of our mission here."

"Okay, that's a reasonable argument, too."

"That's what I was telling my colleagues here. We have two opposing viewpoints with merit, but the fact is, Lovecraft is in charge, and she listened, asked questions and then made an informed decision. And personally, after experiencing her ire firsthand, I can see why she was chosen to head our operation here."

"Why do you say that, Clovis?" she asked, interested in his opinion.

"Because she's no paper tiger. Some of the guys think that just because she's virtually nonexistent in the day-to-day stuff around here, they can convince her to reverse her decision on today's find," he explained. "I disagree."

"What would it hurt to try?"

"Because she's made a decision, and it's final. Questioning that would only ensure that the time we *do* have for study would be taken away immediately. As much as we might wish otherwise, this facility is not run by democracy. The commander calls the shots, and they aren't open for debate. And although I'm more than a little disappointed with her ruling on this, I guess I'd have to admit than I'm also more than a little grateful."

"I don't understand."

"What we're doing here involves a new frontier, Corky," Clovis said. "Discovering technology a thousand years ahead of us, implemented thousands of years before us, is without precedent. We really have no idea how advanced these beings were, and toying with that constitutes an unknown. Who knows how dangerous that could be? I have to agree with her decision."

Corky grunted thoughtfully, recalling Malory's thoughts on the subject from earlier.

"So how is Dr. Ballenger?" Dr. Tanaka asked, changing the subject.

Corky was in the middle of her answer when she saw Malory stand up to exit the room. She hurried through her response, eager to be in the commander's company.

1845 hours

When Corky entered Malory's quarters, it was in time to see her fasten the last button on a Red Sox baseball jersey that hung halfway down her thighs.

"Hey," she said brightly.

"Hey."

"You turning in early?"

"Yeah, but I was hoping you'd join me."

"Of course. You look kinda tired. Is something wrong?"

"Just a strange day. Has me feeling a little weird."

"Want me to make you feel better?"

"Is that a proposition?"

"Maybe," she teased. "Can I borrow a sleep shirt?"

"Sure," Malory replied, bending to pull one out of her footlocker and tossing it over.

"Thanks," Corky said, immediately starting to strip off her clothes. Malory took a seat on the end of her cot to watch the proceedings attentively.

Corky noted the hungry look being cast upon her body and relished the attention. She removed her bra teasingly and let it drop slowly to the ground, smiling as pupils dilated starkly against a pale-blue background. She had never been looked at with such open and needy desire, and it made her feel both attractive and special.

"You're very beautiful," Malory whispered.

Corky pulled the gray Navy T-shirt over her head and grinned. "Nah, I'm just cute. You're the gorgeous one."

"Don't underestimate yourself. You're the most beautiful thing in the world to me."

Corky smiled and quickly came forward to gift her with a gentle kiss. "You're sweeter than you let on, Malory," she said, taking a seat on the other end of the cot and resting her back against the wall. "So tell me what's got you feeling weird," she added, patting her lap invitingly.

Malory didn't need to be asked twice and immediately lay down to snuggle up next to her. "This whole thing, I guess. Sometimes, I think we're messing with something that maybe we shouldn't."

Corky softly stroked the hair in her lap. "If we weren't meant to find it, we never would have."

"I wish I could subscribe to that."

"If you had objections, why did you agree to come here?"

"It was a last minute posting. I really had no idea what it was you guys were digging up. I was dispatched overnight and never bothered reading the textbook they gave me in lieu of a briefing. Not that it would've mattered; I had already committed myself."

"Are you sorry you came here?" Corky asked, suddenly frightened of the answer.

"Not at all. I would have missed out on finding the rest of my life."

Corky sighed. "I would've never figured you for such a romantic."

Malory shrugged and nestled deeper into her lap.

"Are you bothered by that thing they discovered today?"

"A little. It's kinda freaky, and there's no tellin' what the damn thing actually is."

"Hmmm. So what's the rest?"

"The rest of what?"

"You said it only bothered you a little. What else is on your mind?"

Malory grunted.

"Come on; give it up."

"It's dumb."

"What's dumb?"

"I went to watch a movie this afternoon and fell asleep," Malory mumbled. "I had some sort of awful nightmare I can't remember, and I woke up completely terrified. It's been bugging me all day."

"What were you watching?"

"'The Masque of the Red Death,' an old Vincent Price flick."

"There ya go. Vincent Price always spooks me."

"Yeah, well, that's what I keep telling myself," Malory said, bringing up an inquisitive hand to pull out the front of Corky's underwear and peeking inside.

Corky swatted her hand away. "Stop that."

Malory sighed in disappointment. "Yes, Mistress."

"Mistress? What's that supposed to mean?"

"Why, nothing, my little dominatrix," she teased. "By the way, last night was the best night of my life," she added, placing a kiss on the thigh she was resting her cheek on.

"It was the best night of my life, too," Corky whispered. "I sort of lost control. I'm sorry. I just wanted you really badly."

"That's nothing to be sorry for. I enjoy every second of being with you."

"Then what's with the dominatrix comment?"

"I was just teasing."

"Did I do something you didn't like?"

"Of course not. Short of beating me, I'd probably like anything you wanted to do to me. It excites me when you're excited, and my body is as much yours as it is mine."

Corky hummed thoughtfully. "That leaves open a lot of possibilities."

"I hope so."

Corky stared fondly at the head in her lap. "You give yourself so completely, Malory. You're an unbelievable lover."

"Only for you."

"Why me?"

"Because I love you."

"How can you be so sure? We've only known each other for such a short time," she whispered.

"I trust my heart."

Corky debated with herself for a moment. "Then how is it you say you know I love you too?"

"Because your heart shows what your mind is trying to reconcile."

"Huh?"

"Your mind tells you there are a thousand reasons not to love me, but it's arguing a case that's already lost to your heart. It's just being stubborn."

Corky dedicated a moment of thought to that. "And you obtained this magelike wisdom exactly when in your thirty years?"

"The day I fell in love with you."

"And when was this? How did you know?"

"I suspected it from the start, but I knew for certain the day I called you to my office," Malory said, rolling over and beaming a smile.

Corky frowned at the memory. "Uh-huh. Was that before or after you left me in there to converse with your dumbshit doll?"

Malory snickered. "It was when you smiled at me, even though you hated me and suspected I was up to something."

"I remember doing that and actually thinking for a second you were charming."

"I *am* charming. And lovable," she added with a playful smile.

Corky chuckled. "How do you walk through doorways with that fat head?"

"I take a deep breath."

"You're something else, Commander," Corky said, leaning over to place a kiss on her forehead.

"Tell me something I don't know," Malory responded, suddenly turning in the doctor's embrace and nipping playfully at her underwear.

"Stop," Corky exclaimed with a giggle. "That tickles," she added, hastily inserting an obstructing hand between her legs.

Malory grudgingly subsided and threw a quick glance up to meet smiling brown eyes. "Let me see."

"Let you see what?"

"Don't tease. Let me see."

Corky immediately felt the flush of arousal and glanced down at blue eyes that were steadily transfixed on their target.

"Let me see," Malory repeated impatiently.

The flush quickly became all-consuming, and Corky lowered a hand to pull aside her panties, revealing herself to avidly watching eyes. Her nipples hardened in reaction to Malory's audible breath of anticipation, and time dragged on excruciatingly as the commander made no further movement or requests, continuing to study her from close range. She squirmed under the intense scrutiny for as long as she could, but her resolve faded rapidly.

"Malory, please."

The request was all it took. She was instantly caressed by a long and agonizingly slow stroke of Malory's tongue that resulted in a sharp exhale and a shiver that ran the length of her body. Grinding her teeth, she dislodged her lover gently and clasped her legs together in blockade. Breathing deeply in frustration, she turned to look into questioning blue eyes.

"I showed you mine. Now show me yours."

Malory blinked but flopped over almost immediately to wiggle out of her underwear, tossing them across the room. Still on her back, she looked up at the doctor quizzically and received a raised eyebrow in response.

"I can't see you from there. Turn around."

Malory spun around and spread her legs over both sides of the cot to display herself, her eyes dark with expectation.

Corky leaned forward seductively to place both hands behind Malory's knees, slowly forcing her legs up and back until they rested on the panting commander's chest.

"You'll need to hold these out of the way until I'm finished," Corky purred. "I want you to watch me do this."

Malory readily put her knees behind her elbows, placing her hands under her hips to allow herself an even better view. She bit down on her lip as Corky hovered and ran investigational fingers over her.

"God, look at you. You're so excited," she whispered and abruptly descended, receiving a hastily muffled squeal at the contact.

Malory's head lolled back in pleasure but snapped up almost instantly in perceived denial, shooting a pleading look at Corky that begged her to continue.

"You have to watch. If you don't, I'll stop."

Malory nodded urgently in acquiescence, rapt eyes ardently studying the proceedings and grunting in animalistic gratification as lips tenderly covered her. She tried desperately to prolong her release, but the point-blank observation of Corky's attentions brought it forward irresistibly, and when brown eyes glanced up from their task to meet hers lovingly, it was not to be denied.

"Corky!"

Corky smiled in satisfaction at Malory's quick and energetic climax, riding the resulting convulsions out and meeting each thrust of her lover's hips with equal fervor. She waited until Malory's legs dropped in an effort to get away before finally relenting and trapping Malory's body beneath her own, falling forward to place kisses on a belly that still shook with the occasional spasm. She waited a moment for Malory to subside and rose to undo the buttons of her jersey, receiving not a whimper of protest as she nursed at the breasts that her labor had exposed.

"Cor—" Malory started.

"Bend over," Corky interrupted, abandoning the attention she was lavishing on the chest below and rising to kneel on the floor.

Malory swallowed and rolled out of bed. Corky patted a space on the cot, and the commander moved forward obediently to rest her elbows on the spot the doctor had indicated. She meekly allowed Corky to position her as she wished and gasped when a hand seized her hair to pull her head back and the other stroked her skillfully, probing softly for access.

"Yes," she rasped, spreading her legs and arching her back in offering.

The fine hairs on Corky's body bristled with the thrill of Malory's gift, and she placed a soft kiss on her hip before entering her delicately. Her mouth dropped open with desire as Malory gripped the far end of the cot with both hands and thrust backward onto her two extended fingers, embedding them within her and crying out loudly. Malory trembled slightly in aftermath and then renewed her thrusts, her need so passionate that Corky moved enthusiastically to meet her, moaning quietly as her own stimulation increased dramatically.

"Take me, Corky."

The breathlessly uttered words only added to the fire of her own already brightly burning libido, and Corky increased the power and speed of her thrusts, her hand colliding into and against her lover forcefully. Malory responded to every stroke with a hedonistic groan, her arousal so evident that Corky could feel it trickling down her arm.

Her whole body pulsated with a previously undiscovered yearning that clamored for immediate attention. Unable to refuse, Corky released the grip she had on Malory's hair to see to her own urgent demands.

Malory's head fell forward at the reprieve, and she turned a glassy look over her shoulder, climaxing as she surveyed the scene that greeted her. Her whole body shook with the pleasure of it, and she impaled herself on Corky deeply, crying out blissfully in gratification and collapsing to the floor to catch her breath. She sighed in contentment as Corky withdrew from her slowly. After a long, calming moment, she rolled over to watch the doctor pleasure herself.

"I love you," she said.

Corky offered no response but a sharp intake of breath that was accompanied by a rapid escalation of movement from the hand within her underwear.

Malory moved forward, taking her time and watching the activity with fascination. "Let me take these off so I can see better," she requested, pulling on the waistband of the doctor's underwear and smoothly removing them as Corky fell over onto her back.

Malory placed a kiss on the back of an occupied hand. "I like to watch."

Corky responded with a little moan, pulling the hem of her nightshirt up over her breasts and raising her legs to provide a better view.

Malory was quickly captivated, and when Corky began to emit a series of rapid whimpers she eased forward to gently replace the frantic fingers, sighing happily as legs wrapped themselves around her head in ownership. Her eyes rose to catch Corky tasting the ends of her fingers, and the beast within stirred again.

May 8 - 0600 hours

Malory awoke face down on the cot and shot an arm out blindly in annoyance, slapping the harshly screeching alarm across the room to crash into silence. She smiled at the weight still asleep directly on top of her, Corky's breath whispering along the skin of her back.

"She loves me."

"We'll see," Corky mumbled, and Malory chuckled.

"You weren't supposed to hear that."

"Uh-huh," Corky said around a lengthy yawn. "What time did I fall asleep last night?"

"It was right after you sprayed me and declared me your bitch."

"I did not," Corky giggled.

"Speaking of which," Malory said, "I need to use the little commander's room."

Corky chuckled and rolled off to let her up, watching with appreciation as she stretched. Malory's spine popped audibly several times, and she grunted in satisfaction.

"Geez, did that feel good?"

"Yep," Malory said, striding over immodestly to sit down and relieve herself.

Corky observed in enjoyment. "You're not the least bit shy, are you?"

Malory shrugged. "I'm here with you. Why should I be?"

"I dunno. I think it's sort of sexy, actually."

"Watching me go to the bathroom is sexy?"

Corky snickered and rolled her eyes. "So what song are you named after?" she asked over the sound of a flushing toilet.

"What brought that to mind?"

"Dunno. Suddenly curious I guess."

"An old Bob Dylan tune, 'Quinn the Eskimo,'" Malory said as she stood to wash her hands.

"Never heard of it. Are you part Eskimo?"

"How many Eskimos have you ever seen with red hair and blue eyes?"

"Then I don't get it," Corky said, craning her head around to look at her. "How does it go?"

Malory finished drying her hands and turned to Corky with a smile. "Come all without!" she warbled as she gyrated ineptly, and Corky instantly slapped a hand over her mouth. "Come all within! You'll not see nothing like the mighty Quinn!"

"Oh, my God! You're such a boner!" Corky buried her face in the blankets and laughed.

"What?"

Dancing brown eyes peeked out at her. "Was that the Cabbage Patch?"

"What are you talking about?" Malory asked, placing her hands on her hips in annoyance.

"Never mind," Corky chuckled. "Maybe it was funny because I never saw anyone do it in the nude or with such complete lack of rhythm."

Malory stomped her foot, and Corky hid her face again to indulge in a fresh gale of laughter.

"I do too have rhythm," Malory protested.

Corky regarded her lover with a teasing smile. "Whatever you say, Deputy Fife," she snickered and sat up to launch into a comically exaggerated, manic Don Knotts impersonation. "You've got to nip it! Nip it in the bud!"

Corky fell over chortling, and Malory pounced.

Corky shrieked and thrashed about wildly, struggling fruitlessly to get away from the commander's tickling fingers.

"Malory, stop!"

The tormenting fingers gradually came to a halt, and Malory studied her heavily breathing companion, waiting until she let her guard down and then darting forward to capture a nipple between her teeth.

Corky yelped and swatted the top of Malory's head. "Why did you do that?"

"Don't tease me."

Corky grinned. "Somebody can dish it out but can't take it."

"Maybe," Malory admitted, placing a tender, healing kiss on Corky's breast.

Corky petted the head on her chest. "Aww," she soothed. "Don't be such a big baby."

Malory mumbled incoherently and laid her head on Corky's stomach.

"I'm so exhausted," Corky said after a moment. "And my tummy kinda hurts."

"Maybe it's something you ate."

"You think?"

"Could be," Malory speculated. "Maybe from now on, I should wipe front to back."

Corky's face slowly scrunched up in disgust. "That's revolting."

Malory chuckled.

"You would horrify my mother," Corky predicted sadly. "I'll have to train you before you meet my parents."

Malory smiled. "You want me to meet your parents?"

Corky groaned internally at the unconscious slip but forged ahead bravely. "Yeah. Yeah, I do."

Malory squealed girlishly in delight and crushed the doctor in an enthusiastic embrace. "Told you."

Corky rolled her eyes but played along. "Told me what?"

"You love me," Malory stated triumphantly.

Corky grunted indifferently.

"Commander?" the radio squawked.

"Damn it," Malory exclaimed, rolling over Corky to snatch the radio from the nightstand. "Go ahead."

"You said you wanted to look at the second container this morning," McNeely said.

"Yeah, I do. But does it have to be so early?"

"No," McNeely chuckled. *"I just assumed sailors rose with the sun like the rest of us grunts."*

"Is the ship sinking?"

"Not that I'm aware of."

"Then let me take a shit, shower and shave, and I'll get with you later."

"Understood," he said around a laugh. *"McNeely out."*

Corky had listened to the conversation with interest. She opened her mouth to speak but was silenced by a heavy breast that squashed into her face as Malory rolled over her again to put the radio back.

"God, these cots suck," she said irritably. "They're too small."

"Tell you what," Malory said. "If you're a good girl, I'll requisition a larger one for summer."

"Really? Can you do that?"

"Sure," she said, noting the slight scowl being directed at her. "What's with the look?"

"It bothers me a little that you get along with everyone so easily. You can be one of the guys and one of the girls. How do you do that?"

"I never really thought about it. Why would that bother you?"

"I guess it makes me feel like I'm being left out of something."

"Corky, in an official capacity, I'm in charge here, and there are parts of that you can't be involved in. But personally, I'm yours completely and would never intentionally exclude you from anything."

"Hmph."

"Would it make you feel better if I let you have your way with me?"

"Would you let me spray you?"

Malory laughed. "You've already done a pretty thorough job of marking me. I wouldn't be surprised if there was another pack of cigarettes outside my door."

Corky's eyes widened in alarm.

"I'm just kidding," she chuckled. "My quarters are pretty isolated," she added and received a playful swat.

"Ha, ha."

"You never told me. Anyone give you any grief?"

"I took some ribbing," Corky mumbled. "But surprisingly, it wasn't as horrible as I imagined."

"I kinda figured."

"You did, huh?"

"Sure. These guys have been down here a long time. Unless some of them are butt buddies, I would think they all indulge on a regular basis. Of course, you don't hear them scream out in the middle of the night like they're being fucked with a chainsaw. They're much more discreet, unlike someone who shall remain nameless," she said, throwing in an irritating cackle when she was finished.

Corky favored her with a frown. "Do you ever listen to yourself? Your language is appalling, and your terminology is offensive."

"What did I say?"

"You're not meeting my mommy until you clean up your act," she said sternly, crossing her arms over her chest.

1155 hours

Malory took her time getting to the lab, arriving right before lunchtime to pay heed to the gathered scientists. Judging by the expressions of those in attendance, she expected it to be a short meeting. Before hearing them out, she decided to inspect the second container and found it identical to the first, with the exception of an empty interior and missing top panel. She choked down a sudden feeling of uneasiness but kept her expression impassive, not entirely convinced that the vacant cube wasn't an omen of sorts.

"Okay," she said finally. "Let's hear it."

Dr. Lenard cleared his throat. "It seems there's no evidence or theory we can provide that would convince you that the find does not present a danger."

"That's pretty much what I expected."

"However," Lenard continued, "we believe we've found out how to open it."

Her eyes flashed. "That's beside the point, and you know it. Under no circumstances would I allow the contents to be exposed to the populace here without some pretty goddamn convincing assurances."

"No one is suggesting removing the crystal—just exposing it to a more informative study," he explained hastily.

"Out of the question."

Lenard opened his mouth to reply but paused thoughtfully, slowly nodding his consent.

"Very well," Malory said with a nod of her own. "I want both containers secured within the hour," she added on her way out of the room.

"All right, Commander," Lenard said.

"Damn it," Grey mumbled as the door shut behind her.

"We knew what she would say," Lenard sighed. "Let's get them moved. We have a lot more to do in Excavation."

"I told you this would happen," Grey said. "We have what could be the most important find in history here, and she's taking it out of our hands."

Lenard shrugged. "The decision has been made, and right or wrong, there's nothing we can do about it."

"What's wrong about doing our job?"

"Our job?" Lenard asked, looking at him sharply. "We've openly admitted that this isn't our area of expertise. On one hand, I don't like being told no any more than you do, but on the other hand, the commander is right, and our intervention would be irresponsible. I shouldn't have let you cajole me into agitating her with a request for further experimentation."

Grey fumed and glared at his gathered colleagues. "Am I alone on this?"

Lenard let his eyes wander as well. "It appears that you are."

"Fine," Grey said. "Let's rush the cubes to storage so I don't have to look at them and dwell over lost opportunities."

"Let's get it done, then. Dr. Dobson, would you assist me—" Lenard started.

"I'll take care of it," Grey interrupted. "Just send Cohen in to give me a hand.

Have him grab one of the flatbeds so we can haul 'em away."

Lenard gave him a suspicious look but finally nodded and shuffled to the door, waving for the rest of his companions to join him.

Grey watched as Lenard paused to speak to Cohen. Finally, the young airman trotted out of sight, leaving him alone and unsupervised. He immediately approached the cube and ran a hand along one of the top seams, his fingertips deftly locating the small indentations. Knowing that he didn't have much time, he rummaged through a nearby desk for two unsharpened pencils and gingerly pushed them, erasers first, into the small holes.

A second went by, and then two, without result, and he began to think that they had been mistaken after all. Disappointed, he removed the pencils and was in the process of turning away when the clear top panel began to color a strange gray and then separate to retreat into the seams of all four sides.

The brilliant blue light that filled the interior of the cube abruptly faded, revealing the true color of the substance within the crystal to be muddy red. As if sensing the change, the material inside the crystal began to churn violently. Fascinated, Grey put the pencils in his pocket and leaned over to inspect, withdrawing slightly in surprise when the top of the crystal seemed to vibrate and emit a sound similar to that of breaking glass.

1220 hours

Malory was only a few potato chips into her lunch when the alarm brought her out of her seat. She glanced at McNeely and got a shrug in return.

"I have a man down in the lab. Request assistance," Airman Cohen nervously reported over the intercom.

She tried to ignore the fear that clung to her spine and broke into a run, McNeely right behind her. As she raced down the hall, she found several people already gathered outside, and she brushed past them to enter the lab. She came to a halt as she met Cohen standing in front of the glass door and staring inside. She followed his gaze to see both alien containers empty and Grey face down on the floor in front of them. Her fear strengthened its hold on her spine, and for a second, she was unable to find her voice. When she finally did, her tone was furious.

"Motherfucker! What the hell happened?" she asked, turning a glare on the young airman.

"I went to get a flatbed so we could transport the cubes," he said. "When I got here, the cube was empty, and Dr. Grey was on the floor."

"Why didn't you go in?" McNeely asked.

"He was screaming," Cohen said nervously. "He was screaming like nothing I ever heard before. It was…it was..."

"All right, son," McNeely interrupted. "We need to get him out of there."

Malory nodded absently, her eyes frantically searching the interior of the room.

"Commander," McNeely prompted.

She took a deep breath and held out a hand. "Airman, your rifle," she ordered, and he handed it over.

"Commander, I don't think that's a good idea," McNeely said. Then he turned to yell out into the hall. "Hanson! Terrel! Get in here!"

"No," Malory said. "I won't risk anyone else. Just keep the door open and shut it as soon as I get back in here."

"Absolutely not. I'll go in your place."

"I'm not going to argue with you, Sergeant Major."

"Malory, don't," Corky whispered.

The commander turned in surprise, unaware that Corky had entered the room and was staring at her, fretfully wringing her hands.

"Commander, I insist," McNeely said as Hanson and Terrel burst through the bodies crowded in the hall.

"Commander, please," McNeely requested, holding out a hand.

She handed the sergeant major her rifle. "Cohen, clear the hall, and get Percy or Coy in here with a stretcher. Move!" she ordered, turning her attention to McNeely as Cohen raced into the corridor.

"I'll hold the door," she said. "Get Grey out of there as quickly as you can. Don't stop to sightsee."

"Understood," McNeely said. "Move it. I'll cover." He gestured to Hanson and Terrel. "Just grab him by the arms and yank him out of there."

"Wait!" Lenard exclaimed from the doorway.

Malory turned an irate look in the man's direction. "What is it, Doctor?"

"Take some precautions here, Commander," he said carefully. "We don't know what was in the cube. It looked solid, but it might have been some sort of vapor. Rushing in there unprepared might do more harm than good."

This gave Malory pause, and she gave him a terse nod. "You're right. What do you suggest?"

"Decontaminate the room."

"Grey may not have that much time," Corky said.

Malory closed her eyes for a moment. "Okay, here's what's gonna happen. Gas masks for everybody going in and for those waiting in the foyer. Everyone else waits in the hall. As soon as we get Grey out of there and seal the door, we'll get a stretcher in here. Understood?"

Nods all around.

"Everyone not involved, clear the room, and make a hole in the hallway," she ordered, waiting impatiently for everyone to comply. Then she turned to McNeely. "Gear us up, Sergeant Major."

McNeely opened one of the many supply lockers that decorated the interior of the foyer and removed several masks, tossing one to everyone present.

Malory got hers on and cast a look around. "We ready?"

She received nods in response and wrenched the door open, allowing Hanson and Terrel to race through, followed closely by McNeely, who stood by the door, his rifle raised to protect the scrambling men.

It was a quick exercise as both men roughly grabbed Grey by the arms and dragged him across the floor, dumping him unceremoniously as they passed the threshold, McNeely jumping back in after them. Malory slammed the door and sealed it, missing the darting sergeant major by a hair in her haste.

Corky knelt by her patient, rapidly checking his vitals as Percy and Coy rushed in with a stretcher. "He's alive, but his pulse is weak. Let's move him," she said, and Grey was hastily loaded onto the stretcher and rushed from the room.

Malory watched them go. "I want an armed guard posted exactly where I'm standing until I say otherwise. No one is to enter the lab under any circumstances. Have Cohen and Lenard report to my office and then join me there, Sergeant Major."

"Aye, Skipper."

The commander sat behind her desk, glaring at both the young airman and Dr. Lenard as she waited for McNeely to arrive. Her eyes kept straying to Cohen, who was still pale from his earlier experience and seemingly unaffected by the scrutiny being cast upon him by his superior. She hoped that her countenance displayed confidence, but on the inside, she was perilously close to unreasoning fear. It was a feeling that had been growing exponentially since the discovery of the alien within the ice and that had only intensified with recent events.

Finally, McNeely arrived, closing the door behind him and standing quietly just inside the room.

"Grab the chair in my quarters, Sergeant Major," Malory offered, and he gave her a slight nod. He entered her room and returned a second later to seat himself.

"Okay," she said after a deep breath. "What the fuck happened?"

Both men remained silent, so she turned a glare on Dr. Lenard. "Well?"

"I'm afraid I don't know, Commander," he said, removing his spectacles so that he could fidget with them. "Grey stayed behind after you left the lab to transport the cubes to storage. He instructed one of us to have Cohen grab a flatbed, which he did, and that's all I know."

"So he was alone in the lab?"

"I would assume so."

"Airman, how long were you away from your post?"

"No more than five minutes, Commander."

Malory leaned back in her chair. "Doctor, you told me you believed you could open the cube. Do you think Grey might have taken the opportunity to try?"

"I want to say no, but we argued after you left. He was disappointed about your decision to shelve it."

"You argued about it but then left him alone with the damn thing?"

"Regrettably, yes," Lenard admitted. "I've known Dr. Grey a long time. He blusters a lot, but I've never known him to act so recklessly. If he did indeed open the cube, I'll accept full responsibility for his actions."

"I'm not looking to assign blame here. There'll be time for that later. Do you think he could've opened it in five minutes?"

"Possibly. Along the seams of the top panel there are two small holes. The depressions are sized and spaced to accommodate what we theorized was one of the alien's hands—or, to be more precise, fingers. However, I stress that our assumption was just a theory."

"Then our beloved Dr. Grey had more than enough time to test the theory."

"All he had to do was find something small enough to fit in the depressions," Lenard admitted. "But that, of course, isn't a guarantee that he opened the container. It was pretty much a guess on our part that it might be that simple."

"Airman," Malory sighed, "what exactly did you see when you returned with the flatbed?"

"He was lying face down on the floor, screaming," he said distantly. "Screaming like…like…it was indescribable."

"Is that all?"

"Yes, Commander," Cohen answered. "He was just scre..." He paused. "Wait. I think…never mind."

"Please continue."

"It was hard to make out, his voice was so…so strained, but I think he might have said 'worms.'"

"Worms?" McNeely finally asked.

"Yes, I think so, Sergeant Major."

Malory stiffened, almost in panic, and grabbed her radio. "Dr. Rivers, respond immediately!"

A second that lasted ten years followed.

"Go ahead."

Malory almost swayed in relief. "Doctor, does Grey have any signs of being infected by an intruder?"

"What?"

"Cohen believes that Grey might have said 'worms' before losing consciousness."

"Worms?"

"Yes."

"Not to my knowledge, but I'll reexamine his blood sample," Corky said. *"Dr. Grey seems to be uninjured, although comatose. His blood pressure and body temperature are extremely low. I can't find a reason for it."*

"Please let me know as soon as you learn anything."

"Will do. Rivers out."

Malory sat the radio on her desk. "Sergeant Major, dispatch an armed guard to Medical, and round up Reynolds, Alvarez, Hanson and Terrel. We're going to go into that lab."

"Oh, and Dr. Lenard," she added, "you'll be joining us."

1920 hours

McNeely tore off his gas mask and kicked it down the hall in frustration; they had spent the past six hours searching every square centimeter of the lab and had come up empty. Malory echoed the man's sentiments as she slid down the wall she was leaning against and rested her rifle upright between her legs. She sighed and rested the back of her head against the wall.

"I don't get it," she murmured.

"I don't either," McNeely agreed.

"Commander," Reynolds said as he emerged from the lab, "the cubes have been stored. Any further orders?"

"Contact the appropriate authorities, and inform them of the situation."

"Not possible at the moment, Commander. Communications are still down."

"Fix the problem, Chief."

"Commander, the weather hasn't changed. I can't send anyone outside."

She sighed. "How long?"

"According to the last forecast I got from McMurdo, the better part of two weeks."

She ran a hand over her hair in frustration. "Okay, Chief. Let's get someone out there as soon as the weather permits, and you might as well let everybody loose for the evening except those on guard duty."

"Very well, Commander. Have a good evening."

"You too, Chief."

McNeely took a seat beside her in the hall as the rest of the men filtered past, waiting until everyone was out of earshot to speak. "What do you make of it, Skipper?"

"I don't know, but I've got a case of the crawling creeps."

"You think Grey opened the damn thing?"

"Yeah, I do. I feel like an ass for not watching over it with my own eyes until it was stored. The idiot had to have done it right after I left the goddamn room."

"None of this is your fault."

"It feels like it."

"That's because you're the skipper, and a damn good one. You're not responsible for the people who disobey your directives, just as you're not responsible for the unstable conditions in Excavation, and you're most certainly not responsible because some jackass decided to open that damn box."

"But I am. I'm responsible for the actions of everyone under my command, and that includes the civilians."

"Yes, to a point, you are. But you're beating yourself up over something you're not expected to have complete control over."

"Maybe."

He sucked on his teeth. "Tell me, Commander. Why would a sailor with no climbing experience go over the edge of a lethal drop in order to save a life? While you're at it, tell me how a twenty-four-year-old lieutenant with a gunshot wound and ruined arm could manage to keep herself and a man roughly twice her weight afloat in the ocean for over day? And please tell me how a woman who was obviously scared shitless found the courage to prepare to go alone into that lab earlier today?"

She turned a thoughtful look in his direction. "Adrenaline?"

He chuckled. "Don't hand me that shit."

She shrugged. "You obviously had a look at my file."

"Of course I did. I expected them to send a colonel or above."

"Sorry to disappoint you."

"On the contrary, I don't think they could've picked a better person."

Malory smiled. "You trying to get a blush out of me or cheer me up?"

Another chuckle. "I would've liked the blush, but I'll settle for a pick-me-up."

"Looks like you're not gonna let me feel sorry for myself."

"Nope. But I'll sober you up."

"I didn't know I was drunk."

"You keep an excellent poker face, but your girlfriend doesn't."

Malory tensed. "My girlfriend?"

"The good doctor."

"Well, yes. We're friends."

"Don't bullshit a guy who has fifteen years on you," he chided. "I'm pointing this out to you because if it became common knowledge, they'd pull you out of here at the first opportunity. I don't want that to happen."

"Does anyone else know?"

"I imagine I'm the only one."

"How did you find out?"

"I caught the first clue today when she called you by name and looked about ready to cry to keep you from going into the lab. I knew for sure when you sent me into your quarters to get a chair, and I found a set of medical scrubs draped over the back."

"Busted," she admitted. "I take it you don't have a problem?"

"Please," he scoffed. "I was actually kinda hoping you would share your technique with me."

"What?"

"Now that I realize that the doctor wasn't alone in her quarters the other night, I'd like to know how you get a woman to scream like that. An aging stud like myself is always on the lookout for new pointers."

Malory started laughing before he finished. "That is one discussion we will never have."

He laughed with her. "You won't even throw me a bone?"

Malory shook her head. "Try going without for thirteen years while spending half of each day thinking about it."

He chuckled quietly and rose to his feet. "You're a stronger man than I am, Commander."

"That remains to be seen. Let's keep a guard on Dr. Grey. I've got a bad feeling."

"I'll see to it."

She grinned, watching him walk away and letting him go a few steps. "And Doug?"

He stopped and looked over his shoulder.

"Thanks."

"My pleasure."

Corky watched Malory enter Medical and stop to speak quietly with the young, machine-gun-toting Coy, who would be serving as both nurse and guard for the duration of the evening. When the conversation was over, she shot her a wink and went to share a few words with the convalescing Dr. Ballenger. Her rounds apparently completed, she favored her with a bright smile.

"Care to join me for dinner, Dr. Rivers?"

"Sure. Let me meet you there in about ten minutes?"

"Okay. See ya in a few."

Corky tried not to watch the sway of the commander's hips as she walked away. She was only partially successful and mentally chastised herself for the failure. Earlier, she had come to the inescapable conclusion that she was in love with Lieutenant Commander Malory Lovecraft. The idea was so shocking only because of her reluctance to admit it, and the full weight of that knowledge had landed on her without warning when she had watched her openly frightened lover prepare to enter the lab alone. Watching Malory struggle with her fear had scared her as well, and when the sergeant major had intervened, it was all she could do to keep from hugging the man.

With a sigh, she rose and looked in on her patients one last time before relaying last minute instructions to Coy.

When she entered the mess, she was disappointed to see Malory sitting across from McNeely and engaged in conversation. She scanned the room for alternative company and came up empty, as the only other people present were DeSoto and Butler. The two petty officers were the best of friends and had joined the Coast Guard together. How they ended up on the same station was something of a mystery.

Scowling as she realized that she would have to eat alone, she got a tray and made for a vacant table but paused uncertainly when Malory waved her over. She shot a cautious look at her lover and received a nod and another wave, so she padded over, choosing a seat across from her and next to McNeely.

"Hi, guys."

"Good evening, Doctor," McNeely said.

"Dr. Rivers," Malory said. "How is Dr. Grey?"

Their demeanor instantly brought up her guard, and she eyed the smiling commander suspiciously. "No change, but stable. I can't find a reason for his symptoms. I have several tests I'd like to run tomorrow. Hopefully they'll be a little more conclusive."

"I see. No sign of an intruder in his system?"

"None that I can find at the moment."

Malory digested this as she slowly assumed an innocent expression. "Mr. McNeely asked me a question earlier and was quite disappointed when I wouldn't answer it. Perhaps you'd have better luck with Dr. Rivers, Sergeant Major."

McNeely abruptly stopped chewing.

"What question is that?" Corky asked cautiously, not liking in the slightest the look on Malory's face.

McNeely swallowed his food in one large gulp. "Nothing of any real importance, Doctor."

"Would it be easier if I presented it to Dr. Rivers for you, Sergeant Major?" Malory asked helpfully.

He pursed his lips. If the commander presented the question, it would only succeed in embarrassing him and the doctor. In his estimation, it was only fair to include the devious woman in her own trap.

"No, I can handle it," he replied. "I asked the commander earlier if she would inform me as to what exactly she was doing to you the other night that resulted in the screams that woke the entire facility."

Corky gasped in surprise, and McNeely ignored his own blush as he observed the crimson beginning to cover the commander's face.

"You crafty bastard," Malory chuckled, amused at being outmaneuvered. "Oww!" she yelped as her shin was kicked from across the table.

"I can't believe you!" Corky growled

"I didn't tell him anything."

McNeely's blush faded, and he went back to the business of eating his meal, casually observing the entertainment unfolding around him.

Corky fumed, her face now an angry shade of red. "Do you want us both to lose our jobs?"

"That's not something we have to worry about as far as the sergeant major is concerned," Malory explained as she reached down to rub her wounded leg.

"You could have at least given me a little warning."

"Where would the fun be in that?"

Corky huffed and crossed her arms over chest, glaring dangerously at her moronic girlfriend.

"So, to answer your question, Sergeant Major," she purred, "I was screaming because our clueless leader could lick the stripes off an asphalt highway."

McNeely had to bring a hand up to cup his mouth to prevent spitting his food across the table, and he struggled to get himself situated. Risking a quick glance a the commander, he noted that she had her head stooped and a hand covering her eyes, the hand a severe white in contrast to the almost-purple forehead.

Corky smiled and went about finishing her dinner, occasionally casting triumphant little looks at the hiding commander.

"On that note," Malory mumbled, "I'm obviously 0 for 2 this evening and will try to finish my dinner with a modicum of dignity."

"Doctor, is there a series of exercises you could prescribe that might strengthen my skill in that area?" McNeely asked, relishing Malory's sigh of defeat and Corky's fresh blush.

"Well, that could have gone better for me," Malory said as she flung herself onto her cot.

Corky shut the door to Malory's quarters and chuckled. "Ya know, I like that man. He had you twisting and churning."

"Yeah, he kicked my ass. I'll have to think up a suitable punishment."

"Don't be a poor sport," Corky chided. "You started it."

"Yeah, yeah."

"How long has he known?"

Malory rolled over onto her back. "Found out today."

"Is he the only one?"

"Yeah, unless your pal Clovis knows."

"He probably does. He knows about my preference, but he hasn't said anything,"

Corky replied. "How did McNeely find out?"

"You called me by name earlier," she said, sitting up to unlace her boots. "That, and I sent him in here to get the extra chair, and he found some of your scrubs."

"Oh," Corky said. "You scared me today."

"I was scared myself," she said, wiggling out of her pants. "This shit freaks me out."

"Do you think whatever was in that thing got inside Grey?"

Malory pulled her sweatshirt over her head and tossed it to the floor. "I have no idea, but there wasn't a trace of anything left in the lab. Maybe it emitted some sort of gas. I just don't know."

Corky came forward to kneel in front of her lover, embracing her so she could help her out of her bra. "Is that why you have Coy standing guard in Medical with a rifle?" she asked as she tossed the garment to the ground behind her.

"Yeah," Malory said distantly as Corky's eyes roamed over her chest. "Since you can't find anything wrong with him, I thought it prudent."

Corky leaned in to a pull a nipple into her mouth. "Do you love me, Malory?"

"You know I do."

Corky withdrew and flicked at the nipple with her tongue until it hardened. "Then say it."

"I love you, Corky."

"Are you wet?" she asked as she teased back and forth between breasts.

"Yes."

"Do you want me?"

"Always."

With a delicate bite on an erect nipple, Corky rose and began to undress. "Why were you with your first for only one night?"

"Because I was just curious," Malory answered absentmindedly, her eyes riveted on the figure in front of her.

"Not curious enough to see her again?"

"It didn't work out, and I'm glad it didn't."

"Why?"

"Uhm…" she stuttered as her panties fell to the ground. "Because I wanted to wait until I felt what I feel with you."

"Was that the only reason?"

"Turn around."

"Why?"

"Because I wanna see your ass."

Corky smiled and turned around to remove her T-shirt. "You didn't answer my question."

"Uh…yeah," she answered distractedly. "She didn't want to see me again anyway."

"Really? Why?"

"There was…oh, boy." She broke off abruptly as Corky bent over deeply at the waist, letting her bra slide off her arms to the floor.

Corky set her feet farther apart and wiggled her rear provocatively. "You were saying?"

"Uh…I don't know. What was I saying?"

"Do you like?"

Malory could only nod stupidly.

Corky stood and turned around. "Why didn't she want to see you again?"

"Don't tease."

"Tell me, and I'm yours."

Her reply was immediate. "Because when I took her home that night, I ran over her dog when I pulled into the driveway."

A hand rose to hide a smile. "You're kidding me, right?"

"No," Malory said, moistening her lips with the tip of her tongue.

Corky couldn't contain her mirth and slowly went from chuckles to an all-out belly laugh. She carried on long enough that it completely spoiled the mood as far as Malory was concerned.

"It wasn't funny!"

"She had to know it was an accident," Corky chortled.

Malory gave up and flopped onto her back to glare off into space. "She loved that fuckin' dog. She dressed it up in a stupid knitted hat and carried a ridiculous picture of the mutt in her purse."

Corky's eyes twinkled with amusement. "It's not like you did it on purpose."

Malory rolled her eyes and sighed. "After I hit the brakes, she wouldn't move and made me get out to look. It was dark, and the driveway was on an incline, so when I got to the front of the car, I slipped and fell on my ass in a puddle of blood. I freaked out and was hopping all over the place like a big sissy. Anyway, I tried to fling off the little pieces of doggie parts that were on my hands and ended up hurling the pooch's bloody little hat onto the windshield, where it landed with a gross little splat right in front of her face."

Corky brought both hands to her mouth to muffle her delighted squeal.

Malory pretended to ignore her. "Understandably, she never called me again."

"You made that up!" Corky accused.

"Who in their right mind would make up a story like that and ruin a perfectly good turn-on?"

Corky spent a moment working the giggles out of her system before climbing onto the cot to cover her lover's body with her own. Legs immediately wrapped themselves around her waist to trap her, and she tenderly placed a kiss on Malory's lips. "I love you, Malory."

A small gasp was her reward. "Really?"

"Really," Corky confirmed with a whisper, placing gentle kisses on the throat below.

"Say it again."

Corky brought her head up in surprise, and Malory quickly raised an embarrassed hand to wipe away the tear that had escaped. "I thought you knew."

"I did. I just didn't realize how badly I wanted to hear it," she added, moving quickly to catch another tear, but her hand was intercepted, and Corky moved to kiss it away.

"There. All better now."

Malory smiled. "Say it again."

"I love you, Malory."

May 10 – 0218 hours

Petty Officer Coy slouched in his chair by the door and yawned powerfully behind his hand. He scanned the room, his eyes lingering on the still immobile Dr. Grey before moving on to the sleeping Ballenger, noting nothing amiss.

When he joined the Coast Guard, he never pictured himself performing guard duty in an underground complex at the bottom of the world, yet here he was. He ran a hand through short-cropped blond hair and sighed, wondering what had possessed him to volunteer for Antarctica. He had spent six months under the tutelage of Dr. Rivers before being seconded to the Department of Defense and, thus, eventually falling under the command of the newly assigned Commander Lovecraft.

At first, he didn't know what to make of the subtly hostile doctor, although he had to admit that she had certainly loosened up recently. She even flashed a smile in his direction from time to time. He wondered whether it had anything to do with the presence of the easygoing commander—who, rumor had it, was extremely formidable if one were unlucky enough to pull a fuck-up.

A small whisper of noise tickled his ears, and he looked around for its source. Spotting nothing out of the ordinary, he rose to check the status of Dr. Grey.

A few minutes later, he was treading back to his chair, pausing in the middle of his journey to indulge in an another yawn and stretch that brought him to his tiptoes. A raspy gurgle from behind brought him to his heels, and he spun to find himself face to face with Dr. Grey. Fear left him motionless as he met eyes rendered frighteningly insane.

Grey brought both hands up and inserted them into his own mouth, exerting enough force to break his jaw savagely. The corners of his mouth tore like fleshy cellophane, and the sickening crack of bone left Coy mesmerized in terror, trapped inside a motionless body that refused to respond.

Only when a nest of thick, muddy-red worms filled the doctor's mouth, their tubular bodies contorting in a maddening frenzy, did Coy's rifle come up, and he drew a deep breath to scream.

The scream was never voiced. His body was crushed in a macabre embrace, his mouth engulfed by Grey's and filled with traveling worms. The invaders fought through his gag reflex unhindered, forcing themselves forward and tearing through soft tissue like barbed needles. His mouth and throat filled with what he knew was blood, and his agonized cries filtered silently into labored gurgles. He contorted violently as Grey's teeth cut through his cheeks to solidify their union, and he felt his body burning in the wake of the frantically moving intruders. Grey's unholy strength lifted Coy off his feet, and his legs struggled desperately in the air until finally, his activity decreased to a lifeless standstill, and his rifle fell uselessly to the floor at his feet.

0600 hours

Petty Officer Percy strolled carelessly down the hall to relieve Coy. His tour of duty would end with the impending summer, and he had spent many happy hours contemplating how to enjoy his accumulated funds. There were benefits to spending a year underground, and the best one, in his opinion, was the savings plan. Everything was provided for him, and the paychecks added up untouched.

He was so embroiled in his daydream of an irresponsible spending spree that it took him a moment to register the abandoned rifle lying in a congealing puddle of blood right inside the door to Medical. Stopping in his tracks, he leaped backward to place his back against the wall of the hallway and hurriedly pulled the pistol from his holster. He turned his head back and forth to make sure that the hall was clear and reached for his radio, every sense on heightened alert.

His terse report to the rapidly waking sergeant major resulted in the alarm's being activated not five seconds into his explanation.

"Commander Lovecraft and all military personnel, report to the hall outside Medical immediately, with weaponry," McNeely barked over the intercom. *"All other personnel, report to the mess and remain there. This is no drill. Move it, people. I say again…"*

Malory flew out of bed at the sound, dumping a grumpy Corky on the floor.

"What the hell?"

"The alarm," Malory explained, hurriedly slipping into her fatigues and sweatshirt without the benefit of underwear.

Corky sleepily took note of the alarm as McNeely's voice reverberated through the complex.

"Jesus," Malory whispered when he was finished, and she fell to the floor to put on her boots. "Get dressed. I want you to come with me as far as the mess."

"Shouldn't I go to Medical too?" Corky asked, reading the depth of fear etched on Malory's face.

"No! Hurry, now," she added in a softer tone.

Corky frantically hopped up for her clothes, trying unsuccessfully to get into her bra when Malory pulled it out of her hands.

"Just pants, shirt and shoes."

Corky did as she was told, trying to choke down the lump in her throat. She got her boots on and had no sooner stood than her hand was grabbed and she was pulled out of the room.

Malory drew her gun as they entered the hall. When they arrived in front of the mess, she poked her head inside to see people already milling about. "Go on, now," she said, prodding Corky though the door. "Don't let anyone leave."

"Malory—"

"I'll be okay. Please go inside now." She pecked Corky's cheek and turned to run down the hall.

Corky bit her bottom lip, trying not to cry and watching until Malory disappeared around a corner.

As Malory approached Medical, she found the soldiers grouped in the hall on either side of the door.

"Report."

"Coy is missing. His weapon is lying inside, covered in blood," McNeely whispered. "No one responds from inside, and the divider has been drawn, so we can't see the infirmary section."

"Make a hole," she said, waiting for the men to move aside so she could step forward and peek inside.

There was indeed a rifle in the middle of an alarming puddle of drying blood, but more disturbing were the gory footprints tracking from the pool to behind the divider. Even more frightening were the tracks that entered the hall and quickly faded, leaving no trace.

"There are tracks into the hall," she whispered in horror.

"Yeah," McNeely confirmed.

She swallowed. "Alvarez, you're up. Report to the mess, and stand guard."

"Aye, Skipper."

"Staff Sergeant Terrel, Airman Cohen, you're to enter Medical and take positions on either side of the door. Reynolds and Hanson, make sure that they're clear and then mirror their location. Daly and DeSoto, you have their backs. Nod if you don't understand."

No one nodded.

"Do it."

Terrel and Cohen rushed into the room and slammed their backs against the wall, each man dropping to a knee and leveling his rifle forward. "Clear!"

Reynolds and Hanson rushed into the room. "Clear!"

When Daly and DeSoto were in place, she turned to the rest of the men. "Ring, Butler and Percy, watch the hall. Sergeant Major, you're with me."

McNeely nodded and cocked his rifle. "Ready when you are."

"Let's go."

They entered the room slowly, weapons aimed at the curtain. "Chief, Sergeant Hanson, take the corners," she ordered, and they changed positions. "No one fires without orders."

Bracing herself and holding her pistol tightly, she slowly followed the trail of bloody footprints to within a body length of the divider that closed off a large section of the room.

"Sergeant Major, I'll pull it back," she whispered. "You've got the call."

"Understood."

"Say when."

"Ready."

She surged forward and quickly pulled the divider open, folding it in on itself as she crossed the room and dropped to a knee. She shot a look at McNeely, who hadn't moved and was slowly tracking the room with the barrel of his rifle. He held up a steadying hand, signaling that he was preparing to move forward.

Malory nodded and gestured at Terrel and Cohen to move to cover. From her location, she could see only a fraction of the interior and tensely waited for word. It wasn't long in coming.

"Commander, you'll need to see this."

Malory didn't like his tone of voice at all, feeling her backbone begin to fidget. "Everybody clear?"

An affirmative chorus greeted her, and she ventured forward, closing her eyes briefly in preparation as she observed McNeely standing with his rifle in the crook of his arm, his other hand over his mouth.

Reluctantly, she peered around the broad-shouldered sergeant major and instantly turned away with an involuntary gag. "Jesus Christ."

She forced herself not to look at the remains and took a deep breath before reaching for her radio. "Alvarez?"

"Go ahead."

"Status?"

"Everyone safe and accounted for except Grey, Coy and Ballenger."

She sighed in relief. "Stay put, and drop anyone or anything that enters the mess without prior radio contact. Daly and Cohen incoming."

"Understood. Out."

"Daly, Cohen, report to the mess, and assist Tech Sergeant Alvarez. Don't dawdle. We have one dead here and two missing."

"Yes, ma'am," Daly said, and they both ran out of the room, their footsteps pounding down the hall.

She put her radio back on her belt and holstered her weapon, taking a long moment to compose herself before turning to the sight that awaited.

"Is that Dr. Ballenger?"

"Yeah," McNeely confirmed. "They had to break his cast off before they ate him."

"God."

The corpse in front of her had been ravaged almost to the bone. Even the top of his skull had been broken open from the eye sockets to the brain matter inside, his chest cavity reduced to a gaping hole deep enough to expose his spine. His groin and legs were nothing but a few strips of flesh that clung stubbornly to gleaming white bone.

"Percy!" she barked. "Get a body bag. The rest of you, gather around. We got a big fuckin' problem."

Malory averted her eyes as Dr. Ballenger's remains were carried from Medical, trying her best to put aside the horror of current events and formulate a plan of action. She hopped up on one of the exam tables and waited for Percy and Butler to return from their grisly errand.

"All right, people, I'm listening. Let me hear some opinions."

"I think we need to clear the central complex," Reynolds began, "and if a search doesn't uncover Grey and Coy, we should consider initiating computer lockdown."

"Wouldn't that trap us inside?"

"Yes, but if we don't find Grey and Coy inside, it'll trap them outside."

Her brow wrinkled. "Chief, I'm not as familiar with the station as I should be. Walk me through this."

"Okay," he said slowly, gathering his thoughts. "The central complex is basically circular in construction and designed to be self-sustaining in the event of a cave-in, fire or other disaster. The only points of entry or exit are the north and south vacuum doors. Once those doors are sealed by a lockdown command, only those with the correct code can pass through them."

"Won't that cut us off from Operations?"

"Yes, but Operations, although separated from the central complex, is also self-sustaining and seals with its own vacuum door. And in the event of lockdown, all operational functions can be accessed from a secondary workstation."

"Who besides me has those codes?"

"Just the sergeant major."

"Where's the secondary workstation?"

"Mainframe room in the lab."

"Okay. Where do we stand with communications?"

"All external communications are satellite-based, so the dome has to be clear of obstruction, which it currently is not."

"So to talk to the outside world, sooner or later, we're gonna have to send somebody to the silo?"

"Unfortunately, yes."

"How does lockdown affect Mechanical?"

"It functions much the same as Operations and seals with its own door."

"What good does that do us? Mechanical is outside the complex. Even if we seal it, won't someone have to remain behind to maintain the generators?"

The chief shook his head. "No. There's a series of backup generators in place. If there's no one in Mechanical with sabotage on his mind when the lockdown order is given, power to the complex would be uninterrupted."

"For how long?"

"If we conserve, five weeks, maybe six. However, there are emergency generators within the complex proper that could extend that another week."

"And water?"

"We would definitely have to conserve. Our water comes from the ice we take out of Excavation. We have a surplus, but that wouldn't last more than four weeks."

"So let me understand this," she said. "Lockdown would seal the doors to the central complex and to Mechanical and Operations, allowing no one entry or exit without first entering the correct codes."

"Yes."

"We wouldn't lose anything crucial, because operational control would be transferred to a backup workstation and mechanical functions are redundantly controlled."

"Correct."

"Anything else I should know?"

"The only disadvantage is the loss of internal communications."

"Tell me more."

"Lockdown disables the telecom system. We lose the phones and intercom."

"What? That makes no sense. Why?"

"Security protocol in the event of a hostile occupation."

She gaped. "In Antarctica?"

He shrugged.

"Can we bypass it?"

"I can't modify the software. It's encrypted."

She pinched the bridge of her nose and hummed for a moment. "All right, lemme chew on that for a while. In the meantime, I think it might be prudent to assemble some more firepower, so let's break into the arsenal and get Sergeant Terrel equipped with a flame unit. Get ready for a long day, gentlemen, because we're going to search every fucking inch of this place for our missing men. Any questions?"

No one spoke.

"Good. Let's make tracks for the mess, and I'll inform the others of the situation."

Corky sat fearfully next to a concerned Clovis. Over Alvarez's radio, she had heard Malory issue the order to open fire on anyone who entered the mess without announcing himself. She had no idea what could present that much of a danger, and dwelling on it only succeeded in making her more scared than she already was. Since Daly and Cohen had arrived, there had been no further word or any other developments, and she was desperately worried about the commander's welfare.

When the other two soldiers arrived, they conversed quietly in a corner of the room with Alvarez, and she forcefully clamped down on the desire to go ask them what was going on. Not that they would tell her, but the impulse to try to weasel something out of them was hard to deny.

"You okay, Corky?" Clovis asked. "You've been too quiet for a while now."

"Yeah. Just scared."

"I know the feeling. Those guys look pretty damn serious," he said, gesturing at the soldiers.

She glanced at the grim-looking men, holding their rifles at the ready. "Yeah, they do."

"I'm sure it'll be okay."

"I hope so."

He offered her an enormous hand. "Here," he said, and she gratefully placed her hand in his.

"Thanks," she said with a little smile.

"I came by your quarters to get you when the alert sounded," he teased. "No one was home, and the bed hadn't been slept in. Can I make a guess as to where you were?"

"You'd probably get it right."

He chuckled. "She won ya over, did she?"

"Very much so."

"I'm happy for you," he said. "Never fear. I'll keep your secret."

"Thanks, Clovis."

"You worried about her?"

"Yeah. I think that's scaring me more than anything else."

"Don't be. That woman had me believing she was going to kick the shit out of me the other day. No mean feat, considering one of my arms is damn near the size of both of her legs."

Corky chuckled. "She's really not as tough as she lets on."

"No one is, Corky."

She turned a thoughtful look in his direction but was brought up short when Malory's voice came from Alvarez's radio.

"We're coming in, Sergeant."

"Very well," Alvarez replied.

Everyone looked up anxiously as Malory entered the room, followed by a squadron of heavily armed men.

"Two men outside each door, Sergeant Major."

"Aye, Skipper," he said. "Daly and Percy, you're on the east door. DeSoto and Cohen, take the west."

Malory didn't pause to make sure that her orders were carried out. She strode to the front of the room to take a seat on a folding table, placing her rifle between her legs.

"First of all," she started, "get comfortable, because everyone is staying in this room until further notice."

Several questions rang out, but she held up a hand to silence them. "As you may or may not know, the container discovered in Excavation was opened by Dr. Grey, an action that appeared to leave him comatose—that is, until last night, when he apparently attacked Petty Officer Coy, who was standing guard in Medical. It's our guess that Dr. Grey was infected by something from within that container, which he in turn infected Coy with."

"Why do you say that, Commander?" Lenard asked.

"Because Dr. Ballenger is dead. And both Dr. Grey and Petty Officer Coy are missing."

A stunned and horrified silence followed her remark.

"You think they killed Dr. Ballenger?" Clovis braved.

"We know they did. We know this because there were two sets of bloody footprints leading away from and surrounding Dr. Ballenger's corpse."

"Why did they kill him?" Dr. Isaaks asked.

"They didn't just kill him, people. They ate him. We pretty much put a skeleton in a body bag."

"Oh, my God!"

"You can't be serious!"

"They ate him?"

"What?"

Malory again held up a hand. "In case you missed it, there are two people walking around down here with full stomachs who are still unaccounted for. Until they are found and removed, no one leaves this room unless I say so."

She sighed in the silence that followed, noting Corky's shining eyes and realizing that the doctor had lost a patient.

"What are we going to do?" Lenard asked.

"We're going to go looking for our missing colleagues. Until they're found or we can be assured that they are not within the central complex, no one leaves this room without my say-so. Now, I'm in no mood to answer any questions, and we have a long day ahead. I'll only say that I don't ever want to see anything again like I did this morning, and if I have to issue orders to shoot those who disobey my directives from this point forward, I will. There are a lot of lives at stake here, and I won't have one or two fools like Grey endangering the entire group. I hope I've made myself clear."

Her eyes roamed carefully over the assembled crowd and Malory conferred quietly with the soldiers for a moment before addressing everyone again.

"Everyone gather around!" she called out.

She allowed herself a smile when Corky sat down next to her and placed a possessive hand on her leg.

"Lieutenant Ring," she started, "I know I should have asked earlier, but what are the chances of flying out of here if the weather breaks?"

"A fraction above zero. We're too far away from any outpost, foreign or domestic, to hope for a suitable break in weather. There won't be one long enough until summer. The current temperatures would freeze the aircraft's hydraulic systems."

"I guess I knew that," she sighed. "If we haven't located Grey or Coy after we've cleared the main complex, I'll go ahead and lock the place down. That will at least allow us to return to quarters."

"We'll have to secure Operations and Mechanical first, Commander," McNeely said.

"We will."

"Don't you think this may be a little drastic?" Watkins asked. "It's just two guys."

Malory favored him with a blank look. "Dr. Watkins, one of these men is apparently infected with something extraterrestrial and, therefore, outside our experience. I might also point out that Grey was able to overpower a soldier armed with an automatic rifle without raising any alarm. And I should tell you that there isn't a man in this room strong enough to pull the top of Ballenger's head off from the eye sockets with his bare hands."

Corky gasped.

"Jesus," Clovis whispered.

"What did you do with his body?" Corky asked.

"It's in cold storage."

"Dr. Lenard, there is a theory we would like to run by you," McNeely said.

"Okay," Lenard said.

"As you know, we have a dead alien body and two empty containers in storage," McNeely said. "And it was suggested that the aliens were cannibals. We're thinking that our current situation might have been experienced on board that spacecraft."

"Interesting," Lenard replied. "And not very far-fetched. One empty container and a half-eaten space alien. Now we have another open container and uh…well."

"Exactly," McNeely agreed.

"Unfortunately, it appears that our outer-space buddies resolved their situation by crashing almost a mile deep into our planet," Malory pointed out. "Mass suicide isn't an option I'll consider, so as soon as it's feasible, I want that alien body dissected into particles in search of anything that might look like it doesn't belong there."

Malory looked up at the sound of a door opening to see Cohen enter and wave to get her attention. "Commander?"

"Yes?"

"Request permission to secure the head, ma'am," he declared with a pained expression.

She almost smiled. "Do you consider your request to be of an urgent nature, Airman?"

"Very urgent."

"Carry on, then," she said, letting her smile show. "Take someone with you; no one goes anywhere alone."

He disappeared instantly, and she turned her attention back to the group. "Anyone else need to answer the call of nature? Now is the time."

"Uhm…" Corky said uncomfortably. "I don't think I could go with a guy standing watch over me."

A few men chuckled, and Corky blushed.

"I guess I could go with you," Malory said. "It depends on whether you gotta do number one or number two, though."

Corky's blush and the beginnings of laughter vanished in a wave of automatic gunfire that echoed loudly through the room.

"Alvarez and Butler, stand fast! The rest with me now! Move!" she yelled, grabbing her rifle.

Malory stormed out of the mess, the comforting sound of pounding footsteps echoing behind her. She spotted DeSoto a short distance down the hall, hastily inserting a fresh magazine into his rifle. Several yards beyond him stood a bullet-riddled Dr. Grey, clutching a booted and fatigued leg in one of his hands. He was dragging the severed member behind him as he advanced on DeSoto, creating a crimson smear on the floor.

She dropped to one knee and leveled her rifle. "DeSoto! Behind me now!" she yelled, and he ran back several yards to join the firing line.

Grey came forward undaunted, an insane gleam shining in otherwise lifeless eyes. Dried blood covered his face and chest; his jaw drooped at a grotesque angle.

"Short burst," Malory ordered. "Go for the head on my command."

She waited until Dr. Grey was only three body lengths away. "Fire!"

The brief roar of several rifles firing in unison filled the hall, and Grey's head exploded from the neck up, coating the walls around him bright red. Amazingly, he was still on his feet, the headless body still moving forward uncertainly.

"Fuck me," Reynolds whispered.

Several clumps of a fleshy substance fell to the floor from the stump of his neck, and Malory had to fight back a dry heave to speak. "Half on right knee, half on left. I'm on right."

"Right."

"Right."

"Right."

"Left."

"Left."

"Left."

"Fire!"

Automatic gunfire thundered again in the hall, and Grey fell forward, one leg blown off at the knee and the other attached only by flimsy strands of tissue. When his torso struck the ground, a glut of moist, writhing flesh resembling handfuls of ground beef spewed from the exposed orifice of his neck.

"Worms," McNeely said.

"Back up!" Malory almost screamed, transfixed in horror by the contorting piles. "Flamethrower, now!"

Terrel moved forward through the retreating crowd and let loose several bursts, dousing the entire hallway with bright orange flame.

"Get the extinguishers," Malory ordered, watching the fire consume both the walls and what was left of Grey's body.

Hanson and Daly rushed forward to douse the flames, and she reached out to stop them. "Let it burn a little longer."

She waited until she began to sweat through her shirt from the heat. "Go," she said finally, and they rushed forward to put out the fire.

A few minutes later, the hall was filled with the stench of burning flesh, and the only thing left of Grey was a blackened, smoldering lump.

"DeSoto," she said in the silence that followed. "What happened?"

"Cohen went to check the head in Garcia's quarters. He was turning to leave when Grey jumped out of the shower stall and started tearing him to pieces."

"Christ," McNeely said, shaking his head.

Malory suddenly stiffened. "Wait. Who's missing?"

"Percy!" Daly exclaimed in dawning horror. "God, he was right beside me, firing at Grey."

Reynolds snatched the radio from his belt. "Percy?"

Malory grabbed hers as well. "Alvarez?"

"Go ahead."

"Is Percy in there with you?"

"Negative."

"Percy, respond!" Reynolds yelled into his radio.

"Fuck!" Malory yelled in frustration, throwing her radio at the wall, where it shattered and fell to the floor.

"Commander," Reynolds said.

"What?" she snapped, and he gestured behind her with a nod of his head.

"Gimme a fuckin' break," McNeely whispered.

Malory turned to see Cohen pulling himself into the hall, using only the stump of his left arm, his other appendages in tatters or missing altogether. Blood flowed freely from his wounds, complicating his efforts to travel and creating a grisly path on the floor. Even as he tried to slink away, he was ravenously feeding on what she recognized as one of his own severed hands. She wanted to cry; the young airman had been a cheerful soul, someone who always had a smile lurking under the surface. It was a cruel blow to the psyche.

She closed her eyes. The thing looked liked Cohen, but it wasn't. She couldn't let it be. It was an aberration that only looked like the person she once knew and felt responsible for. Now he was only a puppet for a cancerous villain that had not only killed the young man, but also desecrated his remains.

She let her expression crystallize. "Burn it, Sergeant Terrel."

"Ma'am?"

"Burn it. Then burn whatever it left behind in Garcia's quarters."

"Roger that," Terrel said, determinedly advancing down the hallway.

"DeSoto, Hanson, back him up," she ordered, and they followed in Terrel's wake.

"I want all of the remains collected and thrown into the incinerator, including Ballenger's and that alien we found. In addition to Terrel, I want Hanson equipped with a flame unit, and I want a new radio and a shotgun. A big goddamn shotgun."

Corky spent the next three hours on the border of hysterics. She had chewed her fingernails down to nubs, and the urgent need of her bladder only added to her agitation. After the loud and very close gun battle that had taken place earlier, there had been no word other than a hushed radio conversation that Alvarez had engaged in. Overhearing a snippet of Malory's voice had calmed her considerably, but as the time dragged on, her fears had reclaimed their hold on her.

She was more than a little surprised by how her initially reluctant attraction for the commander had transformed into such an engulfing need. The very thought of losing Malory frightened her more than she thought possible, and any reservations she had possessed only a few days before had effectively evaporated.

The rattle of Alvarez's radio startled her, and about a minute later, the soldiers again entered the mess. Her eyes tracked to the one sporting a head of dark red hair, and she breathed a sigh of relief. Malory's shirt was soaked through in several places, and even from a distance, Corky could tell that she was exhausted. She smiled in response when blue eyes searched for her anxiously and then filled with relief.

Malory strode to the center of the room and sat in her previous spot. She sighed and took a deep breath. "At this time, Dr. Grey is dead, as is Airman Cohen. Petty Officers Percy and Coy are now missing."

She let them mumble among themselves for a moment. "We believe that Dr. Grey was originally infected by an alien intruder and then passed this intruder on to Coy. We suspect Percy to either be infected as well or dead."

"What kind of intruder is it, Commander?" Clovis asked.

"Worms."

"Excuse me?"

"Worms," she repeated loudly. "Dr. Grey was infested with them. Now, we have no idea what they do to you if you become infected, but apparently, you develop superhuman strength and an appetite for your own kind. Grey tore Cohen to pieces with his bare hands and took unimaginable damage to his body before we were able to put him down. It also appears that whatever happens to you once you become infected, diminished intelligence is not a side effect."

"Wait a minute," Watkins said, rubbing his forehead nervously. "Grey underwent a medical examination, didn't he?"

"Yes," Corky replied.

"Then why didn't we know about these worms sooner?"

Corky stiffened slightly at his accusatory tone. "I didn't exactly perform an autopsy on the man, because he was still breathing. Blood and tissue samples didn't reveal anything abnormal, and neither did X-ray. His blood pressure was below normal, as was his body temperature, but his condition was stable, and I wanted to monitor him overnight before attempting anything more intrusive."

"You must have missed something, Doctor," Watkins implied critically. "If you'd taken the time—"

"That's enough!" Malory interrupted. "If anyone is to blame for anything, it's the late Dr. Grey. He intentionally and carelessly exposed himself to the contents of the cube, thereby endangering us all."

An uncomfortable silence followed. Eventually, Dr. Lenard dared to break it.

"So what's our situation, Commander?"

"As of this moment, I've initiated a computer lockdown of the entire station. The north and south doors have been sealed and reinforced with a weld. I have guards posted at each one. After a search of the central complex failed to turn up our missing men, we can only assume that they are outside the facility. This means that we can't get out, and they can't get in. This also means we don't have to camp in here and can return to our quarters. So pick a partner, because you're bunking up two to a room tonight and for the foreseeable future. No one is be alone from this point forward."

"And our plan of action, Commander?" Clovis asked.

"Search and destroy. We can't evacuate, and we have almost four months before leaving becomes a possibility. We're stuck in here, and until the threat is eliminated, none of us is safe."

"And communications?"

"Communications are down, and I'm not sending anyone out to the silo until I know they'll be able to come back. And because the complex is under lockdown, the doors to Operations and Mechanical have been sealed, as have all other doors to areas deemed of importance. So you'd better hope that I survive this ordeal, or the sergeant major does, or none of you is going to get out of here."

"I'm afraid I'm a little confused as to what lockdown accomplishes, Commander," Lenard said.

"As I already stated, Petty Officers Percy and Coy are missing. Nobody wanted to go to sleep tonight wondering whether they were wandering around in here with us. So we verified that they weren't inside the facility proper, Operations or Mechanical, and then we initiated lockdown. With the station sealed up, we can rest easy tonight and resume the search for our missing men tomorrow."

"So we have no idea where they are?" Watkins asked.

"We know that they're not inside the complex with us and that they aren't nearly strong enough to breach the doors," Malory said. "So take it easy."

"Choose a roommate, fellas, and see to your needs. Dinner will be at 2100 hours; attendance is mandatory," McNeely said.

"Everyone is to provide a list to the sergeant major as to who you're bunking with," Malory added. "Dr. Rivers, you're with me."

Corky grabbed her hand as soon as they were out of the room. "Are you okay?"

"Yeah," she answered, bringing Corky's hand to her mouth for a kiss. "How are you doing?"

"Scared."

"You got the easy part."

"Was it really bad?" Corky asked reluctantly, not sure whether she really wanted an answer.

"It was unspeakable."

Corky chewed on the words thoughtfully, taking comfort in the hand that grasped hers. She remained silent until they entered Malory's quarters and then let out an urgent squeak, her body giving her an ultimatum. Letting go of Malory's hand, she ran across the room, frantically unbuttoning her pants, and hastily plopped down on the toilet.

Malory closed the door and chuckled. "Would you listen to that? I'm surprised you're not launching yourself into the air."

Corky moaned in relief and ignored her completely, concentrating on her moment of profoundly liberated bliss.

Malory grinned and propped her shotgun against the wall, unslinging the rifle from her back to keep it company. It was followed by a belt of shells and a bandolier of magazines. When she was done unburdening herself, she sat on the cot and began to unlace her boots, her nose wrinkling.

"God, I stink."

Corky emerged from her euphoria. "Are we gonna be okay, Malory?"

"I think so."

"You need to know so. I can't lose you. I won't lose you."

Malory looked at her fondly. "Somebody loves me."

Corky rolled her eyes. "Malory, this is serious."

"You don't need to tell me that."

"Then tell me we're going to be okay."

"I can't tell you that, because I don't know. But I can tell you that I'm going to do my best."

"Your best is good enough for me. I never thought I would hear myself say this, but I can't imagine life without you."

"I shall try and bask in those words and pretend they weren't spoken to me while you sat upon the pot."

Corky giggled. "I guess I could've chosen a more romantic location."

"Wanna take a shower with me?"

"Yes."

Malory stripped off her stinky shirt. "Let's ride."

2145 hours

Dinner was uneventful, the mood very quiet and subdued. A corporeal undercurrent of unease permeated the room, the monotony broken only when Lenard and Watkins approached Malory at the end of the meal.

"Commander?" Lenard said.

Malory looked up from her plate and gestured for the men to sit down next to McNeely and Reynolds. "What's up?"

"Uhm…" Watkins started hesitantly. "We'd like to be issued weapons."

Malory stared at them. "At the moment, that's out of the question."

"May I ask why?"

"Because our enemy looks exactly like us and could be any one of us. I won't create a bigger problem than we already have. Besides, if you encounter one of these things, you can empty a weapon into it dozens of times and not even slow it down."

"You apparently killed Grey," Watkins pointed out.

Malory had to clamp down on an angry response. "Yes, we did. With seven people firing automatic rifles at precise targets. Grey didn't have a head or legs below the knees, yet he still kept coming. Staff Sergeant Terrel had to incinerate him with a flamethrower to finish him."

"God," Corky gasped from beside her.

"Yeah. So unless you want to use the gun on yourself, issuing you one at this time would be a useless gesture."

The two men sat silently, considering her words. "All right," Lenard finally said. "I see your point. What's our plan, then?"

She took a deep breath. "Tomorrow morning, everybody spends the day in the mess while a group of us break the weld on the south door and either confirm Excavation clear or eliminate Percy and Coy."

"That's a lot of area to cover," Watkins said.

"Yes, it is. A lot of it is close quarters, and we can't afford to lose anyone else to death or infection."

"Is there any way we can help?" Lenard asked.

"The best way to help would be to do exactly as we ask," she said, not unkindly. "Stay in groups, and don't let anyone stray."

Lenard nodded his consent. "Are we sure the doors can't be breached?"

"We couldn't dent those doors with a grenade," Reynolds said.

"On that note, I'm going to call it a night. Are you ready, Dr. Rivers?"

"Yes," Corky replied, coming to her feet.

McNeely watched them go, waiting prudently until they left the room to speak. "Chief, who volunteered?"

"Alvarez."

"Tell him to keep it quiet," McNeely advised. "She'll hand him his ass if she catches him watching over her."

Reynolds chuckled. "He knows."

Corky dumped her bag of clothes on the floor and flopped into Malory's chair. "Do you think anyone realized I was wearing one of your shirts?"

"Nah," Malory said as she seated herself on the end of her bunk and yawned.

"I'm glad we went to get some of my things. I don't think I've ever gone a full day in my life without wearing underwear."

"Actually," Malory said thoughtfully, "I kinda like the way my pants ride up on me."

Corky giggled.

Malory chuckled and yawned again. "God, I'm tired."

She blushed. "Sorry."

"Gee, and I thought I was a horny toad," Malory teased.

"Shut up."

Malory stood and closed the distance between them, reaching out a hand to cup the doctor's cheek. "Don't ever be sorry," she said, leaning forward for a kiss.

"Don't you leave me."

"Never," she said, taking her hand and pulling her to her feet. "Now come to bed. It's gonna be a long day tomorrow."

Malory entered the mess the next morning and immediately signaled for the sergeant major as Corky sauntered away to grab a tray for breakfast.

"Commander," McNeely said, gesturing for her to step aside with him.

She followed him to an isolated corner, bracing for news that she knew she didn't want to hear.

"There are six people missing, and they don't respond to radio calls."

"What the fuck? Why wasn't I informed immediately?"

"I only found out a few minutes ago, and I didn't want to start a panic."

She reined in a fit of temper. "Who?"

"Everyone quartered in the north barracks. Jones, Garcia, Gregory, Garret, Blair and Laroux."

"So everyone assigned to kitchen and Maintenance?"

"Apparently so," he replied. "The north barracks is where we put the civilian employees."

"Jesus Christ. Who else knows?"

"People are beginning to suspect, but for now just me, you and Alvarez."

"This is gettin' fuckin' scary, Sergeant Major."

"I couldn't agree more."

She suppressed a shiver and took a deep breath. "So we lost six last night, and we have Percy and Coy still unaccounted for?"

"Correct."

"Who's on the doors?"

"Reynolds and Ring."

"Get them back here now," she ordered. Then she yelled, "Get situated in the middle of the room! We've got trouble!"

McNeely barked into his radio to order the men back.

"What's going on, Commander?" Clovis asked.

"Gather in the middle of the room, and stay away from the doors."

"Reynolds and Ring coming in!" McNeely yelled in warning, and a second later, they burst into the room.

"Pull some of the appliances out of the kitchen to block the east door. Move it, people!" she barked. "DeSoto, Hanson, you're outside the west door. Go!"

The men scrambled into a flurry of activity, most of them running into the kitchen.

"Once the door is blockaded, everyone move to that side of the room."

"Commander," Lenard said, "everyone isn't here yet."

"Anyone not present is now part of the problem," she stated, stepping to the side as some of the men struggled by with an enormous stainless-steel freezer.

"What?" Watkins practically screeched. "Oh, my God! They got inside? Those things are in here with us?"

"Yes. Now shut your mouth, get your shit together and do as you're told!"

He withered under her glare and subsided, wringing his hands anxiously as he crossed the room to join his colleagues.

When the men had the east door effectively blockaded, she chambered a round in her shotgun. "Those with flame units, hang back. These things have the same weaknesses we do. If they can't see or travel, we've got them licked, so concentrate your fire on the head and legs. Understood?"

No one spoke up. "Very well, soldiers on me."

They gathered around her quickly. "Chief, were the doors breached?"

"No. There wasn't a sound all night."

"Did we miss something? How the hell did they get in?"

She sighed. "We're going to have to clear it again and figure it out, people. If they walked through the door right now, I doubt we could drop eight of the things."

"Commander," McNeely said, "I suggest we recruit some more guns."

She released a long breath. "Any objections?"

"I don't think we have a choice," Lieutenant Ring said.

"Very well," she said, turning to face the huddled civilians. "Who knows how to handle a weapon? We have a situation, and it might come down to firepower."

"I can," Clovis said, and several others added their voice to his.

She nodded and turned back to McNeely. "What do we have for them?"

"Nothing unless I can get to the armory."

"We need to do that first, then. All right, we need to—"

"Incoming!" DeSoto warned from the hallway.

"Chief, you're inside with Butler!" she yelled as she dashed for the hall.

She burst through the doors to see DeSoto already on one knee and aiming down the corridor at three figures almost thirty yards away who were approaching rapidly.

"Form a line!" she ordered and dropped down next to DeSoto. "Start on the right, and stay on target until it drops!"

The men crowded into the small hallway, kneeling and standing shoulder to shoulder. "Fire at will," she said, and the deafening roar of gunfire surrounded them.

Blair almost disintegrated under the firepower directed at him, and he fell stiffly, his bodily remains still quivering in the effort to continue forward.

Magazines fell to the floor and weapons were hastily reloaded as the distance between them and their enemies began to diminish rapidly. Malory dropped her empty shotgun and reached around to unsling her rifle, hurriedly taking aim and firing short, three-shot bursts. Even with half of his head torn away, Garcia moved forward resolutely, his body flying away unnoticed in bloody chunks.

Finally, he dropped, leaving only Gregory, who was almost completely untouched and at an alarmingly close range.

Malory inserted a fresh magazine and stood. "Fall back!" she yelled, taking careful aim at the depressingly young body that had once belonged to the quiet and unassuming Gregory.

The men retreated into the mess, and Malory suddenly found herself alone with the rapidly advancing creature. Her finger moved to press the trigger but paused when Gregory stopped and stood unmoving in the middle of the hall. He lifted his hands to his mouth and jerked down savagely, completely unhinging his jaw with a gruesome splintering of bone.

Malory didn't hesitate; she emptied her rifle into the man's face, neck and chest. The assault of bullets only succeeded in knocking Gregory back a stutter-step, and he lunged forward with his arms outstretched.

She dropped her rifle and turned to run into the mess, a scream dying in her throat. Her body was barely across the threshold when Reynolds threw his weight into the door, narrowly missing her as the door met a fleshy, unyielding resistance, and she was seized by an impossibly strong grip on her hair.

McNeely lunged forward to add his strength to the effort. "Get on the fuckin' door!"

Malory's forward momentum was stopped by the power of the grip, and she was ripped backward, colliding with the half-open door painfully.

Alvarez leaped forward with a lightning-fast draw of his knife and brought it down, cutting off a large chunk of her ponytail to free her. Malory staggered forward and turned to put her strength against the door.

Seeing the dilemma, Clovis let go of a frantically struggling Corky and ran forward with a roar. Using all of his considerable strength, he collided into both the startled soldiers and the door.

The force of his arrival slammed the door closed with a sickening crack as one of Gregory's arms was crushed and almost severed. Blood filled the doorframe like glue, and Gregory's fingers twitched madly as the crushed limb dangled precariously from the tissue still exerting a hold on the appendage.

"It won't hold!" Reynolds said.

"Back up!" Malory ordered. "Form another firing line!"

The words were no sooner out of her mouth than the door crashed open with stunning force, scattering the soldiers and Clovis in all directions. The edge of the door caught Malory on the side of her face and knocked her back several feet to land painfully on her back. She groggily rolled over and brought herself to her knees, drawing her pistol.

"Malory!" Corky screamed.

The sound barely registered as she was yanked into the air by the scruff of her neck, catching sight of an abhorrently unnatural mouth filled with grotesquely gyrating worms descending upon her. She screamed and desperately thrust the barrel of her pistol into Gregory's surviving eye. The bullet splattered brain matter on the wall behind him, and the grip holding her aloft was suddenly released. She fell to the floor and collapsed to her knees, dimly aware of McNeely running forward to grab her by the shoulders.

He started to pull her away, but Gregory's wildly flailing arm caught him in the chest and propelled him into the air, dropping him several feet away with a grunt of pain. Malory was struggling to get to her feet when the swing that had dispatched McNeely returned to catch her in the side. The blow lifted her off her feet and sent her careening into a table halfway across the room, where she lay motionless.

Corky screamed again and wrenched free of the men holding her, racing over to her fallen lover.

Alvarez rushed into the hall to retrieve Malory's discarded shotgun and walked back into the room, loading it with shells. He approached the blind and still-thrashing Gregory from behind, coming within arm's reach and shouldering the weapon. The blast removed what was left of Gregory's head, and he followed it up with two more shots to the back of his knees, dropping the twitching body to the floor.

"Burn it, Hanson!" he ordered. "Terrel, get the ones in the hall. Everyone still standing, find something to block the door with when he gets back. Move!"

Corky frantically rolled Malory over and checked for a pulse, tears of relief filling her eyes when she found it strong and steady. She was in the process of searching out any obvious injuries when blue eyes fluttered open.

"Is...is everybody okay?" Malory croaked.

The threatening tears spilled over and ran down her cheeks. "I think so."

"Hey," Malory whispered. "I'm all right."

"You'd better be."

"I just needed a little nap," Malory said. "Now help me up. We've got things to do."

"Okay," Corky said, wiping her eyes.

Malory got to her feet and winced, knowing that she had broken or at the very least bruised some ribs. She shook it off and smiled for Corky's benefit, squeezing the hand in hers tightly before turning to assess the situation.

The men were working busily to block the door. She turned to look at the broken table that had borne the brunt of her impact and spotted her gun on the floor several feet away. Not caring whether anyone might be watching, she released Corky's hand and leaned over to peck her on the cheek.

"We're gonna be okay."

Twenty minutes later, Malory gingerly sipped a cup of coffee and surveyed the prison they had created for themselves. She had pointedly ignored everyone since obtaining her java, and the men had finished shoring up the doors to their satisfaction. She personally thought the task was a waste of time. If the creatures wanted in, they were going to get in, and a confrontation within the small confines of the mess hall was a prelude to disaster.

She shot a glance over her shoulder at Corky, who was going about the task of getting ready what food she could. No one had much of an appetite after witnessing Gregory's bloody demise firsthand, yet she realized that the doctor was coping with things in her own way. A smile came to her face as Corky stuck an experimental finger into her concoction and brought it to her mouth, nodding slightly in satisfaction. Suddenly, the situation became intensely personal, and she was overcome with grim determination. She recognized it for what it was: resolve.

It was do-or-die time.

"Everyone gather around," she commanded, waiting patiently for them to congregate and taking Corky's hand when she came out of the kitchen. "We can't stay here. You all saw what just one of those things did. We're sitting ducks, and I'm not going to sit here and play with myself until one of those things decides to make a meal out of me. We have to make some choices."

"What choices do we have, Commander?" Lenard asked.

"There's only one. We flush them out and destroy them. I won't order anyone to come with me, but that's exactly what I'm going to do."

"Where do we start, Skipper?" Alvarez said. "I'm with you, and I believe I speak for everyone in uniform."

"Hear, hear," McNeely chimed in.

"I'm with you," Clovis said.

Every head in the room began to nod.

"It looks like we all are," Lenard observed.

"Okay," she said. "What do we have in the armory, Sergeant Major?"

"Standard compliment of M4's and 1911's. About six Benelli M1's and a thousand rounds for each weapon, minus what we've already used."

"Nothing heavier?"

"Afraid not. This is a scientific outpost. We have a dozen flame units because they're excellent for creating tunnels in the ice. Other than that, we have some small explosives. That's it."

She hummed. "Lemme hear some opinions."

"I think we need to find out how the hell they got in here," Reynolds said. "As strong as they are, they're not strong enough to break the seals on the fire doors. There has to be something we missed."

"I suggest that we reestablish the perimeter once we determine how they got in," Alvarez said. "Then I recommend we travel as a group, rifles up front, shotguns in reserve for close work and flame units to finish. Fire teams in front and behind."

"I have no objections to any of that, Skipper," McNeely said. "But if we can manage to reestablish a perimeter, we still have to count on them getting in sooner or later."

"I agree," Ring added.

"Let's run it down," she said. "How many hostiles do we figure we're dealing with at this time?"

"Percy and Coy still unaccounted-for, Commander," McNeely said. "Garcia, Gregory and Blair are dead. Jones, Garret and Laroux still missing."

"So five probabilities."

"Yeah, unless some of them were dinner."

A chill ran up Malory's spine. "Jesus," she murmured, shaking her head. "Let's make the armory our first stop so we can get everybody packin'. Then we inspect the quarters of those dead or missing from last night. I'd be willing to bet at least one of those rooms can tell us how they got in. Once that's done, I intend to hunt them down. Anyone disagree?"

She looked around. "Good, because it wasn't up for debate. Let's get it together. I don't want to be caught in here. Stock up on the C-rations, gear up and clear one of the doors."

Corky squeezed her hand. "I'm coming too, right?"

"You're not getting out of my sight."

0738 hours

Malory stood in the hall outside Laroux's quarters with her army of civilians gathered behind her. They had proceeded to the armory without incident and had cleared a path to Laroux's room thus far.

McNeely and Alvarez had point and stood on either side of the door, waiting for her signal. She nodded and waited tensely. McNeely pushed open the door and fell back to a cover position as Alvarez dropped to a knee in the open doorway. After a careful inspection, he entered slowly, only to emerge seconds later.

"Laroux is dinner scraps. No sign of Garret."

Malory sighed, slightly ashamed that it was a sigh of relief. One meal meant one less enemy. "Garret share quarters with Laroux last night?"

"Yeah," McNeely confirmed, peering into the room. "We need the chief up here."

"Very well," Malory agreed. "Alvarez, relieve him, and send him up front."

Alvarez nodded and began making his way through the crowd gathered in the narrow hall toward the rear.

"What's up?" Malory asked, reluctant to look inside the room. Viewing Ballenger's remains had been enough.

"They came in through the floor."

"Say again?"

"There are service tunnels under the complex that contain heating ducts, electrical cables, network cable and so forth," McNeely explained. "They used those tunnels to get in."

Malory closed her eyes as the information sank in. They could be anywhere, including the places they'd already searched. "Jesus. Where are the access points?"

"I only know of the one outside Operations. The chief knows them all," McNeely said. "Here he comes," he added as Reynolds came forward.

Malory turned to him immediately. "Chief, where are the access points to the service tunnels?"

He looked at her in sudden horror and understanding. "Shit!" he exclaimed. "One outside Operations, one in Receiving and another in Mechanical."

"Why didn't I know about this earlier?"

"It didn't occur to me, Commander. The doors are usually sealed, and lockdown didn't detect anything amiss."

"Can they be breached?"

He shook his head. "No. Those doors are vacuum-sealed as well."

"So why didn't they seal when the complex went into lockdown?"

"They should have. I can only assume they were propped open."

"Did we do that?"

"No way."

"Would they seal automatically if the prop was removed after lockdown?"

"No," Reynolds replied. "After the computer verifies lockdown, it won't send any further commands until lockdown is rescinded."

"Why didn't the computer tell us the damn doors were still open down there?"

"It should have. I can only assume that whoever kept them from closing blocked the sensors on the lock mechanism. It's the only way I know to fool it."

She looked at him with an expression of disbelief. "So someone was down there when the command was given and was smart enough to block the sensors?"

"That would be my guess. Or someone knows a trick I don't."

Malory chewed on that in dismay, suddenly feeling terribly exposed. "Where would the safest point in the complex be that is not vulnerable to entry through use of the service tunnels?"

"The lab," Reynolds said. "All heat and power are routed in from overhead. The service tunnel is cut off from entry to that area by another vacuum door. The door itself is permanently sealed. Only you can open it, via computer command."

"Then let's roll," she said. "That's the only safe place in the entire compound right now."

"Commander," McNeely said, "the lab is huge. It'll take some time to clear it."

"Do we have another option at this time?"

McNeely considered. "No."

"Then let's go there directly. Chief, you're on point with the sergeant major."

"Aye, Skipper."

"But first," she added, "Sergeant Hanson, burn what's left of Laroux."

Hanson nodded grimly and stepped forward, illuminating the hall as he sprayed fire into the room.

The going was excruciatingly slow, as they treated every door they encountered as a potential threat and darted two at a time past each one. They made no effort to conduct a search and traveled grimly toward their destination. Finally, as their objective came into sight, their movement became quicker, as they all hoped to get behind the relative safety of the laboratory's pressure door.

Within twenty-five yards of the entrance, Malory had begun to harbor the small hope that they would arrive unscathed. That hope vanished as the floor suddenly rushed up in the middle of their party, immediately dropping two men into the tunnel below. The pit in the floor created two groups, one in front and one behind. The screams started from below instantly.

"Leave them! We can't help!" Malory yelled. "We're running for it! Everyone over as fast you can!"

Those trapped on the other side didn't ask questions and took several steps back, initiating a running start to propel themselves over the four-foot gap in the floor.

"Sergeant Major, form a firing line in front of the lab!" Malory ordered, darting around the running bodies and grabbing Corky's hand.

"Stay with me," she said, pulling her down the hall toward the assembling men.

McNeely barked orders to get everyone positioned, and Malory ran toward him with Corky in tow, turning to look behind her in time to see Dr. Isaaks seized in midair from the tunnel below. His face crashed grotesquely into the edge of the floor with a grisly thud that left behind teeth and blood before he disappeared into the tunnel.

His fate went almost unnoticed as the remainder of the men jumped across the void without hesitation and ran forward. As Alvarez passed her and joined the firing line, she released Corky's hand and dropped to one knee.

"Sergeant Major! Clear the lab! Use as many as you need to get it done as quickly as possible. Everyone else, shore up and hold the corridor."

McNeely turned at once, slapping several men on the back to follow him, and within seconds, a deadly quiet descended upon the hall.

"What do we do, Commander?" Watkins muttered nervously.

"Keep your head, and blast anything that moves until the sergeant major gives us the go-ahead to enter the lab."

The sounds of nervous breathing and restless fidgeting were the only things to be heard for the next twenty minutes. Malory's eyes vigilantly scanned the hall down the barrel of her rifle, and she tried very hard not to linger on the teeth scattered indiscriminately on the floor a dozen yards away. A hand touched her shoulder, and it took every ounce of willpower she had not to scream and rain gunfire down the hallway.

Corky felt the body under her hand tense, and she squeezed Malory reassuringly. "Easy."

"Commander," Clovis whispered, "if we get into the lab, I need to talk to you."

Malory nodded, afraid to glance away from the hall for even a second.

Her concentration was so intense that she periodically had to wipe the sweat away from her eyes with her shirtsleeve, and she felt the beginnings of a powerful headache. Finally, as she began to believe that she had spent a year of her life rooted to the same spot, McNeely called out.

"Inside, people! Move!"

Everyone scrambled to get inside, and Malory breathed a long sigh of relief as the pressure door was sealed behind her.

"Commander," Clovis said.

She turned to him tiredly. "What is it, Dr. Stokes?"

"We need to change the entry code on that door immediately. I don't think we can take the chance that it might not be remembered."

Malory closed her eyes. "Who knows it?"

"Everyone but you, most likely."

"Why is that?"

"Because you're the only one who never comes in here. Everyone else knows it. It's common knowledge."

She sighed. "How do we change it?"

"Has to be done by computer. I'm sure the chief knows."

Reynolds overheard. "He's right, Skipper. I'll get on it right now." He slung his rifle over his shoulder and headed through the door that led to the mainframes.

She followed him. "McNeely, Ring and Alvarez, join us, please."

When they had all gathered around Reynolds, she spoke softly. "Can you change the codes on all the doors, Chief?"

"Yes."

"Do it. Make them all the same. The five of us are going to be the only ones with the new code. If one of us falls, it needs to be changed again. Who else knows how to do this, Chief?"

"Only me."

"Very well."

"How do you suggest we proceed from here, Skipper?" McNeely asked.

Malory took a deep breath and fell into a nearby chair. "Obviously, we need to clear the service tunnels and seal the tunnel doors, or we can't clear the ground we've already covered."

"Only one person at a time can fit down there," Reynolds pointed out. "Unless we travel single-file."

"I kinda figured," Malory said.

McNeely scrutinized her intensely. "No way."

"We don't have a choice, Sergeant Major. We can't survive in here until summer."

"I agree. But you're not going to be the one going down there. We'll draw straws."

"Rank hath its privileges. And unfortunately, it also has its responsibilities."

"No."

"Sergeant Major," she rumbled, "I'll admit your dick is bigger than mine, but this isn't your call."

"I'll do it," Alvarez interjected.

Malory's eyes tracked to the formidable tech sergeant. "Your offer is gratefully acknowledged. But I won't allow it."

"May I speak freely?" he asked.

"Sure."

"Neither you nor the sergeant major can be spared. You two are the only ones capable of bringing the complex out of lockdown. Lieutenant Ring can't do it, because he's our only pilot, and the chief can't be chosen, because his knowledge of the facility is too valuable to lose. And honestly, I'm probably the only one who stands a modest chance of surviving. I spent my previous two tours with Special Operations."

Malory studied him thoughtfully. "All good points. But you're not going to change my mind."

"Commander," he continued, "your survival is paramount. In addition, you are physically the weakest among us and the most injured. I've seen you try to hide it from Dr. Rivers, but you took a hell of shot in the ribs this morning. You'll have to stoop to maneuver in the service tunnels and even crawl in certain areas. Your injury will only hinder your ability to act in the event of a confrontation. Not to mention that you risk further injury to yourself by attempting to negotiate the terrain down there."

"Sergeant Alvarez—"

"Let me also point out that if you die down there, you'll kill Dr. Rivers, who has been afraid to take her eyes off you since this began."

She shot out of her chair. "That's not only extremely manipulative, but also way out of line."

He stood his ground. "It's also true, Commander."

She opened her mouth, taking a deep breath to get some steam behind her tirade. "He's right, Commander," McNeely cut her off. "On all counts."

She slowly closed her mouth and studied the men silently for a moment. "I'll let you know in the morning. At that time, I'll brook no further argument. Regardless of my decision. Right now, I could use some rest."

They nodded silently, and she began to walk away.

"Commander," Reynolds said, "the entry codes have been changed. You'll need to memorize the number."

She stopped and turned to view the monitor, committing the code to memory. "Thank you, Chief. Let's keep everybody close to the foyer this evening. Just in case."

"Understood," McNeely replied as the commander left the room and the men moved to follow her.

Corky was leaning against the wall with her knees drawn up to her chest when Malory reappeared.

"Hey."

"Hey," Corky replied quietly. Malory slid down the wall to take a seat next to her. "You okay?"

"Yeah," Corky said, reaching out a hand to pet the back of her head. "Your beautiful hair."

"Huh?" Malory asked, bringing a hand up to check and finding the stub of a ponytail. "Shit," she said, pulling the useless band out. "How bad does it look?"

Corky grinned and studied the now-shoulder-length hair. "Kinda cute, actually."

"Really?"

Corky ruffled it playfully. "You look great."

Malory eyed her suspiciously.

"Really, it looks good."

Malory shrugged. "I guess I'd rather lose a hunk of hair than my ass."

"Your hair will grow back if you don't like it," Corky said and then whispered, "But I want that ass to remain where it is. It looks good on you."

Malory smiled slyly. "It does?"

"Uh-huh. Perhaps I should take a look at it, to make sure it's okay."

Malory beamed. "As much as I would love to indulge you, I'm afraid our situation isn't as private as I would prefer."

Corky giggled. "I suppose that would ruin your command image."

Malory chuckled. "Pretty much," she agreed and then winced.

The grimace didn't escape notice. "What's wrong?"

"Nothing."

Corky didn't buy it and glared at Malory stubbornly until she reddened. "Take a deep breath for me."

Malory sucked in a gulp of air and blew it out with a triumphant smile. Corky frowned, and her hand darted forward to probe Malory's side. She received a sharp hiss of pain for her effort.

McNeely had been watching them for the past few minutes and turned to his comrades. "Check this out, guys," he said, gesturing in Malory's direction.

Four sets of eyes covertly studied the scene, watching as the little doctor began to scold the commander quietly, eventually rising and pointing authoritatively to an adjoining room. Malory offered what was apparently an unacceptable response, and the doctor bent over to pull her to her feet, again pointing to the next room. Shoulders slumping, Malory sighed and turned to walk through the door Corky had indicated.

McNeely chuckled as the women disappeared. "Looks like someone outranks her."

"I'll be damned," Reynolds said. "Are they together?"

"Yeah."

Ring grunted. "I was wondering what was going on with them."

"Who gives a shit?" Alvarez said. "I'd follow her orders to the gates of hell."

"You might have to do just that," McNeely said.

Corky pointed to a table and turned to lock the door. "Take a seat, and strip off that shirt."

Malory did as she was told, sitting down on a metal work table and pulling her sweatshirt over her head. Corky gasped and rushed forward.

"Jesus, Malory," she said, eyeing the massive purple-yellow bruise covering most of her side. "Lift your arm."

Malory raised an arm in the air and tried not to wince as Corky gently probed her side, failing twice and receiving extra attention in that area.

"Take a deep breath."

"I can't."

Corky sighed. "Oh, baby. Take a big breath, and hold it for me. This might hurt a little."

Malory nodded and did as she was asked, grimacing as Corky pressed a hand against her in examination.

Corky dropped her hand. "They're not broken, but I wouldn't be surprised if they weren't cracked," she said with a measure of relief. "I'll need to wrap them."

Malory blew out a puff of air. "Well, that's good news."

Corky frowned at her. "No, it isn't. You're all beat up, and I don't like it one bit. One side of your face looks like someone clubbed you with a hockey stick; you've got cracked ribs and are minus a foot of hair."

Malory brought a hand up to her hair self-consciously. "I thought you said it looked good."

Corky slapped her on the knee. "I can't believe you," she said, shaking her head. "Out of all that, you're worried most about your hair? Don't be such a girl."

An indulgent smile. "I thought you liked girls."

Corky rolled her eyes. "I do. But I love you, and I don't like to see you hurt."

"I love you, too, Corky."

"I was so scared for you today," she mumbled.

"Corky," she said softly, "I have to go outside in the morning."

Brown eyes looked at her sharply. "No."

"I have to."

"No, you don't! You send someone else."

"I can't send anyone else."

"No!" Corky exclaimed, gearing up for combat. "You *will* send one of the other guys. You're not going," she added, stomping a foot for emphasis.

Malory reached out and grabbed her hands. "Corky, I have to go. I can't and I won't order anyone else to do it. Neither will I allow someone to go in my place."

Corky stared at her fearfully. "Then we'll stay in here until summer."

"We don't have enough food to last us the week, and no matter how secure things are, these things are smart. They'll find a way in here by summer."

"Don't ask me to let you do this," Corky pleaded.

"I won't ask. Because it's going to happen anyway."

Corky's face crumpled, and the tears started. "Please don't go."

Malory pulled her into her arms, embracing her tightly and ignoring the pain in her side. "It'll be okay," she whispered into her hair. "You'll see."

McNeely looked up when the women emerged from the other room, noting the doctor's puffy eyes and the commander's look of sad resolution. He knew what it meant, and he nudged the napping Alvarez, who sat beside him.

"What's up?" he said, coming awake instantly.

"She's going."

Alvarez looked across the room and watched as the commander took a seat against the wall and the doctor snuggled up to her desperately, burying her face in Malory's chest.

"I knew she would."

McNeely sighed. "I did, too. Think she has a chance?"

Alvarez took a moment to consider. "Better than average."

Corky slumbered fitfully, snapping awake several times to make sure that Malory was still in her embrace. Finally, she gave up trying to sleep altogether and lay still in her lover's arms, listening to her heartbeat and soft breathing. She had tried frantically to get Malory to change her mind, but it had been all for naught. She had even considered throwing herself to the floor in the morning and pitching a fit but discarded the idea reluctantly, figuring that Malory would have someone drag her into the other room and lock her inside. The fear for both Malory and their situation was making her irrational.

She sighed and opened her eyes, slowly tracking around the room cluttered with sleeping men, her entire body growing ice-cold as she met a pair of eyes staring at her from the other side of the door. Her scream echoed around the room, jolting everyone awake.

Malory went from a dead sleep to standing at rigid attention in a nanosecond, her hands white on her shotgun, eyes flying around the room. "What the fu—" She trailed off abruptly as she met Coy's hopelessly insane stare.

He was standing as if in a trance on the opposite side of the transparent door, his broken jaw drooping hideously.

"He's alone, Commander," Alvarez said. "Let's let him in. We can finish him quick, and it'll be one less to worry about." There were several nods of approval.

Malory also nodded. "Form a firing line," she ordered, and the men scrambled.

"Love…craft," Coy gurgled gruesomely, his devastated jaw slurring his pronunciation.

Everyone in the room froze in their tracks, all eyes slowly turning in Coy's direction.

Malory squeezed Corky tightly against her, her grip on her lover steady to keep her hands from trembling. She didn't want to believe that she had heard the thing speak.

"Love…craft," Coy repeated.

Feigning a confidence that she didn't feel in the slightest, she let go of Corky and stepped forward. "What can I do for you?" she asked, feeling proud of the question.

His eyes focused on her, his jaw convulsing. "Love…craft."

"That would be me. What is it you want?"

"Only…for you…" He coughed a mouthful of worms onto the glass that separated them. "For you…to…die."

Malory fought back a gag, only barely succeeding. "Why me?" she forced herself to ask.

"Without…you…no hope."

"There's always hope."

"Very…little hope…I assure…you."

Malory's heart skipped a beat, and her face paled.

"Y…yes," Coy rasped, apparently delighting in her obvious fear.

"Malory," Corky said, taking a step forward in concern.

Malory raised a hand to stop her. "What is it that you want?"

"To be…fruitful…and…multiply."

"I can't allow that."

"No…choice."

"We'll fight you."

"You…will… die."

"Will not happen."

Coy's head twitched violently to the side several times. "The…time is…near, " he replied. Then he turned to stagger stiffly into the hall, slowly disappearing from view.

Stunned silence reigned in his departure, and Corky came forward to embrace Malory from behind.

"Commander," McNeely said finally, "you are not leaving this room. If you try, I'll have you subdued."

"It doesn't matter, Doug."

"What doesn't matter?"

"Those…things. They'll get in here sooner or later."

"What are we going to do, Commander?" Clovis asked.

"Survive."

"How do you propose we do that?" Watkins asked.

"By taking the fight to them."

"That's suicide! They could be anywhere!" Watkins said, his eyes darting around anxiously.

"We stay here and wait for them to get in, and starve, or we move forward. Either way, I'll bet my last dollar that we're not as important to them as the rescue team would be."

"Why do you say that?" Lenard asked.

"They don't want to stay here any more than we do. They want to travel."

"Oh, my God," Corky gasped. "If even one of them reached a city—"

"We'd be fucked," McNeely finished for her. "It would be next to impossible to stop them. They'd…uh…reproduce too fast."

"Commander, come take a look at this," Clovis requested from the door.

She walked over to join him, following his eyes to the clump of worms Coy had coughed up. "Unfortunately, I've seen them up close before, Dr. Stokes."

"They're dead," he said. "They're already decomposing."

Malory allowed herself to inspect the grisly pile on the other side of the door as Lenard and Tanaka came forward. Dr. Tanaka dropped to his knees to get a better look and hummed thoughtfully for a long moment.

"It would be my guess that they can't survive for long without a host," he said finally.

"I'm inclined to concur," Lenard added. "Or maybe they need tissue to sustain themselves."

"That might also explain why they eat some and infect others," Tanaka speculated. "Perhaps they can't inhabit a body that is too heavily damaged. Or perhaps they use the tissue they consume as needed fuel to keep the host functional. Then there's the possibility that—"

Malory followed their conversation until visuals began to take form. She quickly slammed the door on them. "Seems now we have something new to think about," she interrupted. "Chief, if one were traveling from here in the service tunnels, which door is closest?"

"Operations."

"And the farthest?"

"Receiving."

"I'll need one volunteer, the chief, the lieutenant and the sergeant major excluded."

"That would be me, Commander," Alvarez said.

"You've already got a job, as do I. We need one more."

"I'll do it, Skipper," Hanson said.

She nodded. "Lose the flame unit, and gear up. You have Operations. Alvarez, you're on Mechanical. I'll take Receiving."

"When are we leaving?" Alvarez asked.

"Five minutes."

She turned to place a kiss on the top of Corky's head, bending to whisper in her ear. "See you in a bit."

Corky smiled bravely. "You'd better come back, Commander."

Malory beamed her best smile and turned to the crowd. "When you get your door sealed, radio in to the sergeant major and then get back here as fast as you can. Chief, give us a flight plan."

Reynolds stepped forward. "I assume you'll be entering the tunnels from the entrance the creatures created with yesterday's ambush?"

"Yes."

"It's a straight shot for about thirty to forty yards before you come upon an intersection. Operations will be to the left. The next intersection will be to the right; it leads to Mechanical. From there, the tunnel curves around to the left, eventually leading to Receiving."

"Alvarez, Hanson, any questions?" Malory asked.

"Got it," Alvarez said.

"No questions," Hanson replied.

"If you succeed and are able to head back, radio your status prior to arrival. You'll have to be able to get back in here with a reasonable degree of safety for the people inside. Understood?"

The men nodded, and she walked over to don her gear.

"Commander," McNeely said. "A quick word in private, please?"

Malory gestured to the next room and followed him.

"Your orders, in the event that you do not return?" he asked as soon as the door closed behind her.

"One way or the other, Doug, I'll seal my door. If the other guys succeed, clear the complex. Then, at the very least, you'll need to clear the area outside the north door so you can either leave the facility at the first opportunity or admit reinforcements in the summer."

"And if things go south?"

"If that happens," Malory said, "I want you to do me a favor."

"Name it."

"First, you cannot allow a rescue to arrive without warning. The dome will have to be cleared. Get it done, even if you have to take everyone out to the silo."

He nodded. "And the rest?"

"The rest is personal," she whispered. "If the situation calls for it, I'd like you to put Corky down so that she doesn't end up as a meal—or, worse yet, one of those things."

He took a deep breath. "Malory, I don't—"

"Please, Doug," she interrupted softly, tears hanging on the precipice. "I can't bear the thought of her suffering like that."

He closed his eyes and nodded.

Malory breathed a sigh of relief and brought a hand up to wipe her eyes. "Don't let her see it coming, okay?"

Another nod, and he extended a hand. "You watch your ass out there."

She took his grip with a smile. "You can count on that."

0610 hours

Malory walked back through the door, McNeely emerging a second after her. "We ready?" she asked and got nods from Alvarez and Hanson. "Let's blow this pop stand."

She let her best cocky smile fly at Corky and shot her a wink, receiving an affectionate smile in response.

"Okay," she said, cocking her shotgun and inserting another round. "Open the door. I'll take point. Alvarez, you've got flank. Don't stop to smell the roses."

"Good luck, all," Clovis sounded off, prompting a round of well-wishing.

Reynolds nodded and came forward to punch the code into the door. "Ready?"

"Do it," Malory ordered, taking off at a run as soon as she had enough room, pounding through the foyer and into the hall.

Within seconds, they approached the missing floor plates from the last attack. Taking a running start, she slid the last few feet on her knees and dropped headlong into the tunnel. It was a longer fall than she anticipated, and she landed on her hands and knees with a grunt. She rolled away quickly so that the men following her had room to enter and found herself face to face with the ravaged corpse of Dr. Isaaks, her hand and shotgun resting in the devastation of his chest cavity. She bit down on the impulse to squeal in disgust and rolled over him with closed eyes as Hanson dropped into the tunnel beside her.

She had to bend over at the waist to keep her head from scraping the ceiling, and she leveled her gun down the hallway. As soon as Alvarez joined them and gave her a thumbs-up, she proceeded as quickly as she could manage, eyes and ears straining to detect anything of import. Their anxious breathing and hurried footsteps in the ice seemed conspicuously loud.

Within minutes, she cautiously approached the first intersection and signaled the men to halt. Taking a deep breath and holding it, she rushed forward and leaped across the gap, coming to her knees and signaling it clear. Hanson nodded and gave a two-fingered salute before making his way down the adjoining tunnel alone. Alvarez motioned her forward, and she turned to continue on, mentally wishing the young sergeant well.

Ten minutes later, she did the same for Alvarez as the man disappeared toward his destination, finding herself suddenly alone and feeling terribly vulnerable. After a determined sigh, she was on her way again, her breath coming in visible puffs of white as the cold inside the tunnel only added to the apprehension consuming her.

The tunnel began to veer off to the left, and her gaze became even more agitated, the curvature in front of her slightly obstructing the path ahead. The ducting and conduits lining the wall, which she ordinarily wouldn't notice, took on a sinister appearance as obstacles to be avoided, and she was afraid to let any part of her body brush against them.

A lifetime later, she spotted the door beckoning to her in the distance, and she went stock-still, afraid to let herself hope that she might actually succeed. The walls closed in on her as she hurried forward, her focus reduced to nothing but the objective in front of her. Twenty more yards, and she could sprint back to safety. Soon, it was fifteen yards, and then ten.

Eight yards from her destination, she screamed in terror and surprise as the floor from the compound above fell in on top of her. The scream cut off abruptly as the wind was forced out of her by the obscene strength of the grip that yanked her into the hallway above. Stars danced in front of her eyes as her face collided painfully against the wall, bloodying her nose with a crunch. She went limp in her captor's grip and found freedom as she sank to the floor. Her arms and neck burned from having her sweatshirt torn forcibly off her body, and she rolled to the side, surprised to find the shotgun still in her hands.

Coy stared stupidly at the rag of her shirt dangling from his fist and turned to recapture his target.

The point-blank blast from her shotgun severed his left leg from the knee down, and he fell almost comically to the ground. His hands made no move to break the fall, and his head hit the ground with the sound of a melon being split.

Malory followed the blast with two more quick shots. She would have fired a fourth, but the impact from the rounds forced his body into the hole he had created in the floor, and he disappeared from view. Sounds from behind brought her swinging around to see Percy lumbering up the hall from about twenty feet away.

Not wasting any time, she emptied the shotgun at Percy and dropped it to the floor, instantly swinging the rifle around from her back and firing it until it locked open empty. The clatter of the magazine hitting the ground was quickly followed by the insertion of another and the loud clack of the bolt being snapped closed. Her finger pressed the trigger, and a salvo of bullets tore into the ceiling as the floor panel she was kneeling on surged upward, flinging her back down the hall. She fell into the hole she had emerged from, landing on her left shoulder with an audible pop and emitting an ear-splitting scream of pain that echoed off the walls.

The sudden grip around her ankle brought her back to the moment, and she brought the rifle up with her right arm, aiming through tearing eyes. The bullets slammed into Coy's face, neck and chest, tearing away flesh and splattering the ice walls haphazardly with blood and tissue. Worms began to drop in clumps from one side of his ruined head, and Malory screamed again, frantically kicking away from him as his grip left her boot.

She scrambled backward wildly and bit her tongue hard enough to draw blood when her back connected with something solid. Her head whipped around, and she found herself against the frame of the pressure door. In a second of clarity, she knew that she had no other option and crawled through hurriedly, pulling the door closed behind her. She caught a glimpse of Coy relentlessly pursuing her, using his arms to propel himself forward, before the door closed with a satisfying electronic chime.

The tears started in earnest as she entered the code to seal it, effectively locking herself out of the central facility. She fell back against the wall and dropped the magazine from her rifle, digging another one out of her bandolier with her right hand and slapping it home. The agony radiating from her left arm was crippling, and it sent waves of misery coursing through her when she tried to make a fist. She brought a hand up to wipe her nose, and she flinched in pain.

Angrily, she took stock of her situation. She had lost her shotgun but still had her pistol and radio. Other than her rifle and the bandolier of magazines, she was dressed from the waist up in a pale-blue bra, the sleeves of her missing sweatshirt gathered at her wrists. The bandage around her ribs that Corky had diligently applied the night before was missing, and she suspected that her nose was broken. She didn't even want to think about her shoulder.

It took a moment, but it slowly dawned on her that she was still in possibly hostile territory, and she considered the alternatives. The only place available that offered her a safe haven was Operations, and getting there would require running across the cavernous room that housed the platform and down a long ice hallway, up two flights of metal stairs and another short hallway. Then she had to enter her code and seal the door. If she managed to get there, she would find herself trapped in a small room with no food or water. Sadly, she realized that it was her only choice, and she rose with a whimper to travel the few yards that led to the end of the tunnel.

She adjusted the stock of her rifle to make it easier to handle with one arm and poked her head out cautiously, rapidly glancing around and finding it clear to emerge into Receiving. The wide-open space of the cavern allowed her the small liberating feeling of having room to maneuver. It was a drastic change from the cramped quarters of the tunnel, and for a moment, at least, she could look around and feel confident of her safety. It was much colder, as heat was applied sparingly to this part of the compound, only enough to keep equipment from freezing over. Her eyes took in the long column that led to the platform and the world above, and she wished that escape were as simple as taking an elevator ride. The distinctive outline of the helicopter rested silently on its skis, and her gaze roamed over the room's other machinery. The scene reminded her of a hastily abandoned ghost town.

A flicker of movement caught her eye, and she froze, watching intently as Dr. Garret lurched out from between several barrels of fuel. He was far enough away that she didn't feel immediately threatened, as she was confident that she could outrun him. She began a slow jog toward the hall that led to Operations, crossing the open space and keeping a wary eye on her pursuer. Her path widened as she approached the hall, and she kept a distance between herself and the entrance, in case it was providing refuge to anything that she didn't want to encounter.

Finding no sign of company, she looked over her shoulder to see Dr. Garret moving along at an alarming pace, closing the distance between them. She considered trying to slow him down or take a leg from him, but she didn't have much confidence that she could aim the rifle accurately with one hand. Shrugging it off, she hurried down the hallway, pausing at the foot of the stairs to check on Garret's progress. He hadn't reached the hall yet, and she suddenly remembered her radio. She let go of the rifle and pulled it from her belt.

"Sergeant Major?"

"Go ahead," he responded immediately, his relief evident.

"The door is sealed," she said, glancing up sharply as Garret appeared to pick up speed and advance faster than she thought possible.

"Understood. Your status?"

Garret began to jog, the stiffness she associated with the creatures beginning to show signs of wearing off. She brought the radio to her mouth but thought better of it as Garret began to cover more ground, and she turned to run up the stairs. Two steps from the top, the radio flew from her hands and dropped to the ground below as a stair collapsed under her. She fell, the impact of her chest against the next step knocking the breath from her body. Her waist hanging precariously in the air below the staircase, she struggled madly to pull herself up with her right arm. The rifle dangling from her side hindered her progress, and she began to flail around in panic.

The sound of footsteps in the ice sobered her, and she struck out with her injured appendage, using both arms to pull herself up and emitting a piercing scream of pain. Finding her feet, she didn't look back and ran up the second flight of stairs at a breakneck pace, flying down the hall so fast that her feet barely touched the ground. Her momentum brought her up against the door to Operations with a thud, and she frenetically punched in the entry code, her finger jabbing forcefully into the keypad.

She thanked God that she got it on the first try and threw herself into the room, slamming the door shut behind her. Her eyes came up to see Garret's face ram into the porthole hard enough to leave behind a blood smear, and she quickly reentered the code to seal the door. The rifle came up, and she backed away from the door slowly, riveted on the face staring at her blankly through the window. Her calves bumped up against a chair, and she spun, her eyes flying around the room in terror. Still hyperventilating from her close call, she needed several minutes to restore any semblance of calm and composure.

Eventually, she balanced herself with a deep breath and unslung her rifle, placing it on a desk. She sank into the chair that had spooked her and gingerly poked at her shoulder, whimpering at the pain her examination produced. A sleeve from her ruined sweatshirt became a washrag, and she tenderly wiped the blood from her face, throwing the soiled garment across the room when she was finished. Starting to fume at the situation she found herself in, she lifted angry eyes to meet those that still gazed at her maddeningly through the window.

A hand came up to reveal her right breast. She cupped it defiantly. "Suck me, bitch."

Her display elicited no response. Garret just stared.

Corky positioned herself in a corner of the lab and brought her knees up to her chest as soon as Malory left, praying desperately for her safe return. Clovis joined her a few minutes later. She appreciated the comfort his presence provided, offering him a weak smile of gratitude.

The time stretched on, and she schooled herself not to cry, telling herself that if Malory could find the courage to do what she had to do, she would be brave enough not to break into tears—at least until she had the benefit of a little privacy in which to conceal her breakdown. She was determined to give the appearance of strength, knowing that everyone looked to Malory for leadership, and she wasn't going to tarnish that by playing the part of the hysterically inconsolable girlfriend. It was going to be a hard sell, even to herself.

Her eyes rose to the nervously pacing McNeely and stayed focused on him intently; he would be the first to know. The sergeant major prudently kept his distance, not wanting anyone to overhear any communications he might receive. However, she studied his body language carefully for any clue that he might unconsciously reveal.

A little over a quarter of an hour after Malory and her party had left, she caught the rapid motion of McNeely bringing his radio up and speaking into it tersely. She tensed as the man walked over to address everybody.

"Hanson got his door sealed and is on his way back. Let's get ready in case he arrives in a hurry."

The men began to assemble in front of the door, and Clovis got up to join them, leaving her to maintain her vigil alone. The minutes passed in silence, one melting slowly into another. Finally, the radio in McNeely's hand barked urgently.

"I'm in the hall," Hanson muttered. *"It's clear. Let me in."*

"Open the door," McNeely ordered. Hanson ran into the room, the door closing behind him immediately.

Hanson sighed dramatically.

"Well done, Sergeant," McNeely said. "Any trouble?"

He shook his head. "Any word from the commander or Alvarez?"

"Not yet. But they had farther to go than you," he said, retreating again to his private corner.

Corky looked at the young sergeant and scolded herself for wishing that it were Malory who had returned instead of him. Her worry was giving her a powerful headache, and she lapsed back into her thoughts, eyes again straying to McNeely and taking up residence.

After another ten minutes of oppressive silence, McNeely paused his nervous pacing to raise his radio, crossing the room hurriedly.

"Alvarez is on his way back," he said. "His door was already sealed, and he's got company."

The men scrambled to their former positions.

Sooner than expected, McNeely's radio crackled. *"I've got distance. ETA less than a minute,"* Alvarez reported.

McNeely waited almost thirty seconds. "Open the door."

Within the span of three heartbeats, Alvarez raced into the room. "It's right behind me," he said, and the door was quickly closed.

All eyes scanned the anteroom anxiously, and the sound of plodding steps gradually became audible, eventually revealing the figure of the former kitchen manager.

Mr. Jones entered slowly on an almost-ruined leg and missing a good portion of his face. White teeth were visible through chunks of flesh that had been savagely torn away, and the wounds moved with a life of their own as worms labored to find undamaged tissue.

Corky noted this with unseeing eyes, suddenly rising to her feet. "We need to kill it. Malory can't get back in if it's standing there."

McNeely stared at her in understanding and then turned in Jones's direction as if summing the creature up. "Right. Looks like he's been chewed on. Back away from the door, and form up in the corners," he ordered, and the men started moving. "His right leg is barely there. Everyone on that first. When he drops, burn him."

He turned to verify that everyone was in place. "I'll open the door. Give me a second to get clear."

His finger had pressed the first key when they heard the unmistakable sounds of a shotgun being fired in the distance, and he froze. Corky's hands came up to cover her mouth in comprehension, and the room went deathly silent. A few unbearable seconds later, the long, steady burst of an automatic rifle echoed off the walls.

"Oh, God," Corky whispered in horror.

Another abbreviated burst was followed by a long automatic salvo. All ears listened expectantly, waiting for anything that might provide more information, but the silence weighed heavily and showed no sign of letting up.

"Love...craft," Jones gurgled, his voice drawing everyone's attention. "Love...craft is...dead," he finished and turned to lumber back into the hall.

Corky's resolve floundered at the words, and her face altered from horror to despair. Her sob was startlingly loud, but no one could turn to look at her. As the sob was followed by another, Clovis put his weapon down and walked over to embrace her.

The men moved away from them respectfully, and McNeely crossed the room to sit down angrily in a chair, spinning in his seat to face the wall.

"Sergeant Major?" Malory's voice crackled through the radio.

"Fuck me!" McNeely exclaimed in surprise, the radio moving from his belt to his mouth in a blur. "Go ahead."

Corky's head rose sharply to peer out from behind one of Clovis's arms, hope shining in her eyes.

"The door is sealed."

"Understood. Your status?"

No answer was forthcoming. "Commander?"

Corky snatched the radio from her belt. "Malory?"

"Commander?" McNeely repeated and did so several times, his frustration growing with every unanswered call. Finally, he threw his arms in the air and made as if to throw his radio against the wall, barely restraining himself at the last second.

"I want a gun," Corky stated quietly.

McNeely took a deep breath and turned to face her. "Why?"

"Because she's alive, and we're going to find her."

"Fuckin' A," Alvarez piped up in agreement.

McNeely nodded. "How many are we up against?"

"I figure six," Hanson said. "We found what was left of Dr. Isaaks in the tunnel. We know of Coy and Jones for certain. Garret is still missing, as is Percy, and we lost Gallagher and Dobson yesterday."

"Six?" Watkins said in distress. "We almost lost our ass to just three yesterday."

"We have a lot more guns now," Reynolds said. "And the complex is secure. Whatever is out there is trapped in here. Just like us."

"We can't leave her out there," Corky said. "We won't leave her out there."

"We're not going to," McNeely said. "However, we'll need a group to stay behind. All of us walking around out there creates too big a target, as we found out yesterday."

"Who stays behind?" Watkins asked eagerly and received several derisive looks.

"I guess you do," Alvarez said with thinly veiled contempt.

"Knock it off," McNeely said. "Ring, Hanson, Watkins and Rivers get to keep the home fires burning. The rest form up."

"I'm going," Corky stated. "She may need help."

"Doctor," McNeely said, "if we find her and she's injured, you can't treat her out there. We'll get her back here on the double."

"I want to go."

McNeely sighed. "You're staying here, because if she were present, she would never allow it. And I won't, either. You would be a liability."

"I'm going, and you can't stop me."

McNeely raised an eyebrow. "Oh, yes, I can," he rumbled. "Although I'd rather not. Please don't make me."

"I will *not* stay here! And we don't have the time to be talking about it."

McNeely eyed her carefully. "You're right. We don't have the time," he agreed suspiciously and turned to whisper in Reynolds's ear.

The chief turned to leave the room, returning a minute later, carrying several long strands of network cable that he handed to several of the soldiers.

"Do you wish to reconsider, Dr. Rivers?" McNeely asked.

Corky bared her teeth.

With a nod from the sergeant major, the men began to advance on the little doctor.

Several minutes later, McNeely sealed the lab door and joined the rest of the men in the hallway, ruefully dabbing at the scratches on his cheek.

"Jesus. She fought like a fuckin' Comanche," he muttered, getting several nervous chuckles of agreement. "Okay, DeSoto and Daly, you're on point with me. Chief, Terrel and Butler, bring up the rear. Alvarez, you got tunnel duty. Use your radio. The rest of you, form up between us single-file."

"Right," Alvarez agreed, moving forward quietly and dropping through the hole that had been created in the corridor. *"Clear,"* he added a moment later through McNeely's radio.

McNeely nodded. "Remember, boys, head and legs. Anything else is a waste of time."

Malory considered her alternatives, not particularly fond of any of them. She cursed herself for losing her radio, knowing that if she had retained it, she could at the very least let everyone know that she was okay. She considered using the intercom, but doing so would require bringing the complex out of lockdown, and that wasn't an option, as it would release the seal on the doors. The worry about her own situation was only slightly less than her concern for those who were still among the living, a diminutive brunette principal among them.

She assumed herself to be the only one in immediate dire circumstances, as she had overheard no shots being fired, either before or after her own. She felt sure that she would have heard them if any had occurred. Being underground almost guaranteed that the resonance and echo of gunfire would travel undiminished from one end of the complex to the other, and she considered the lack of such noise to be a good sign. Unfortunately, if she wanted to look for bad signs, she had to look no farther than her own body.

Her shoulder was definitely dislocated, and she determinedly ignored any thought beyond that complication. The mere idea of undergoing a repeat of the surgery and therapy she had endured with her past injury made her want to cry. Her ribs were definitely broken now. She could feel the ends grinding together when she moved, and she could only hope that she wasn't bleeding internally. Breathing in through her nose was an exercise in stinging pain, and even the thought of a gentle breeze wafting over it resulted in throbs of misery. But the biggest kick to the head—the one that really pissed her off—was the telltale cramps that alerted her to the early arrival of her period.

It was just too much.

Angry blue eyes rose to find Garret still staring at her through the window as though she were a rack of lamb, and a plan began to form. The creatures were smart, but they were not infallible.

Intending to prove it, she rose stiffly and spent a few minutes foraging through the desks and cabinets, eventually accumulating all the necessities to implement the first stage of her plan.

Scotch tape and paper in hand, she approached the door and began to cover the porthole, obscuring her activities from the unnerving eyes on the other side. The thud of fists pounding on the door informed her that the results of her labor were not appreciated.

"Don't worry," she mumbled. "I'll be getting back to ya."

"Untie me," Corky demanded from her hogtied position on the floor.

Hanson rubbed his watering eye, still stinging from its collision with the toe of the doctor's errant boot. The woman had put up a furious fight, kicking and screaming wildly. More than one of his colleagues had suffered an impact from her madly flailing hands and feet before they finally managed to subdue her.

"I said, untie me," Corky fumed, wiggling violently on the floor.

Hanson shot a look at the lieutenant and almost laughed, knowing that if the situation hadn't been so grave, he would have. Ring was seated with his elbows on his knees and his head in his hands, looking as though he might vomit or cry, or perhaps both. The man had taken a vicious blow to the groin at the onset and was still suffering the repercussions.

"Untie me, goddamn it!"

He rubbed his eye again. "Promise to behave if I free you?"

"I promise to kick your ass."

Watkins chuckled from across the room, and he tried to ignore him. "Then I'm afraid we'll have to wait until the sergeant major gets back."

Corky went completely still and growled her frustration. "Okay, I promise," she ground out reluctantly.

"You sure, now?"

"I said, I fuckin' promise!"

"That language isn't very ladylike."

Corky craned her neck to glare murder in his direction.

Ring finally emerged from his exile of affliction and chuckled. "Cut her some slack, Sergeant."

"Oh, all right," he relented, moving forward and drawing his knife.

Corky fought the urge to charge the man as she threw the cables still dangling from her wrists to the floor in irritation. She straightened her clothes with agitated hands and snarled at the smirking sergeant.

He acted quickly and extended a finger in reminder. "You promised."

Her lips tightened into a thin, tense line, and she reached for the only weapon she could think of. "When the commander gets back," she said, "I'm telling on you."

Her comment only succeeded in generating a chuckle from all three men.

Corky huffed and stomped off through the nearest door.

"Alvarez, we're halting," McNeely said into his radio and signaled a stop to those behind him.

"Understood."

McNeely wiped his forehead with his sleeve. "Chief," he called out with a wave.

Reynolds came forward and kneeled next to him.

"We've cleared half the complex and seen no sign. They've got to be close," McNeely said quietly.

"Yeah, I figured we'd have run into at least one by now," Reynolds replied, searching the hall in front and behind with a cautious gaze, his eye suddenly freezing on the ceiling behind them.

"Doug," he whispered and pointed to the roof.

McNeely followed the finger to a ceiling tile that was slightly ajar and directly above a large group of men. "Jesus," he said, flying to his feet. "Butler, Terrel, above—"

His warning came a second too late as the roof abruptly rained down on them and Gallagher fell from above, landing on his feet with unnatural grace. Terrel rolled away as fast as the flame unit strapped to his back would allow, bringing his weapon up but hesitating to fire for fear of enveloping Butler and a group of civilians in flame.

Butler was not as fortunate. Gallagher landed directly behind him, and he screamed as his arm was wrenched out of the socket. A spray of blood jutted from the fractured bone protruding through his bicep.

The men closest scrambled to get out of the way, and Butler's scream morphed into a warbling gurgle as Gallagher's teeth seized his esophagus and tore through his throat. In his convulsions, Butler's finger clamped down on the trigger to his rifle, and he sprayed gunfire wildly down the hall, several rounds catching Terrel in the chest and knocking him onto his back.

Gallagher threw Butler aside like a rag doll, the corpse colliding with Dr. Lenard so powerfully that he left his feet with the impact and landed on his back. He struggled to his feet, covered from head to waist with Butler's blood and clutching his broken eyeglasses possessively to his chest.

"Behind me, now!" McNeely roared.

The sergeant major watched in horror as the fleeing Dr. Tanaka was caught from behind and Gallagher slammed his head into the wall with an audible crack. McNeely bobbed and weaved in the hall as the men rocketed to a position behind him, trying unsuccessfully to get a bead on Gallagher that didn't further endanger the unfortunate Dr. Tanaka.

"Two behind us!" Reynolds yelled.

McNeely yanked his head around to see Jones and Dobson casually advancing on them from a distance. His attention returned forward at Tanaka's scream, and he turned in time to see the man's jaw completely torn away from his skull. His hand flashed to his radio.

"Alvarez, fall back to the lab! We're overrun! The rest of you, drop that fucker now!" Then he let loose an automatic burst that humanely tore through the dying Dr. Tanaka and plunged unnoticed into Gallagher's body.

The men followed his example, and the now-dead Tanaka was reduced to tatters in a hail of gunfire. Clovis leveled his shotgun and emptied it at Gallagher's knees. He fell to the floor, only to be surrounded by half a dozen men who vengefully emptied their weapons into the creature, blowing it apart by inches.

Reynolds darted past the conflict and slid to his knees next to the unmoving Terrel, cursing when dead eyes stared unseeing into his own.

"Move!" McNeely ordered, indiscriminately shoving the remaining men back the way they had come. "Run for it, boys! "

The men took off at a dead run, with the exception of DeSoto, who calmly reloaded his rifle and took the time to empty it again into the quivering pulp that Gallagher had been reduced to.

"DeSoto, with me now!" Reynolds yelled, and the young man turned to spare a last look at Butler's corpse, allowing himself a mere second of lament over the death of his friend before running to join the fleeing men.

McNeely again reached for his radio as they pounded down the hall. "Ring, we're coming back on the double! Get on the door!" he yelled. A minute later, he was caught up in the swell of bodies struggling to get inside into safety.

The chief and DeSoto were the last to enter, and Ring pushed the door closed with the assistance of several panicked hands.

"Wait! Is Alvarez here?" McNeely asked.

"I'm here! Seal the fucking door!" Alvarez yelled.

Ring punched the code into the door. A general sigh of relief followed, and McNeely threw his rifle across the room to take out a computer monitor. "Goddamn it!"

Corky ran back into the room at all the commotion and looked around fearfully, not spotting the one she had hoped to find and noting with sadness that there were only eleven people in the room.

Watkins observed the lack of bodies, too. "Great," he said sarcastically. "Maybe we should build a fire and sing some songs."

"If I were you," Reynolds warned, "I'd shut the fuck up."

"I have the right to speak! The commander's dead, and we're dropping like flies. Are we sup—"

His words were cut off by the butt of Alvarez's rifle slamming into the side of his face. He crumpled to the ground in a silent heap.

"Well done, Sergeant," Corky said mildly.

Malory heard the gunfire and cursed, momentarily halting work on her preparations as she listened intently for several minutes after the last shot had been fired. Fighting a gnawing feeling of urgency, she went about finishing her work.

She had painstakingly rearranged the room's three desks in front of the door to create an obstacle course, leaving only a few feet between each one. She was thankful that the infrequently used room was narrow enough to make each desk a tight fit. When Garret entered, he wouldn't be able to go around and would have to climb over each desk individually, which she hoped would give her enough time to get away. As an afterthought, she had used her rifle to knock the casters off the legs on one side of each desk. Her plan would fail if the creature simply shoved the desks together and crushed her at the far end of the room. With the casters removed, that possibility would be much more difficult, because each desk now leaned into the floor at an angle.

Feeling ready, she checked the magazine of her pistol and chambered a round. Leaving the handgun on the last desk, she slung her rifle and slowly began negotiating the furniture on her way to the door.

She had no doubt that Garret was still on the other side. The sound of his fists pounding relentlessly on the door had proved to be a constant source of anxiety and irritation. Steeling herself with a deep breath, she leaned over the last desk to enter the code that would unseal the door. As her finger pressed the last key, she scrambled madly back to the rear of the room, leapfrogging the desks as quickly as she was able. She retrieved her pistol as her feet hit the floor behind the last one and waited for her guest.

The pounding ceased when the entry light turned green, and Garret wasted no time in throwing the door open, lunging into the room with insane glee. His waist slammed into the first desk, and Malory took careful aim, letting a round go as he rebounded slightly from his collision. The bullet entered his eye and snapped his head back violently, a red splatter flying into the air behind him. Undeterred, he bowled forward determinedly, the desk scraping loudly as its legs dug into the floor. Her second shot missed its target and struck him in the bridge of his nose, managing to remove a good portion of his brain pan with an impressive patch of hair still attached. Garret rammed the first desk into the next, and his momentum came to a jerking halt as he encountered the second obstacle. The .45 roared again, and his vision was extinguished in a red mist.

Malory grunted in satisfaction as he began to flail around blindly, and she holstered her pistol. Garret's movements became frenzied, and he lost his bearings, spinning around in a circle and lashing out in a desperate attempt to capture his quarry.

She brought the rifle up and kneeled to steady it against the top of the desk, taking deliberate aim. She fired the bullets one at a time, each one slamming into Garret's right hip. When the rifle locked open, she inserted another magazine and continued firing upon her target until his ruined hip could no longer support the weight of his body. She stood to insert a fresh magazine when he fell, and she cautiously moved forward, clearly aware of the still-thrashing body. With a deep breath of preparation, she hopped onto a desk and ran into a short leap that brought her clear of Garret's body and into the open doorway. In relative safety, she again raised the rifle and fired several automatic bursts into his good leg until the calf hung from flimsy strips of tissue. Satisfied, she reloaded her rifle as she stared at the writhing body.

"Make yourself at home. I'll be back in a little while to crispy-critter your ass."

She pulled the door closed, entering the code to seal it, and then turned to make her way carefully down the steps. When she reached the bottom, she hurried under the staircase to retrieve her radio, pausing when she found a hacksaw lying next to it. Her eyes rose to examine the step that had collapsed under her weight. It had been sawed through to a fraction, and one side now hung perilously from a small strand of twisted metal.

"Devious little fucker," she mumbled, and reached to pick up her radio. "Sergeant Major?"

Agitated when she received no immediate response, she was about to call again when she noticed that the power light was off. She tossed the radio into the snow, realizing that it had been on when she lost it, and the battery had run dry. Resolutely, she rose to her full height and twisted her head around until the vertebrae in her neck cracked.

"Here comes trouble."

In the lab, the sound of gunfire brought sagging heads up all around the room.

"That was a handgun," Alvarez said, coming to his feet.

Several of the men joined him, and they listened intently as slow, repeated reports of rifle fire echoed through the complex.

Corky smiled. "It's Malory."

McNeely snatched his radio. "Commander?"

The only reply was a hail of automatic fire that ended quickly.

"Commander?" he asked again, waiting several long seconds for a response. He was about to speak again when a body suddenly stepped into the foyer.

He lowered the radio slowly as Percy walked to within arm's reach of the door. There was expectant silence as all attention was focused on the brutally disfigured man.

"He's been shot up," Clovis said.

"This is the first we've seen of him since he went missing," Reynolds said. "I bet he had a run-in with the commander."

"Unless they decided to start playing with guns, I would guess she got away from him," McNeely said.

"We—" Reynolds started but ground to a halt as Percy extended a finger and pressed a number on the keypad. "Shit!"

"Form up in the corners. Move!" McNeely yelled.

Percy hit another button, slowly picking up speed and rapidly entering a series of numbers on the keypad.

"Oh, this is fucking great," Watkins murmured.

McNeely watched the entry light signal red repeatedly. "What are the odds of him hitting the right numbers?"

"A million to one," Reynolds replied. "But he could hit the right combo any minute, or not for months."

McNeely sighed and leaned against the wall. "Looks like we ain't gonna get any sleep."

"Let's let him in, " Alvarez said. "He's alone."

McNeely considered. "I don't know. They move a hell of a lot faster now than they did at the beginning."

"No shit," Reynolds said. "Gallagher was all over us. We'd lose somebody before we could put him down."

"Leaving him outside is good," Watkins said.

Several sets of eyes strayed to the man contemptuously.

"Rigor mortis," Corky said.

"Excuse me, Doctor?" McNeely asked.

"They're moving faster because rigor mortis is wearing off," she explained. "It must take a while for everything to loosen up again."

They absorbed her speculation in silence, and she continued. "Perhaps there's a stage of dormancy when they first take over a host. Maybe that's why I didn't detect any worms in Dr. Grey."

"They're planning now, too," Reynolds added. "They must've decided that an all-out assault was too costly. They ambushed us this time."

"Fantastic," Watkins murmured. "Maybe we should just surrender."

"Watkins," Alvarez growled.

Malory sealed the tunnel door and reentered the complex, spending a moment studying the carnage from her earlier encounter with Coy. A remarkable amount of blood colored the inside of the tunnel for several feet, the red standing out against the white of the ice walls, but there was no sign of a body.

Carefully, she moved forward several feet until she could poke her head through the missing floor panels, her eyes landing happily on her discarded shotgun. She pulled herself up into the hall with a series of painful grunts and made tracks for the weapon, snatching it up with a grin.

She loaded it to capacity and chambered a round. "Groovy."

Moving cautiously forward, she came to a gradual halt as she turned a corner and spotted a slowly moving body several yards ahead. Coy was pulling himself down the hall with his hands, the stump of his leg keeping him from walking.

Malory closed in on him from behind, a little surprised that he was unaware of her presence. As she came to within a few feet, she could see that his leg had clotted. Looking closer, she took note of the worms working their way in and out of the flesh industriously, laboring to keep the tissue they resided in functional.

She took careful aim. "Hey," she said. "What's that on your face?"

Coy spun wildly on the floor, most of his head and face missing, using his hands in a flurry of motion to thrust himself toward her.

The blast dissolved what was left of his skull in a crimson squall, and the decapitated body contorted viciously on the floor. Eight rounds later, she mechanically reloaded the shotgun, carefully stepped around the ruined pulp of Coy's corpse and continued her journey down the hall, humming softly.

Eventually, she arrived at her quarters, and she opened the door cautiously, a cruel blue gaze scanning the interior carefully. Satisfied that no one was lurking, she entered her office and, shotgun poised at the ready, flung open the door to her room. Her eyes immediately tracked to Little Lovecraft's severed head, and she snarled in fury, bending to pick it up and glancing around angrily in search of the rest of her doll. She found the body under the cot and gently put the two pieces of her beloved companion on top of her footlocker.

"Bastards," she hissed.

With a sigh, she stripped off her rifle and bandolier, setting the shotgun on her cot so she could pull on a sweatshirt carefully. After several gasps of pain as the shirt made contact with her nose, she forced her wounded arm through the sleeves and then pulled a belt from her closet. The belt became a sling as she strapped it around her waist, trapping her left arm inside the loop and snugly tightening the limb to her side.

Feeling considerably better, she reclaimed her weapons and walked back into her office, pausing at the door to snatch her hat from its hook before stepping into the hall.

1741 hours

Tension filled the lab as Percy continued to punch numbers into the keypad calmly. Anxiety rose sharply and then fell minimally every time the entry light flashed red, denying him access.

"We're gonna have to let him in," McNeely said. "We can't just sit here and wait for him to chance upon the right code, and we should do it before one of his friends shows up."

"We'll need some bait," Alvarez said. "I suggest someone expendable and therefore nominate Watkins."

"I second that," Ring said quickly, and hesitant chuckles sounded around the room.

"Fuck all of you," Watkins said. "I'm not moving from this spot."

"Knock it off," McNeely chided. "Besides, with any luck, it'll go for him first."

The resulting snickers turned into nervous laughter, and even Corky joined in. The echo of a gunshot penetrated their moment of mirth, and the laughter subsided swiftly. Eight more reports sounded in quick succession, and then silence reigned again.

"That's got to be the commander," Alvarez said.

"I know it is," Corky said.

"Did those rounds sound any closer?" McNeely asked.

"Hard to tell inside, but they seemed louder," Hanson replied.

"It didn't seem to bother our friend out there," Reynolds pointed out.

Indeed, Percy hadn't paused in his mission and continued to key numbers into the door.

"Could they be using weapons out there to break the seals on the doors?" Lenard asked, his spectacles now repaired with an unsightly wad of medical tape that rested on the bridge of his nose.

"We don't have a weapon in inventory that could break the seal on those doors," Reynolds said.

"Could any of our weapons break through this glass?" Lenard asked, gesturing to the transparent partition separating them from the foyer.

The chief looked at the glass thoughtfully. "I seriously doubt it."

"But you're not sure?"

"There's a slim chance that concentrated fire could weaken it. Why do you ask?"

"Not to rain on anyone's parade, but the chances of Lovecraft's still being among the living are remarkably slim," Lenard said. "These things have shown signs of astonishing intelligence. Perhaps they're experimenting."

"Malory *is* alive," Corky said.

"I hope so, Doctor," Lenard said. "But we should be prepared for anything at this stage."

"Well, gee," Watkins muttered, "the thought of those things with weapons gives me a warm fuzzy."

"Watkins," McNeely rumbled, "if we didn't need the extra gun so badly, I'd feed you to those things myself. Do yourself the favor of remaining silent unless you have something productive to add."

Watkins rolled his eyes, falling back against the wall heavily, and McNeely studied him carefully for a long moment.

"Sergeant Major," Lenard said, "you said we have some explosives. Could they use those to penetrate the room?"

"Yes," McNeely replied. "But to use them requires a knowledge I would assume no one else has, except for me and possibly Sergeant Alvarez."

"Even the commander?" Lenard asked.

McNeely paused. "Perhaps."

"Have any of you considered the notion that if Lovecraft is one of those things," Watkins began, "she has the knowledge to effectively destroy us all? She could walk right up and open this door or bring the entire complex out of lockdown."

"Malory is *not* one of those things," Corky growled.

McNeely shared a look with Reynolds and nodded.

Corky cast wary eyes on both of them. "What are you doing?"

"Doctor," McNeely sighed, "unfortunately, Watkins has a point. We have to at the very least change the door codes again."

"No! She won't be able to get back in!"

"That's the whole point," Watkins said.

"She is not one of those things! She's out there fighting them! You've all heard the shots!"

"Doctor, if she falls," McNeely said, "she could endanger us all."

"You don't know anything! She would kill herself to keep from being taken by those things!"

"That is unarguably true, Dr. Rivers," McNeely agreed. "But even if she were to do that, we've all seen the dead get up and walk."

Corky opened her mouth to reply and then brought a hand up to cover a sudden sob. She turned away from everyone and faced the wall.

McNeely watched her sadly for a moment and then turned to the chief. "Do it."

Malory walked boldly down the hall, making no attempt at stealth. She fought bravely through occasional bouts of wooziness that she knew were the result of her injuries. When she found her attention wandering, she hummed in an effort to keep herself grounded, often softly singing the words to the few songs she remembered snippets from.

Her steps came to a faltering halt as she spotted the remains of several bodies in the distance. Her shotgun came up in preparation, and she advanced, noticing movement as she got closer.

Jones was so intent on his meal that he was unaware of her approach until the last second. He raised his head from the grisly hole in Terrel's belly with an expression of morbid surprise, only to find the barrel of a shotgun three inches away from his face. A ravaged piece of meat fell from his mouth as his eyes rose to meet a pair of blue ones almost as insane as his own.

"Let me wash that down for you."

Jones would've found the blast deafening if he had retained the necessary anatomy. Grim intent fueled the next eight rounds, and Malory paid no attention to the blood that splattered her from indulging in the close-range massacre. When the gun was empty, she casually shook the worms and tissue off her boots as she reloaded the weapon.

Out of the corner of her eye, she caught movement, which turned out to be Butler approaching stiffly from a few dozen yards away, one mangled arm dangling uselessly from his side like a slice of raw bacon and his clothes soaked with blood from a ragged wound to his throat. She watched his advance indifferently as she chambered a round and inserted another shell to load the shotgun to full capacity.

The sound of another footfall alerted her to the presence of Dobson, advancing from behind her. Trapped between them, she gloomily assessed her situation. She couldn't drop them both in time to prevent one from reaching her. It was going to have to be a running battle. She smiled.

"You'll not see nothing like the mighty Quinn," she sang softly and turned to run in the direction of Butler, leveling her shotgun as she closed the distance.

Her rate of movement and the one-handed grip on the shotgun affected her accuracy, but the nine semiautomatic blasts were devastatingly effective—the last two especially, as they removed Butler's head from the nose up, leaving him blind and flailing around aggressively.

She ran the last few feet as fast as she could, screaming in rage as she ducked her right shoulder and ran into him with all the strength she had. The collision proved to be fruitful, and Malory managed to knock him off his feet. But she couldn't keep her balance as she bowled over him and fell painfully to the ground a few yards behind him, her shotgun skidding away from her.

She fought to overcome a powerful spell of nausea and floundered several times in the attempt to regain her feet. As she fell to the floor on her third attempt, the impending blackness of unconsciousness threatened to take over, and she struggled to stave it off.

The struggle ended with an agonized rasp as she was lifted into the air by the belt that strapped her injured left arm to her side. Disorientated and helpless, she was manhandled in the air until she found herself face to face with the demonic features of the late Dr. Dobson. A terrified power surged through her, and she brought her good hand up to claw into his eyes, digging in and tearing several nails off with the ferocity of her attack.

One of his hands clamped around the back of her neck, and she felt herself being drawn inexorably forward. She went into a frenzy of resistance, contorting madly in his grasp and screaming as his mouth began to advance on her own.

Suddenly, she went limp in his embrace, and her head lolled backward in apparent unconsciousness. An expression of macabre surprise crossed Dobson's ruined features, and he paused in obvious curiosity, studying the limp form that lay helpless within his grasp.

His remaining eye blinked when blue orbs snapped open and regarded him savagely as a cool, unyielding object made contact with the roof of his gaping mouth.

"All sales are final," Malory rasped.

The blast of the .45 scattered the back of Dobson's head all over the ceiling, and Malory landed on wobbly legs as the grip on her was released. Wasting no time, she backed up a step and took careful aim, extinguishing what was left of his vision with another roar from the handgun. She emptied the remaining rounds into his head with precision, moving a step with each shot in the direction of her misplaced shotgun, kneeling to retrieve it when the pistol was empty.

Keeping a careful eye on the sightless Dobson as he cavorted recklessly around the hallway, she reloaded the shotgun and chambered a round. "I hope like hell that you feel pain," she said hoarsely. "Because I really want this to hurt."

Corky looked up sharply at the sound of gunshots and blew out a relieved breath. She refused to subscribe to any theory suggesting that Malory wasn't the source of all the gunfire.

McNeely approached the door to the lab thoughtfully, leveling a hard stare at the determined Percy.

"She's out there," Corky said. "Let that fucker in and blow him away so we can go help her," she added with a dismissive gesture in Percy's direction.

"Fuck that," Watkins said. "If Lovecraft is alive, there's nothing we can do for the bitch."

Several of the men rose angrily, and Corky shot a homicidal glare in his direction. "You worthless, yellow pussy," she hissed, striding over to stand in front of him and extending a hand. "Give me your rifle, you spineless shit."

He clutched the weapon to his chest possessively. "Fuck off, you little queer. You ain't got the balls for it."

The sound of several rifles cocking was startlingly loud, and Watkins looked up to see every gun barrel in the room pointed directly at him, the eyes behind them shining with deadly intent.

"Give her the weapon," McNeely growled. "Right now."

Watkins froze, excruciatingly aware that the threat outside now paled in comparison to the danger immediately confronting him.

"I said *now!*" McNeely barked.

He slowly extended the rifle in Corky's direction, and she snatched it out of his hands. "Asshole!"

"Chief, we're gonna need some more cable," McNeely said, still looking down the length of his gun barrel at Watkins. "And a chair," he added as an afterthought.

"With pleasure, Sergeant Major," Reynolds said, lowering his rifle and making an exit.

Watkins's eyes widened. "Wait a minute, now. You can't—"

"Shut the fuck up," McNeely said. "I can think of about twenty people I wish were here with us now instead of you."

"That ain't no lie," Alvarez rumbled. "We lost some damn good men, and I'd grease you myself right now if I thought it would bring any of them back."

Reynolds walked back into the room, guiding a rolling chair in front of him, which he shoved into Watkins's knees. "Have a seat, Dr. Watkins."

"You can't do—"

His words were cut off by the impact of the chief's backhand, and several men rushed forward to force him into the chair, binding him tightly in place.

"Don't do this!" he screamed in panic.

"Gag him," McNeely said. A few seconds later, Watkins was silenced. "Place him against the wall in full view of the door."

Watkins whimpered helplessly through his gag as he was rolled into place, his eyes darting around fearfully.

"Form up. I'm going to let Percy in," McNeely ordered. "If a stray round strikes Watkins, I'll consider it an accident."

Alvarez and Reynolds turned sinister smiles on the bound man.

"Head and legs. Everything else is a waste of time," McNeely reminded.

He looked around to receive nods of readiness and walked for the door, closing to within three feet before freezing in his tracks. His eyes riveted on the instantly recognizable black hat as Malory stepped into the foyer and leveled a shotgun at the back of Percy's head.

"Malory!" Corky exclaimed.

Percy turned as if perceiving a threat, and the occupants inside the lab found themselves viewing a graphic portrait of blood, tissue and bone as his head exploded onto the glass.

The gore obscured the details of the resulting carnage as eight more rounds thundered through the room. At the last shot, McNeely overcame his paralysis and lunged forward to open the door.

A tense moment later, Malory stepped in on shaky legs and attempted a weak smile in Corky's direction. "Hail to the queen, baby."

Corky's hands came to her mouth in concern as she got a close look at her lover, not knowing what injury to start fussing over first. Both of her eyes were blackened from an obviously broken nose, the bruises so large that they melted into the previous contusions she had suffered. Her left arm was strapped tightly to her body with a belt, and her complexion was sickly pale, not to mention the blood covering her from head to toe.

She took a hesitant step forward and then broke into a run as Malory's eyes rolled back and she began to collapse, saved from hitting the deck only by McNeely's quick embrace.

The sergeant major lowered her gently to the floor, and Corky fell to her knees beside her, hands flying over her body in diagnosis.

"Get a stretcher," she ordered a moment later. "She's in shock. We need to get her to Medical right now."

"DeSoto! Daly!" McNeely barked. "On the double!"

The men rushed from the room, and McNeely turned to Hanson. "Burn that piece of shit," he said, gesturing to Percy's quivering remains. "The rest of you, gear up. Let's make sure she got them all."

Corky barely heard the commotion going on around her as she tried to detach herself professionally from Malory's injuries. She failed miserably, and the tears fell from her eyes freely as she struggled to find a spot on her lover's body that wasn't beaten or bruised.

As the flames from Percy's body were extinguished, the stretcher arrived, and the commander was loaded onto it quickly. Corky raced behind DeSoto and Daly as they hurried her lover out of the lab and down the hall.

May 13 - 0100 hours

Four hours later, McNeely watched dispassionately as Garret's remains were reduced to ashes and Reynolds walked up beside him.

"Fuckin' A, Doug," the chief whispered. "She got every one of 'em."

"Yeah," he said quietly. "Yeah, she did."

Reynolds let out a long breath. "Think she'll be okay?"

"I dunno. I fuckin' hope so."

"So do I."

McNeely sighed. "Let's get this place cleaned up and stowed away. We still have a few months before we can get the hell out of here. Start with the mess. I'm sure I'm not the only one hungry enough to eat the ass out of a rhino."

"Watkins is still in the lab," he reminded McNeely amusedly.

"Have someone tighten his restraints and wheel him into his quarters. Let him work his way free."

Reynolds grinned. "I believe Alvarez would volunteer for that."

"No doubt," McNeely said around a chuckle. "We might also want to look after the belongings of everyone we lost."

"I'll see to it. What are you going to do?"

"I'm going to Medical. Have someone bring me a plate when chow is available."

"Will do. I'd imagine everyone will be there as soon as they can."

McNeely nodded and turned to walk out of Operations, leaving Hanson and Ring to see to their grisly task.

He found himself alone when he arrived at his destination, the divider drawn across the room. With a tired sigh, he seated himself to wait, all too aware of the steady beep of monitoring equipment hidden behind the curtain.

0345 hours

McNeely was startled awake by a nudge from the chief, who offered him a plate of food and sank into the chair next to him. He rubbed the sleep out of his eyes and was surprised to find everyone but Watkins present.

"Thanks," he grumbled. "What time is it?"

"Almost 0400."

"Any word?"

"Not yet."

"Everything squared away?"

"It's a work in progress," the chief said. "It'll be a few days."

He nodded. "I guess it's time to bite the bullet," he announced reluctantly, setting his plate on the chair before warily slipping behind the divider.

His eyes instantly landed on the unconscious commander, and he winced in sympathy. She was rendered almost unrecognizable by the metal cast taped across her nose. A thin sheet was tucked meticulously around her body, and he followed the IV trail to her arm, where he found the doctor asleep. Corky was slumped over in a chair by the bedside, her face resting on the mattress next to Malory's hand. He approached quietly and knelt next to the slumbering doctor, nudging her gently.

She snapped awake instantly. "Malory," she said hopefully, her eyes anxiously searching.

"Doctor," he said softly, alerting her to his presence, and she jumped in surprise. "I'm sorry."

"It's okay," she mumbled.

"How is she?"

She turned tired eyes in his direction. "She's gonna be fine," she choked out, her voice cracking.

He exhaled in relief, not getting the chance to speak as Corky's face fell and she launched herself into his arms, crying tears of worry and relief.

"Oh, hey," he soothed, surprised to find the little doctor clinging to him desperately. "It's all over now."

The men waiting nearby overheard snippets of the conversation and recognized the unmistakable sounds of Corky crying.

"If the commander doesn't make it," Alvarez rumbled darkly, "I'm going to execute Watkins just for the fuck of it."

A few mumbles of agreement met his words, and several minutes later, the sergeant major emerged from behind the divider. All eyes rose expectantly.

McNeely smiled, and shoulders slumped universally in relief. "She's gonna be out of it for a while, but she'll pull through."

"Is there anything we can do, Sergeant Major?" Clovis asked.

"I'm glad you asked that. Dr. Rivers will be staying in Medical for the foreseeable future, so I'd like you to pack her a bag and grab her a cot. Also, someone go grab her something to eat; I'd imagine she's pretty hungry."

The men jumped to their feet.

"Oh, one more thing," he added. "Someone go tighten the ropes on Watkins, and put a plate of food just out of his reach."

"I'll do that," Alvarez said quickly, turning to leave the room.

"Sergeant Alvarez," McNeely said before he could leave.

"Yes?"

"Make sure you leave the faucet dripping, too."

Corky bent over her patient studiously, squinting through magnifying lenses as she carefully placed the stitches. She had never sewed a head back on, mostly because the act itself seemed like an exercise in futility, but this was a special case. It was her hope that the endeavor would leave undetectable scars, and she went to great pains to make her stitches as small as possible. So intense was her concentration that she failed to notice the blue eyes that fluttered open behind her.

Malory immediately squinted in response to the bright light situated above her, and she spent a few minutes adjusting. When she was able to open her eyes completely, the first thing she noticed was the obstruction on her face, and a hand rose to investigate.

"Oww!" she squeaked when she poked herself harder than she intended.

Corky's head snapped up at the sound, and she turned in her chair, her face lighting up as she met Malory's eyes.

"Hey!"

"Hey," Malory rasped, trying a grin that rapidly turned into a frown. "It hurts to smile."

"I know," Corky said, turning to discreetly cover her other patient with a sheet. "Let me get you some juice."

"Okay."

Malory crossed her eyes in an attempt to view her nose until Corky returned and placed a kiss on her forehead. "Apple juice okay?"

"Sure."

She was instantly force-fed a straw. "Suck."

Malory did as she was told, watching the doctor with wary eyes.

When Corky had determined that she had consumed an acceptable amount, she withdrew the straw.

"You're smiling at me," Malory said. "I take it I'm going to live?"

"Yep."

"How bad is my shoulder?"

"It was dislocated. Some slight tearing, but nothing that won't heal."

Malory looked at Corky suspiciously. "Then why do I feel so bad?"

"You broke three ribs. They were piercing you on the inside."

"Oh," Malory whispered. "So what's with the shit on my face? Will I end up looking like the Elephant Man?"

Corky giggled. "Nope. In a few weeks, you'll be as pretty as ever."

"Really?"

"Really."

"Do you have a mirror?"

"Why?"

"I want to see."

"No, you don't."

"Please."

Corky rolled her eyes. "You won't like what you see."

"You said it would heal, right?"

"Yes."

"Then let me see."

Corky wavered, but sighed and crossed the room to retrieve a hand mirror. "Remember, you'll soon be as good as new. I promise," she said, reluctantly holding the mirror in front of Malory's face.

Malory gasped and swatted the mirror away. "I look like the ass end of a roadkill," she said babyishly.

Corky smiled. "You're beautiful."

"Whatever. How long do I have to lie here?"

"A while yet."

Malory sighed like a child.

"I missed you," Corky said softly, leaning over to place another kiss on her forehead.

"Do you love me?"

"More than anything in the world."

"Okay, I'll lie here for a few days."

Corky chuckled. "You don't have much choice in the matter."

"But what if I need to…uhm…shake the dew off my lily?"

Corky smiled and reached down to produce a bedpan.

Malory's eyes widened in horror. "No way."

"Give it a rest. I've already changed it for you a couple of times," she teased. "And the sergeant major did it once."

Corky broke down instantly at Malory's expression.

"Okay, I was just kidding," she admitted with a snicker.

"No fair picking on me. I'm convalescing."

"Oh, all right. I couldn't resist."

"Hmph."

"Speaking of the sergeant major, I should call him. I know he wanted to talk to you when you woke up."

"No."

"Huh?"

"Is everything okay?"

"Yeah, thanks to you."

"Then I don't want to see him unless it's an emergency."

"Why not?"

"Why not?" she asked. "Look at me. I'm so ugly, I could make a train back up and take a dirt road."

Corky chuckled. "So? Its not like he's gonna make a pass at you or anything. Don't be such a little prom queen."

"Fine, but I'm not using the bedpan. I'd rather teach my asshole how to chew gum."

Corky laughed. "I love you, Malory."

"I love you, too."

"I know you're feeling moody," Corky said. "I have something that might cheer you up."

"What's that?"

For an answer, Corky walked over and, with a flourish, pulled the sheet away from the room's other occupant.

"You fixed her!"

Corky grinned like an idiot at Malory's delight and carried Little Lovecraft over to be clutched in an impatiently extended hand. "She's a tough little bitch, just like her mommy. Although, she did learn some manners while you were sleeping."

Eyes sparkled with amusement. "Is that a fact?"

"Yep."

Malory seated the doll on her chest and pulled the string.

"What happened to your nose? Did your parents lose a bet with God?"

Malory scowled. "It's going to be a long winter."

It had been six days since Corky had seen Malory, something that she had been quietly warned to expect on the flight to Washington. So it didn't come as a surprise when Malory and the servicemen were spirited away as soon as the plane had landed. From that point, Corky had been separated from her colleagues and had become an unwilling guest of the government, spending three full days undergoing an interrogation conducted by six stern-looking men who had absolutely no sense of humor. On the fourth day, she was given a room key and an escort to a nearby hotel, with instructions to remain there until called upon.

She had spent the time since in a long haze of worry and concern, wondering what would happen to Malory and the others. They had discussed the situation at length in the month before their rescue, both in public and in private. As commander, Malory was the one who would be held the most culpable, and speculating about her fate was a constant source of unease that consumed Corky to no end.

Finally, the call had come and had been greeted with relief and apprehension. Now the Pentagon loomed in the distance, and she looked disinterestedly through a car window as the scenery passed her by.

As the vehicle pulled to a stop, she recognized several of the men who were waiting to greet her as her erstwhile interrogators, and she got out reluctantly. Unexpectedly, another man emerged from the crowd, and her eyes lit up as she rushed forward to embrace him.

"Larry!" she exclaimed. "It's so good to see you."

"Well, hello there," Larry replied after receiving his mauling.

"What are you doing here?"

"They wanted to talk to me, too."

"What's going on?"

"Not quite sure yet."

A throat cleared, and their escort gestured them inside. Corky fell in with the pace of the procession, more than a little irritated with all the secrecy. The entourage traveled silently through what seemed like never-ending miles of corridor until they arrived at a door manned by a pair of grave-looking Marines, one of whom opened the door.

"Dr. Rivers, Dr. Daniels, please make yourselves comfortable," he said, gesturing them inside.

Warily, Corky entered the room and smiled at her friends, all of whom were wearing their dress uniforms.

"Hi, guys. Don't you all look handsome," she said, looking around hopefully but coming up empty. "What's the scoop?"

"Don't know," McNeely said. "This is the first we've seen of each other since we landed."

"Where's Malory?"

"No idea," McNeely said. "But I'll bet we find out today."

"Is she in trouble?"

"She better not be," Clovis rumbled, and she smiled at him fondly.

"We were all run through the wringer," Reynolds said. "I can guarantee it was much worse for her."

"So what are we here for?"

"To wait," McNeely said.

"For what?"

"We'll have to wait to find out."

1510 hours

It had been almost seven hours, and the sound of the door opening startled everyone. Corky looked up and was disappointed to see an older man in a Navy uniform enter the room.

"Attention!" McNeely barked as he sprang to his feet, prompting the other soldiers to follow suit.

"At ease, and good afternoon," Admiral Eaton said amiably. "Dr. Watkins, would you come with me, please?"

The ostracized Watkins, who had been sitting by himself in a corner, reluctantly preceded the admiral out of the room. The door was left open in their wake, and Corky did a double take, hardly recognizing Malory as she walked through the door in her uniform.

"Attention!" McNeely said again, and Malory closed the door behind her, turning to find a roomful of salutes directed at her.

"Oh, cut it out," she chided, accepting a flying embrace from Corky.

"Would you look at those legs?" McNeely asked in wonder.

"You owe me money," Reynolds said. "I told you she shaved them."

"Look at those ribbons," Alvarez said. "I've seen generals who didn't have so many."

Malory rolled her eyes and leaned over to kiss Corky on the top of her head. "If everyone is finished having fun at my expense, I'll tell you what's going on," she said, belatedly noticing Daniels. "Nice to see you again, Dr. Daniels."

"Good to see you, Commander."

Everyone found a seat and looked at her expectantly.

"First of all, everyone has been cleared of any malfeasance, including myself," she announced, to communal relief. "And the powers that be have approached me with a proposal to present to you all."

"What's that, Skipper?" McNeely asked.

"You have thirty days to decide whether you'd like to continue on to other duty assignments or remain under my command. Those of you with the Coast Guard will be seconded to the Navy permanently. Those of you with the NSF have the option to become DoD employees under my purview."

A rapid exchange of surprised glances followed.

"Wow," Reynolds exclaimed. "That's a bag of tricks."

"I don't get it," McNeely said.

"As improbable as it seems, our government doesn't have an abundance of people experienced in what one would call the supernatural. The DoD will provide a base of operations for us, and we'll be deployed nationally and internationally to investigate…uhm…paranormal phenomena."

"You're kidding, right?" Clovis asked.

"No, I'm not. I was as surprised as I'm sure all of you are now."

"Does that include me?" Daniels asked.

"It includes everyone in this room and any staff we care to bring into the fold. However, our mission and objectives are to remain classified."

"I'll be damned," Alvarez muttered.

"You have a month of leave to decide. Those of you who are interested need to report back to me here at the end of that time."

Corky pulled on her sleeve, guiding her to a private corner of the room.

"Malory, what does this mean for us?"

She gave her a bright smile. "We can do whatever you want. I don't have to be involved in this, and neither do you."

Corky peeked around Malory at the men muttering among themselves. "I want to do it."

"Then that's what we'll do."

"Just like that?"

"Just like that."

"Can we go see my parents first?"

"Sure."

"Where will we live?"

"Don't know yet, but I used to work in this building. I have a condo in town," Malory said. "It has a king-size bed," she added rakishly.

Corky giggled. "I can hardly wait."

"Me either. I've been wondering for months what sex would be like in a real bed."

Corky favored her with a gentle smile. "I'm so proud of you," she said. "Let me go talk with the guys. You wait here."

"Okay," she said, watching as the men huddled around the doctor and they mumbled quietly for several minutes.

Eventually, she wandered over to the window to watch the traffic in the distance, becoming lost in her own thoughts.

"Commander?" McNeely asked, and she turned to find everyone lined up in the middle of the room.

"Yes?"

"We've already decided."

"And?"

Daly began to whistle, and her eyes widened in recognition, a hand rising to cover her mouth as a group Cabbage Patch began.

"Come all without. Come all within," they sang. "You'll not see nothing like the mighty Quinn..."

Also by the Author

ENGRAVINGS OF WRAITH
BY KIERA DELLACROIX

Bailey Cameron is a woman with secrets. The reclusive owner of a successful corporation, she is also hostage to a covert life she neither wanted nor asked for. One that refuses to become a part of her past.

Blackmailed into a return to her deadly role as the Wraith, a frightening entity in the world that lives in the shadows, Bailey decides to break free. She settles in for a brutal game of chess with her former employers, prepared for every eventuality but one -- Piper Tate, her new assistant, who decides that the dark, mysterious Bailey is someone she wants to know better. A lot better.

The stakes continue to rise, as Piper discovers in Bailey a gentle, innocent heart. A heart that beats within the body of a killer who can't be tamed and who is prepared to do whatever it takes to preserve the new world Piper has introduced her to.

ISBN: 0971815054

Now Available from Fortitude Press

THE BLUEST EYES IN TEXAS
BY LINDA CRIST

Kennedy Nocona is an out, liberal, driven attorney, living in Austin, the heart of the Texas hill country. Once a player in the legal community, she now finds herself in the position of re-evaluating her life - a position brought on by a personal tragedy for which she blames herself. Seeking redemption for her tormented past, she loses herself in her work, strict discipline of mind and body, and the teachings of Native American roots she once shunned.

Dallasite Carson Garret is a young paralegal overcoming the loss of her parents and coming to terms with her own sexual orientation. After settling her parents' estate and examining her failed past relationships, she is desperately ready to move forward. Bored with her state of affairs, she longs for excitement and romance to make her feel alive again.

A chance encounter finds them inexplicably drawn to one another, and after a weekend together, they quickly find themselves in a long distance romance that leaves them both wanting more. Circumstances at Carson's job develop into a series of mysteries and blackmail attempts that leaves her with more excitement than she ever bargained for. Confused, afraid, and alone, she turns to Kennedy, the one person she knows can help her. As they work together to solve a puzzle, they confront growing feelings that neither woman can deny, complicated by outside forces that threaten to crush them both.

ISBN: 0971815003

CASTAWAY
BY BLAYNE COOPER & RYAN DALY

Where "Survivor" meets "Gilligan's Island" in "The Twilight Zone." Sixteen men and women are stranded on a tropical island–with an intrusive camera crew and a psychotic producer, where they fight for survival, TV ratings, and a million dollar prize. The winner is anyone who loves thrill-a-minute misadventures, gut-busting laughs, and 'broad'-minded women.

The premise may be familiar, though the contestants are anything but, when a desperate network owner is hell-bent on blockbuster ratings and casts the show accordingly. Shannon, a budding novelist and former network employee, falls deeply in lust with tall, dark, paranoid Ryan, a Kentucky survivalist who is determined to win. "The course of true love never did run smooth," Shakespeare said. Even he couldn't have imagined the road bumps Shannon and Ryan will encounter en route to love and hot monkey sex.

The women are not only star-crossed, but insect infested and sand crab bitten. In this irreverent spoof, which focuses on an industry where nothing is as it seems, and no one can be trusted, Shannon and Ryan pull out all the stops to 'get the girl' – and win the prize. Join them as they discover the best thing about 'Paradise' is each other.

ISBN: 0971815089

Now Available from Fortitude Press

FIRST
BY KIMBERLY PRITEKEL

Emily Thomas is a successful New York attorney who enjoys a happy homelife with her beautiful partner. Beth Sayers was the childhood best friend with whom she shared big dreams as they grew up in Pueblo, Colorado. Inseparable by age nine, together they learned about life, each other, themselves, and most importantly love.

When Emily hears of Beth's death at the age of 34, after more than a decade of estrangement, she must piece together her tumultuous past and come to terms with the defining relationship in her life. Why had her friendship with Beth deteriorated and what part of herself had she lost with it?

First is Emily's journey back to Colorado, back to her childhood, and back to face the ghost of a woman who had captured her heart and never really let it go.

ISBN: 0971815070

I FOUND MY HEART IN SAN FRANCISCO
BY S.X. MEAGHER

Despite the questions of her roommates and the objections of her fiancé, Jamie Evans persists in enrolling in a college course that seems an odd choice for a young woman of her background. What no one can know is that the course, The Psychology of the Lesbian Experience, will propel Jamie onto a journey of self-awareness and realization.

For the required fieldwork, Jamie is paired with the darkly beautiful Ryan O'Flaherty —a boldly "out" and sexually adventurous lesbian. This somewhat unlikely pair slowly, and sometimes painfully become aware that what they feel for each other is more than just friendship.

The temptation to live life on her own terms is great, but so are the costs, as Jamie struggles to break out of her establishment-fashioned, pre-ordained mold. If she can summon the courage, however, she might find out that love, and life, have so much more to offer than she had ever dreamed.

ISBN: 0971815038

THE LIFE IN HER EYES
BY DEBORAH BARRY

Real love is not for the faint of heart, and the courage it takes to survive its loss, and love again, is more than the average soul can bear.

Rae Crenshaw does not lack for companionship. The tall beauty radiates charm and confidence, but this attractive combination conceals a vulnerable heart that has known far too much pain. She finds solace for her emptiness in casual trysts, maintaining a severe emotional distance, all the while seeking that which she feels can never be found again.

Evon Lagace's young life has been one of extremes - a failed dance career, a precious, beautiful relationship, and a traumatic, crippling loss. Once so full of exuberance and happiness, she must now struggle to find peace amidst the despair and loneliness.

Share the tears and the triumphs of these two remarkable women as you celebrate their journey to the realization that perhaps, for a lucky few, second chances can exist.

ISBN: 0971815046

To Order:

Title	Quantity	Cost per Unit	Total Cost
At First Blush		$21.99	$
The Average of Deviance		$12.99	$
The Bluest Eyes in Texas		$15.99	$
Castaway		$13.99	$
Conspiracy of Swords		$19.99	$
Engravings of Wraith		$18.99	$
exChanges		$13.75	$
First		$13.99	$
Hell for the Holidays		$13.99	$
I Found My Heart in San Francisco		$18.99	$
Icehole		$13.99	$
The Life in Her Eyes		$13.99	$
Lorimal's Chalice		$18.99	$
Warlord Metal		$13.99	$
Shipping and Handling	First Book	$4.50	$
	Each Add'l Book	$2.00	$
Texas Residents Add 8.25% Sales Tax			$
Total			$

To order by credit card, please visit our Web site at: www.fortitudepress.com.

To order by check or money order, please mail the above form to:

Fortitude Press, Inc.
PO Box 112
New York, NY 10268-0112